MIND *of* WINTER

A NOVEL

LAURA KASISCHKE

HARPER ● PERENNIAL

NEW YORK ● LONDON ● TORONTO ● SYDNEY ● NEW DELHI ● AUCKLAND

HARPER ● PERENNIAL

A hardcover edition of this book was published in 2014 by
HarperCollins Publishers.

P.S.™ is a trademark of HarperCollins Publishers.

HarperCollins books may be purchased for educational, business,
or sales promotional use. For information please e-mail the Special
Markets Department at SPsales@harpercollins.com.

FIRST HARPER PERENNIAL EDITION PUBLISHED 2015.

Designed by Fritz Metsch

Printed on acid-free paper

Library of Congress Cataloging-in-Publication Data has been applied
for.

ISBN 978-0-06-228440-2 (pbk.)

15 16 17 18 19   [RRD]   10 9 8 7 6 5 4 3 2 1

PRAISE FOR
LAURA KASISCHKE AND *MIND OF WINTER*

"Leave-the-lights-on-tonight frightening, with a quiet edge of horror that is much more effective than gore." —NPR

"A nightmare-inducing domestic mystery. . . . Kasischke's background as a poet is clear in her use of language, particularly the repetition of certain phrases and images. The suspense and horror in *Mind of Winter* is largely created by these rhythms, and by her choices of what to leave out as much as to state. . . . Kasischke knows that what lurks hidden in the shadows is scarier than any monster we can see. She also knows that, scared as we may be, we can't resist a peek." —*Boston Globe*

"A terrifying brew of family drama and horror. . . . The awesome ending doesn't disappoint." —*Entertainment Weekly*

"Shocking." —Vogue.com

"Impossible to put down." —*BookPage*

"It is not enough to say that Kasischke's language is 'poetic,' a word that has come to mean 'pretty.' Rather, her writing does what good poetry does—it shows us an alternate world and lulls us into living in it. . . . [T]he language catapults us into another plane of existence, one of façade and reflection." —*New York Times Book Review*

"An unknown horror hovers just out of reach in this gripping psychological thriller. . . . Kasischke skillfully mixes an insightful look at a damaged woman with a twisty plot that builds to a shocking ending." —*Publishers Weekly* .

"A book that will haunt you for days and long, long nights after reading." —*Booklist* (starred review)

"Thought-provoking and chilling, M*ind of Winter* will have you looking over your shoulder as you tear through the pages to the shocking and heartbreaking conclusion. It will leave you questioning not only what is real but also what it means to be a good mother."

—Kimberly McCreight, *New York Times* bestselling author of *Reconstructing Amelia*

"A genuinely disturbing tale, each layer perfectly crafted, stacked together like a set of Russian nesting dolls, the tiniest one at the center the horrific secret that everything else depends upon. It's rare and wonderful to find a book like *Mind of Winter* that is both a masterwork of evocative prose and a bone-chilling page-turner."

—Jennifer McMahon, *New York Times* bestselling author of *The Winter People*

"*Mind of Winter* is a tightly coiled story of suffocating love and undeniable horror. Its grip is remarkably chilling, masterfully poetic, and psychologically unrelenting."

—Ivy Pochoda, author of *Visitation Street*

"If I could stand on a mountaintop and shout over the land, I would do it now: This book is magnificent! It's a gripping psychological thriller, at once both charmingly domestic and flat-out terrifying. Laura Kasischke writes so well that she leaves me inspired and very, very jealous."   —Elin Hilderbrand, author of *Beautiful Day*

MIND *of* WINTER

For Bill

Which is the sound of the land
Full of the same wind
That is blowing in the same bare place . . .

—Wallace Stevens, from "The Snow Man"

MIND *of* WINTER

CHRISTMAS, 20--

SHE WOKE UP late that morning, and *knew*:
Something had followed them home from Russia.

This scrappy bit of information had been offered up to
Holly in a dream, she supposed, a glimpse into a truth
she'd carried with her for—how long?

Thirteen years?

Thirteen years!

For thirteen years she'd known this, and not known—or
so it seemed to her in her half-awake state on Christmas
morning. She rose from bed and went down the hallway
to her daughter's bedroom, anxious to see that she was
there, still asleep, perfectly safe.

Yes, there she was, Tatiana, one pale arm thrown over
a pale coverlet. Dark hair spilled over a pillow. She was so
still she could have been a painting. So peaceful she could
have been—

But she wasn't. She was fine. Holly felt reassured and
went back to the bedroom, slipped into bed beside her
husband again—but as soon as she did, she thought it
once more:

It had followed them home!

This was something Holly had known, apparently, in her heart, or in her subconscious, or wherever it was inside her where bits of information like this hid themselves for years, until something made her aware of what she'd forgotten, or repressed, or—

Or was it something she'd willfully overlooked? Now she saw it:

Something had followed them home from Russia!

But what?

And then Holly thought, *I must write this down before it slips away.* It was that feeling she used to have when she was younger—the almost panicked desire to write about something she'd half glimpsed, to get it on the page before it dashed away again. Sometimes it had felt nearly nauseating, that desire to yank it out of herself and put it into written words before it hid away behind some organ deep inside her—some maroonish, liverish, gillish organ she'd have to pry behind, as if fingering it out of a turkey carcass, ever to get at it again. That's what writing a poem used to feel like to Holly, and why she'd quit writing poems.

My God, though, this thought was like a poem—a secret, a truth, just out of reach. Holly would need time to pluck this out and examine it in the light, but it was in her, whether she'd known it or not until now. Like a poem that wanted to be written. A truth insisting on recognition.

Something had followed them home from Russia!

It was the explanation for so many things!

The cat, crawling off. Her back legs, her tail.

And her husband. The bump on the back of his hand, like a tiny third fist—a homunculus's!—growing. They'd said it was benign, but how could such a thing be *benign*? They'd said to ignore it, but how? Something was bearing fruit inside her husband, or trying to claw its way out. How were they to ignore it?

(Although, to be fair to Dr. Fujimura, they *had* learned to ignore it, and it had eventually stopped growing, just as she'd said it would.)

And Aunt Rose. How her language had changed. How she'd begun to speak in a foreign language. How Holly'd had to stop taking her calls because she couldn't stand it anymore, and how angry her cousins had been, saying *She loved to talk to you. You were her favorite. You abandoned her while she was dying.*

And then the hens. Ganging up on the other one, on the hen she'd so stupidly, so cavalierly, named Sally. Six weeks, and then—

Don't think about Sally. Never think of that hen and her horrible name again.

And the water stain over the dining room table in the shape of a shadowy face—although they could never find anywhere that water would have seeped through their skintight, warranty-guaranteed roof. The roof company men had stood around in their filthy boots and stared up at it, refusing to take any blame.

Also, without explanation, the wallpaper had curled away in the bathroom. Just that one edge. You could never do anything to keep it in place. They'd tried every adhesive on the market, but the daisy wallpaper would stick fast for exactly three days and nights before it peeled away again.

Holly needed to write down these things, this evidence! The cat, Aunt Rose, the bump on her husband's hand, the hens, the water stain, the wallpaper—along with the clue provided to her by her dream:

Something had followed them home from Russia.

How long had it been since she'd woken up needing to write? God, how Holly used to *need* to write. Now she needed to write again. What time was it? She was still in bed, or in bed again. Had she already risen, looked in on her daughter? Or had that been a dream? She'd come back to bed and slipped again into sleep? Perhaps. Now she didn't need to open her eyes to know that it was morning, that it was snowing.

Was there a pen in this room? If she found a pen before Eric and Tatiana woke up, would she be able to actually sit down and write? That broken habit. That abandoned necessity.

Holly thought she could. She would be able to write. She could feel it—the bitter ache of it. There was some awful pressure on her lungs. There was, she felt, something stoppered up in her torso. She imagined vomiting it out of herself, like vomiting up a swan—something with a long, tangled throat nestled inside her own throat—choking on its feathers and all its bony quills. How relieved she would feel afterward, lying on the bedroom floor beside the swan she'd vomited out of herself into the world.

Outside, the wind sounded like a nerve being yanked through the tree. It was Christmas morning, but late. It must be nearly nine o'clock. They never slept this late on Christmas morning! Far too much rum and eggnog last night. Was Tatty still asleep in her bed? Her pale arm, pale coverlet, pale pillow with a splash of dark hair, still. Holly had looked in on her, she remembered this, but it had been hours ago, hadn't it? Surely Tatty would be up by now, ready to open presents. Where was she? Why hadn't she come into the room to wake them up?

Because she was fifteen, of course. She was probably also still asleep. There would never again be a Christmas morning, crack of dawn Tatty coming in to slap their faces lightly with her damp, new, tiny hands. Instead, they'd all overslept on Christmas morning, and Holly had woken up with this little horror in her mind, that something had followed them home from Russia.

Something evil?

Well, perhaps not evil. But it had sapped them. It continued to sap them.

"Oh, that's motherhood," Thuy would say. "You're just talking about motherhood. Children, they're energy vampires . . ."

But don't forget the cat. The wallpaper. Aunt Rose. Even when she was semi-lucid, even when the words were familiar English words, Aunt Rose had seemed to Holly to be reciting lines from "The Fire Sermon": *On Margate Sands I can connect nothing with nothing the broken finger-nails of dirty hands my people humble people who expect nothing la la . . .*

And there had also been their CDs, hadn't there? All their favorites had been scratched, as if overnight—although, surely, it had been over a long period of time? *Every one* of their favorites had been ruined, and they'd never even bothered to replace them. They'd just left them there on a shelf, like their books, which they never took down to read now, or even to blow the dust off.

And speaking of the dust! My God, it was everywhere. It *was* Holly's exhaustion. It was floating and impossible, still bearing cat fur in it after all these years without the cat, as well as strands of Tatiana's long black hair. When Holly complained about the dust, Eric claimed he didn't see it, that he had no idea what she was talking about, but that if it bothered her that much she should hire a housekeeper again.

And yes, she could have hired a housekeeper again, but she'd never even found the energy to do that, not after the last one, and her accident on the back steps, slipping on ice while taking out a bag of garbage. And even before that, her allergies, her rashes, and Holly's guilt at paying another woman, a poorer woman, a Spanish-speaking woman, to do this intimate work for her that she should have been perfectly able to do for herself.

Dust, exhaustion, it was in the air:

Something had followed them home from Russia.

Repeat it, Holly thought. It is a refrain. As in a poem. *Write it down.* Write down the way some shadow face is finally peering around a corner on this Christmas morning (they'd slept so late) and shown itself.

Something that was here all along. Inside the house. Inside *themselves.* It had *followed them all the way home from Russia.*

❋

BUT NOT THE baby! Not Baby Tatty! Of course not the *baby.* They'd *brought* the baby Tatiana home from Russia. She was no follower, no revenant, no curse from another country.

No. Of course not Baby Tatty wrapped in her Ratty Blankie. Not Tatty the Beauty. Gorgeous Russian dancer, howler monkey, sweetheart, wanderer, love of their lives. Not Tatiana.

No. Some Thing. And the only thing it had in common with their daughter was that it came back with them from Russia.

Holly was still simply trying to wake up, imagining a pen in her hand, writing it down . . . How late was it? Ten o'clock?! Why was she still asleep, or asleep again, on Christmas morning? She patted the place beside her for Eric. *Please, God*, she thought, *let him be gone*. Let him be gone so I can have a few moments alone to write. She'd almost managed to open her leaden eyes. *Please, God, let Eric have taken Tatty with him to the airport to pick up his parents. Please give me half an hour to write it down, to make sense of it, to look at this thing.* Otherwise she would forget it, she knew, and then she would never know it, this thing she knew. It would never be a completed thought, let alone a poem, this thing that—

That had broken three of her mother's iridescent water glasses! And scratched every one of their CDs, as if with a penknife. Left them unplayable. Unreplaced. Not even downloaded onto iTunes yet (but would they ever have gotten around to *that*?). The Water Music. The Four Seasons. The Patti Smith. Even the Beatles. Had Holly even *heard* those Beatles songs since then? Even on the radio of a passing car? It was as if those songs ("Norwegian Wood," "I Want to Hold Your Hand") had never been written, or played.

And the cat. The horror of that. And before that, the hen, their favorite. How the other chickens had turned on her. Not even pecked her to death, but just pecked her so close to death that she was only a forgotten brokenness, left behind them, as they went on with lives.

And the notebook full of poems snatched with her purse from the coffee shop, and her laptop full of poems from the hotel in California—from the *safe*.

And the housekeeper, Concordia, whom Tatty had loved, but who'd suffered from allergies and rashes she'd never before had when she began housekeeping for them, and then twisted her ankle on ice on the back steps (taking out their garbage, full of plastic bottles Holly should have recycled) and never come back.

And, my God, Holly had almost forgotten the daughter of her coworker Kay—a twenty-two-year-old hit by a car while crossing the street with the light at a crosswalk on a perfectly sunny day. How irrationally and completely Holly had felt that she herself should take some blame for that. After all, Holly had never liked Kay, and the day before the accident Holly had slapped an employee handbook onto Kay's desk and told her to read it (she'd been so sick of Kay's tardiness, her long lunches, her personal phone calls, but what difference did any of that really make?) and that night Kay had gone home with the handbook, in tears, and (who knew?) maybe she'd told her daughter that she was having trouble at work, maybe the daughter had been hurrying across the street the next day, worrying about her mother, and hadn't looked both ways?

"That's insane," Eric had said to Holly. "If the universe works that way, it means that you yourself are God. I thought *you* were the atheist, the one who had no superstitions."

But what if it hadn't been insane? What if they'd brought something back with them from Russia? Something malevolent. Or something desperate to return to its origins? Maybe it wanted to go back!

Hadn't one of the nurses in Russia warned them? *Tried* to warn them? That one with the drooping eyelid and the hair like a Renaissance princess, all down her side in a braid made of gold, seeming slicked with oil.

Had her name been Theodota?

She'd been the one who'd worn some strange thing in a bubble of glass pinned above her breast. It was a dried rose, she'd told Holly, that had been touched to the tomb of some saint—the patron saint of stomach ailments, one of which had plagued Theodota most of her life. The thing in the bubble had looked, to Holly, like some kind of tumor, something shriveled and internal, and she'd complained bitterly to Eric about the religious mania of the Siberian nurses. Weren't they supposed to be done with religion in this godforsaken place?

"No. That's us," he said. "You're confusing Russians with Americans. Americans are the ones who've forsaken God. The Russians have found Him again."

He'd always defended religion, hadn't he? Although he

himself attended no church, prayed to no god. It was a way of defending his parents, she supposed, whom he always felt she was criticizing whenever she criticized religion or old-fashioned values or pickled foods.

Had it been in Siberia that the thing on Eric's fist had begun to sprout, to grow just under the skin? Holly had a vague memory of one of those nurses, perhaps Theodota herself, at the Pokrovka Orphanage #2 taking a long look at his hand, shaking her head, trying to communicate something to him by speaking slowly and carefully in Russian, not a word of which Eric or Holly understood.

About Tatiana, Theodota had said, "No. Don't name her Russian. Name her American. Or she'll be back."

The nurses had called her Sally. They had explained to Eric and Holly, "We give her American name so that in her life and in her death she will not be restless in America, try to return to Russia."

"But we want her to be *proud* of her Russian origins," Holly had tried, in turn, to explain, not sure if any of her English was being understood. "We want to call her Tatiana because it is a beautiful Russian name for a beautiful little Russian girl."

The nurse had scowled and shaken her head vehemently. "*Nyet, nyet,* no," she said. "Sally. Or"—here she softened, as though sensing that they might be able to compromise—"you name her Bonnie. Bonnie and Clyde, no?"

Holly had been smiling, but she was having a hard time keeping the spirit light. She said, "No. Tatiana."

"No," the nurse had said right back to her.

"Oh my God," Holly had said, later, to Eric. "What is wrong with these people?"

Even Eric, at that point, had regained his sense of humor enough to shake his head in disbelief at the superstitions of these people in Siberia.

But that had been almost the least of it! On their second trip back to the orphanage, this time by train from Moscow, the conductor, wanting to practice his terrible English, had explained to them that he always wore, under his uniform, a *cilice*—which, it turned out, in his case, was a barbed cross on a chain. The conductor undid the buttons of his shirt to show the cross to them— primitive and the size of a child's hand, hanging from a piece of twine—along with the scratches on his sparsely haired chest (could he have been even thirty years old?) that the cross's barbs left there. He explained that the tracks of the Trans-Siberian Railway were laid over the graves of the prisoners who'd built it, as if that explained the need for the punishing barbed cross he wore against his skin.

Holly was appalled, while Eric had been charmed. Neither of them had expected this sort of thing from the Russians. They'd expected, maybe, searchlights and vodka bottles and barbed wire and an unfriendly, militaristic citizenry—although, in truth, they'd not even gotten that far in their imaginings. Had Eric and Holly even believed that Russia, that *Siberia*, existed until they were in it? Hadn't they thought that the adoption agency was just being descriptive, calling it "Siberia"—which to Holly had always been a way to *describe* a place, not an actual place. She'd perhaps actually thought, even as the adoption agency arranged plane tickets for them, that by "Siberia" they just meant "off the beaten track" or "desolate." Not that the orphanage was actually in Siberia.

But it was Siberia they found themselves in. Siberia existed. There were vodka bottles and searchlights and barbed wire, as Holly had expected, and there were women wearing babushkas, wagons full of straw, grim men in uniforms, some beautiful young girls with fur hats—none of which surprised her. Although Holly was surprised by everything else. Everything. And, particularly, the superstition. At the Pokrovka Orphanage #2 the babies had coughs and fevers, so the nurses had asked Holly and Eric to wear cloves of garlic around their necks. They'd handed Holly and Eric actual cloves of garlic dangling from pieces of gray twine. To ward off germs? Or . . . ?

In any other place, Holly would have balked, but, inside Pokrovka Orphanage #2, she slipped the garlic over her head happily, gratefully. She would have done anything at that moment—opened a vein, gorged on ashes, pledged her soul to Satan—to hold this baby they'd come all this way to hold.

Whose name would certainly not be *Sally*. Holly and Eric had known all along that they would call her Tatiana. It meant *fairy queen* in Russian.

Baby Tatty.

"THIS IS THE baby," a nurse said, appearing suddenly in a doorway. Holly had expected an hour of paperwork first, or a long walk through a corridor. She'd pictured herself and Eric standing behind a vault door while a guard twisted a lock. Instead, they'd no sooner slipped the necklaces of garlic over their heads and sat down in the waiting room than they heard the words, heavily accented but in a musically feminine voice: *This is the baby.*

Holly had looked up to the open door to find that an astonishing amount of light was pouring from a window, or from a great wall of windows, somewhere behind that nurse, and the nurse's hair, pale and cut close to her head, was glowing like a halo. That nurse (whom they never saw again, although they asked to) had a cherubic face, a stunning smile—straight teeth and glistening lips. She could have stepped off a cloud or out of a movie screen, bearing this child. She could have passed for any number of supernatural beings—angel, fairy, goddess—or an actress hired to play the part of one that day. It was hard to look away from her face, to look at what she was holding in her arms.

Eric always claimed that Tatty had been wrapped in a blue blanket, but Holly knew she hadn't. Their daughter had been wrapped in a dirty-gray blanket, and it had looked to Holly as if the sun were trying to launder it, bleach it white, bless it. The sun was trying to make the baby shine. The sun wanted Holly to love the child, to take pity on her, to take her home. The sun couldn't have known that no effort on its part was needed for that. Looking from the nurse's face to the baby wrapped in gray in her arms, it was all Holly could do not to fall to her knees, not to cry aloud. Instead, she grabbed Eric so hard that, later, walking away from their first trip to the orphanage, they would laugh that she'd left him battered and bruised—and, in fact, she *had*. When Eric took off his shirt that night they saw that he had a purple mark in the shape of a small conch shell just above his elbow.

When the nurse had stepped fully into the room, Holly stood, and the baby was placed in her arms.

Holly took her daughter in her arms, and before she saw or felt or heard her, she *loved* her—as if there were an organ and a part of the brain that was love's eye or nose or ear. The first sense. It had never been needed before. Now Holly realized that it was, in fact, the sharpest of her senses.

The second sense: smell. Holly would always associate her daughter and her love for her daughter with that secondary sensory impression—the ripe, rich *Allium sativum*, muddy hoofprint of that clove in its torn papery wrapper around her neck, at her chest, between herself and her baby. And a dirty diaper. And the scent of sour milk and cereal soaked into the damp neckline of the ratty, tatty gown they'd dressed her in, as if to sell her to them—as if they'd need to be persuaded to snatch her up!—with a few faded daisies on it for good measure.

And Holly remembered how, then, too, she'd wanted to write it down. She'd wanted to say something about it on a piece of paper before she lost the words. But, of course, there was no time then. Even in the bathroom after they'd had to return their daughter to that nurse and walk away, Holly couldn't write it down. With her naked ass on the cold porcelain, fishing through her purse while her husband paced around outside the thin door, she couldn't find a pen.

❋

NOW, SHE NEEDED to find a pen to write *this* down:

Something had followed them home from Siberia.

From the orphanage. Pokrovka Orphanage #2.

Holly needed a pen and a half hour alone before the in-laws and the roast in the oven and the Coxes. God, the Coxes. Who would sit at the table waiting for her to entertain them. And their terrible son, who seemed to have been born without a soul. Holly had not wanted to write in so many weeks, months, years—and if she didn't do it now, if she could not wake up fully and find a pen, if she did not have a half hour alone, it would pass, and perhaps the desire would never, ever, come back.

She moved her hand over to Eric's side of the bed, to the place she hoped to find empty, the place she *needed* to find vacant beside her, the sheets cool, Eric gone, so that she could have a few moments alone—

But he was there, and Holly felt him twitch awake, and then Eric sat up so fast the headboard slammed against the wall behind him, and Holly was fully awake then, too, realizing that there was far too much light in the bedroom, and Eric, realizing it, too, was out of bed fast, standing over her, shouting, "Jesus Christ. We overslept. *Fuck.* It's ten thirty. My parents must already be sitting at the fucking airport, and the fucking Coxes will be here in an hour. Where in the hell is Tatiana? Why didn't she wake us up? Jesus Christ. Holly. I gotta go!"

Then he was gone:

Holly had barely put her feet on the floor when she heard the sound of Eric's car in the garage, and the garage door opening. Eric was not the kind of man to squeal his tires on the way out of the driveway, but nevertheless he did, and Holly heard it for what it was—the implication of blame. Of course. Of *course* if his parents were already waiting at the airport, worried or sick or complaining, it would somehow be her fault. When Eric's siblings arrived later they would say, "Why in the world was Eric late to get Mom and Dad?"—as if the question were the answer because both were directed at Holly.

And, as Eric had said, where the hell was Tatiana? Could she still be asleep? Had Holly peeked into her daughter's room only an hour or two ago (pale arm, pale coverlet?) or had that been a dream? Was it before or after that when she'd woken, knowing that *something had followed them—*

Holly still felt the need to write it down, and felt surprised and pleased that she still felt the need. But what, exactly, had she wanted to write down? That something had returned from Siberia with them? That it had somehow followed them? Was that the explanation she'd woken up with, the Thing that accounted for the unexplained tragedies of the last thirteen years?

And what were those? Nothing! They were all still alive, after all, weren't they? What else was there, then, beyond the ordinary misfortunes one suffers in thirteen years in a typical American town? The average calamities of a normal family? There'd been a great many more joys than sorrows in these thirteen years!

Sure, she'd had her notebook and her laptop stolen. But the thief who'd snatched her purse at the coffee shop hadn't been after her poems. He'd been after her cash. Purse snatching happened to a lot of women who left their purses on their tables when they got up to refill their coffee cups. And how stupid had it been to leave a laptop (hard drive not backed up!) in a big-city hotel and expect it to be safe in a *safe*?

And the rest of it? The housekeeper? Kay's daughter's accident? The cat had suffered the usual death of a domesticated animal, slipping out the door and dashing into the road. And the hen, Sally. What did they expect? Holly and Eric had known nothing about chickens and their habits when they'd gotten them. It was something the whole neighborhood had figured out at the same time when their town full of clueless academics and software company employees had passed the ordinance allowing backyard chickens.

And the changes to her marriage? Well, she and Eric were, simply, older. Holly sometimes forgot that. Instead of looking hard at Eric's face, or her own in the mirror, on a daily basis, Holly had gotten used to looking, every morning, into the faces from the past that were framed on the wall in the hallway outside the bathroom:

She and Eric thirteen years earlier, standing with their backs to the bare institutional wall of the Pokrovka Orphanage #2, while, in Holly's arms, the wide-eyed Baby Tatty looked up into her new mother's eyes. In this photograph, each of their images held the suggestion of who, in thirteen years, they would be. Eric's red hair was already a little gray at the temples, and his fitness, his physique (all that running and basketball: he'd been only forty-two then) was already beginning to diminish a little with his bad knee. His torso looked thin under his white shirt, and it was easy to imagine that the man in this photograph would grow even thinner as he aged instead of fatter.

And herself. Holly had been thirty-three, and her hair was still naturally blond. She hadn't yet needed glasses, really (or had still been too vain to wear them), and although she, too, had weighed more then than she did now, that weight had been arranged differently on her. She'd worn her soft padding in other places.

And Baby Tatty already had the gaze that made her *Tatiana*. Those eyes were fiercely black, and her hair was already longer than Holly had ever seen on such a young child. In the Pokrovka Orphanage #2 the nurses had called her Jet-Black Rapunzel. Anyone looking at the photograph framed and nailed up in the hallway would have known that she'd become what she was now—a long-legged teenage beauty, still with that silken hair around her shoulders, and those dark eyes.

"Tatiana?" Holly called as she stepped into the hallway, rubbing her forehead. It was, she realized, true. She had a hangover. Not a serious one—but she feared that last rum and eggnog might haunt her all day.

"Tatiana?" she called out again. There was no answer. Could Tatiana have left the house? But where, why? If not, she couldn't still be asleep. Now, she would have to have been willfully determined to make no sound in response to Holly's calling her—which would have been some kind of punishment, perhaps, for Holly, for sleeping. Holly rubbed her eyes with a thumb and forefinger, sighed, readied herself to call out to her daughter again and then gasped, startled nearly to screaming when she found her daughter only inches away, staring at her, disapprovingly it seemed, and standing completely still in the bedroom's threshold. "Tatty, Jesus," Holly said. It took her a second to catch her breath. "You scared me. How long have you been standing there?"

"Merry Christmas," Tatiana said. "Sheesh. I thought you and Daddy were going to sleep until New Year's Eve." She sighed that dramatic teenager sigh she'd perfected in the last year—a sigh that managed to convey in a single breath both bitterness and detachment, a sound that never failed to remind Holly of the snow in Siberia. Holly had expected that snow to accumulate, as it did in the northern Michigan of her childhood, and to organize itself into banks and walls. But it didn't. It just drifted. Endless drifting. There was nothing, it seemed, that could stop it. It was snow, it was solid, it could be seen, but it was one with the wind. Exactly like that teenage-girl sigh.

"We were tired," Holly said, trying not to sound overly apologetic. Why should she be?

"I guess so," Tatty said.

"I got up a couple of hours ago, and you were dead asleep, so I went back to bed."

"I wasn't asleep," Tatty said. "I haven't been asleep for hours. You know that."

"Well, you sure looked asleep." Always an argument, Holly thought. She passed by her daughter in the doorway, smelled mint on her, and tea tree oil shampoo, and L'Occitane Verbena, two bottles of which they'd bought at the mall because Tatty didn't want to share a bottle with Holly, although Holly couldn't wear it anyway, as it turned out. It gave her a headache. She added verbena to the list of flowers she couldn't wear the scent of for more than ten minutes without feeling sick—lily of the valley, magnolia, gardenia.

"Are we going to have breakfast? So we're not opening gifts? Did Daddy go to the airport already? Wasn't he supposed to take *me*?" Hostile, rhetorical questions. Tatty wasn't whining. The tone was reproachful, challenging.

"Look," Holly said, turning around at the kitchen island, trying not to sound as defensive as she felt. "Why didn't you just wake us up if you've been so anxious for all these things? Daddy flew out the door because Gin and Gramps are probably already at luggage claim. And I've got ten million things to do. Can't you eat a bowl of cereal or something?"

"What about presents?"

Holly parted her lips, shook her head, exhaled, turned to the coffeepot, punched the blue eye to turn it back on—the coffee had been set to brew at 7 a.m., and had long since grown cold in the glass decanter.

"Presents will have to wait until Daddy gets back. You know what your presents are anyway."

Tatiana turned then, and headed back toward her room. Her white tank top was almost too bright to look at with all her dark hair between her shoulder blades, and her hips swayed, and her white yoga pants were so high and tight between her legs it was almost obscene. The cheeks of her sweet baby bottom. Pulling against her crotch. Holly hated thinking what a man would think, looking at that beautiful bottom. And then she remembered, with the swiftness of a slap, that although her daughter might pretend to be, and look like, a woman now, she was, truly, just a child. And it *was* Christmas. Holly should have set an alarm. "Sweetheart," she called after Tatty, softening, sorry, but her daughter was already closing the bedroom door behind her.

❄

IT HAD BEEN Christmas, too, the first time they went to Siberia, first saw Tatty, although, after all their exhaustion and elation and the weeks of preparation for their travels, Eric and Holly had completely forgotten about the holiday, or the significance of arriving at the Pokrovka Orphanage #2 for the first time on the morning of December 25.

But there were no signs of Christmas at the orphanage that day, since, for the Russians, Orthodox Christmas was still thirteen days away. Eric and Holly might have forgotten about it entirely, themselves, if it hadn't been for the other American couple staying at the hostel run by the orphanage. That couple had thought to bring gifts for their new baby—blankets and booties wrapped in green and red paper—and fancy soaps and chocolates and silk scarves for the nurses. It was, Holly realized, exactly what they should have done themselves, but by then it was too late. They were seven thousand miles away from Macy's.

"It's okay," the other American mother-to-be said to Holly. "They don't really do Santa here or anything. Mostly they celebrate New Year's, not Christmas. Just a lot of drinking. No one is expecting a present."

But arriving at the orphanage bearing not a single gift for their child or her caretakers on December 25 mattered to Holly. Terribly. Unforgettably. Her first failure as a mother. What difference did it make if she was the only one who knew or cared about it? She was the only one who needed to know or care.

HOLLY LOOKED TO the tree. Tatty must have plugged it in. The miniature lights glowed dimly, like electrical pencil tips, in the brightness pouring in through the picture window. Those lights looked futile to Holly—not really lights in all this brightness. Just little nubs of effort. Overly effortful. She wanted to unplug them again, until later, when the darkness gave them some reason for being lit, but she didn't, because Tatty wanted them on.

Tatty was excited, it seemed, for Christmas, although that was hard for Holly to appreciate. These days her daughter was so rarely excitable about anything except Tommy, being at that age where, if she'd been offered a million dollars, she would simply roll her eyes and languidly offer up her hand to take it. She'd managed to infuriate Holly the other day by saying "one of the reasons" she'd been "dreading Christmas" was that Tommy and his father would be in Jackson Hole the entire week. "No Tommy. Tommy's my Jesus Christ."

"Tatty," Holly had said. "Don't be blasphemous."

"Oh. Okay," Tatty said, and then pretended to hold a joint to her lips and inhale.

Holly had turned her back on her daughter fast.

But despite the fact that Eric and Holly had still been asleep, Tatty must have gotten out of bed and come to the living room to plug in the Christmas tree lights. Like a little girl again. And her disappointment that Eric was already gone indicated that she'd wanted to open her presents, as they'd always done, first thing on Christmas morning, before the relatives had to be picked up and the guests arrived—although this year there were no surprises for Tatiana under the tree. She knew perfectly well what her presents were, having been careful to write down the specifics (even with the ISBN numbers for some of them!) so that Holly could order them off the Internet.

Still, Tatty had woken up before Holly and Eric, and she'd come out here, alone, to turn on the Christmas tree lights, as if, despite her teenage "dread" of family and holidays and Tommy out of town, she was excited about Christmas.

Holly went to her daughter's closed bedroom door and said, "Honey? Tatty?"

No answer. Of course. There was never any answer at first, any longer, when Holly came calling. These days Tatty liked to make her mother work for it.

"Tatty. Can you open the door?"

There was the sound of her daughter's chair legs scraping against the wood floors. She must have been pushing herself back from her desk, away from her computer. It was such a familiar sound to Holly that she sometimes heard it in her imagination when her daughter wasn't even in the house.

"The door's not locked," Tatiana said loudly enough for Holly to hear her but not so loud it would sound like Tatiana was actually inviting her mother in. It was intended to sound begrudging, and also exasperated, indicating that Holly should know full well that the door wasn't locked. It was what she always said when Holly knocked on her door. Tatty made a point of insisting that she didn't lock her bedroom door—that she did not *now*, nor had she *ever*, nor *would* she ever have a reason to lock her bedroom door—ever since Holly had secured a hook and eye to the door and jamb so that her daughter could be assured of privacy.

"Be *assured* of *privacy?*" Tatty had said, sounding affronted, when Holly had installed the lock. "Huh?"

"Well," Holly had said. "When I was your age I was always worried that someone would walk in on me in my bedroom, so I wanted to make sure you felt that your privacy was being respected in our house."

"Uh, gosh, thanks," Tatty had said, narrowing her eyes and shaking her head. "And what would I be doing in here that I'd need privacy for, Mom?"

Holly had actually flushed then, as if some dirty thought she'd had was being read aloud. She shrugged. She said, "I don't know. That's the point! Now you can lock your door so Daddy and I can't barge in."

Tatiana had turned her back to her mother, returning to her computer, the screen of which displayed a half-written paper on the Twenty-Fifth Amendment to the U.S. Constitution—an amendment so dull and obscure that Tatiana had been given extra credit for being willing to take it on.

Holly had simply stood and looked at her daughter's

shoulders, all that lovely, innocent hair cascading down her back.

❄

JET-BLACK RAPUNZEL, THE nurses had called her.

So much lovely, inky, straight long hair, even at nineteen months of age.

And all these years later her skin was still like an infant's—poreless and pristine. Even when she spent a summer day outside without sunscreen, Tatiana didn't tan or burn. Her complexion was the color of milk stained with a drop of blue food coloring. At her temples, a darker blue, and sometimes under her eyes and around her mouth.

"Yeah, but when has Tatty ever once spent a summer day outside without sunscreen?" Thuy would have asked, laughing.

Locked up. In a tower. As if she *were* Rapunzel.

No. That had *not* been Holly's mothering modus operandi. It had never been her MO. What she'd wanted for Tatiana, from the very beginning, was freedom. Wasn't that why she'd installed the hook and eye for her, so that Tatiana could have secrets? So that she could—

What?

Conceal some kind of contraband?

Such as . . . ?

Condoms?

Look at pornography on the Internet? Is *that* what

Tatiana had thought her mother was giving her permission to do? *Was* that what Holly was giving Tatiana permission to do?

Christ, not consciously. None of those things had consciously crossed Holly's mind. It was a symbolic gesture, wasn't it? It was meant to let Tatiana know that she was trusted, that she had rights in their house.

And even if she *did* do something for which she needed privacy in her room, why not? Why not offer up that freedom to her? What would the point be of trying to dissuade a teenager from such things? Tatiana had friends whose parents tried to vet every image their children saw. Their neighbor, Mary Smithers, whose daughter used to wander over to play with Tatty until they moved away a few years ago, had asked Holly to please give her a call before she allowed Bethany to watch anything on the television. "We want to control what she's seeing," Mary Smithers had said, not even shying away from the word *control*.

Eric and Holly had felt almost scandalized about this, as if they'd found out that Mary Smithers was sending Bethany to a nunnery. It was not the way they wanted to raise their child, not in this day and age. They wanted Tatiana to feel she had her own agency, a right to make her own decisions. This was something they'd determined together before they'd even brought her home from Russia, that they would raise their child to be a freethinker and that they would discuss all things freely. They pitied little Bethany, having a mother who didn't trust her enough to be in the presence of a television. And Bethany had confided in Tatiana that "we don't have Internet at our house because my parents don't want me to see it."

What sort of message did *that* send? That the outside world was obscene? That you should hide your child from it rather than give her the tools to protect herself?

"Tatiana, you're at the age when you might have things you don't want your parents to know about!" Holly had said to her daughter, wishing she didn't sound as animated as she knew she sounded.

Tatiana didn't miss a beat. She said, "I thought you said I never needed to keep any secrets from you."

Holly could no longer recall how she'd responded to that, but Tatiana had never, it seemed, used that hook and eye, and whenever Holly knocked on her door Tatiana said, "God, Mom. Just come in. It's not locked. I'm not ever going to be doing anything in here you're not going to be able to witness."

❄

NOW HOLLY TURNED the doorknob, and pushed her daughter's door open to find that Tatiana had already changed out of her white tank top and yoga pants into the hideous red velvet dress that Grandma Gin had given to her for Christmas the year before. Eric's mother was, unfortunately, a seamstress. And a knitter. And for every birthday and for every Christmas she made clothes for her loved ones, and loved to see her loved ones dressed in those clothes.

"Oh, Tatty," Holly said. "You don't have to wear that! Grandma Gin won't even remember!"

"Maybe I want to wear it," Tatiana said, turning to glare at her mother. "Maybe I love it."

Holly stepped all the way into her daughter's room to the familiar clash of scents—the sweet natural smell of Tatty's hair and skin mixed with the perfumes and lotions she used, fruits and flowers and oils, and something else this morning, something slightly fetid, or rotten. Maybe Tatiana had left a banana or an apple in a drawer? Something fermented. Not putrid, but headed in that direction.

Her bed, at least, was neatly made. On her floor and desk were dozens of photographs of Tommy that Tatiana had printed up from her phone and left strewn and curled everywhere, but that was the only messiness. Everything else was folded, dusted, tucked away—tidying that Tatiana must have done because there were guests coming over. Although Tatty had grown testy and impatient with her parents in the last year or two, she was ever respectful of the other adults in her life, adhering strictly to all the codes of conduct one followed in deference to them—even the ones Holly found ridiculous, like calling Tommy's father Mr. MacClean after all this time. Holly and Eric had insisted right away that Tommy, and all of Tatiana's friends, call them by their first names.

Holly made a little circuit around her daughter, looking at the red dress:

The velvet was cheap, heavy—not really velvet. Some kind of polyester Gin must have bought at some thrift fabric shop. She would have bought a whole bolt of it, Holly knew, and made napkin rings or placemats with the leftovers. The dress went down to Tatty's ankles like some kind of Old World costume. No neckline. Fake pearl buttons up the back. And the shoulders were ruffled. The pattern must have been from the eighties. It was awful.

"Honey, how can you even get into that? You've filled out so much since last year—" Her daughter had gone from an A cup to a C in the last twelve months, and they'd had to buy all new bras, and had taken half a dozen of her old tops to Goodwill since then.

"Obviously, I let it out," Tatiana said, shaking her head.

"What?" Holly asked.

"I *let it out*," Tatiana said. "You know, with scissors, with thread?" She pantomimed sewing, and then Holly looked at the dress. It looked, in its way, flawless. Ginny was all about precision. The clothes she made were ugly and out of fashion, but they were meticulously constructed.

"How?" Holly asked.

"Jeez, Mom. Like I said, with a needle, okay? It's called sewing! Just forget it. What did you come in here for anyway?"

"I just wanted to say Merry Christmas," Holly said, wishing she could sound more apologetic, less exasperated. She tried to soften it. "And I'm so sorry we overslept. When Daddy gets back with Gin and Gramps we'll open presents right away, okay?"

There was a little twitch at the corner of Tatiana's mouth. It broke Holly's heart to see it! That was Tatty at four years old being told that she couldn't go to the birthday party because she had a fever! Tatiana had never been the type to burst into tears. Instead, she bore emotions like—

Like an orphan, like a child who'd been abandoned and who'd understood, fully and early, that life was not fair.

"Oh, Tatty, I wish I'd woken up earlier—" Holly felt it this time, sincere remorse and sorrow.

"Mom, jeez, I'm a big girl."

Tatiana turned her back, as if on the whole idea that it had mattered—the oversleeping, the disappointment.

But it was Christmas morning! And maybe Tatty had thought this Christmas would be like all the Christmases of those early years—all those mornings that had started at dawn with Tatty's clammy hands on their cheeks ("Mommy! Daddy! It's Christmas!") and the ripping open of presents that were complete surprises. The stockings magically stuffed with little plastic animals and butterfly barrettes. That whole Santa hoax, which Holly had put an end to early, against Eric's wishes—but, honestly, who thought that was a healthy myth? An intruder, bearing gifts. And then to find out it's all been a lie, perpetrated by your parents?

But maybe Tatty, this morning, had wanted to relive those early years, and the excitement, but then her parents, exhausted from their jobs and a late Christmas Eve dinner with too much wine and then the rum and eggnog, had practically slept until noon!

"Sweetheart," Holly said, and stepped over to her daughter. She reached out her arms and took the faux red velvet package of her daughter into her arms. Tatty was stiff, but she didn't pull away. Holly breathed in the musky citrusy flowery scent of her. Some of that was store-bought, but some of it was just Tatty, the scent she was born with, that sweetness even the garlic around Holly's neck hadn't managed to extinguish. To Holly, that baby had smelled as if she'd been plucked from a nest made of viburnum switches in the branches of a balsam fir. It even occurred to her that the nurses might have sprayed the baby with something to cause her to smell like this. Since they'd seemed so eager to sell Tatiana to Holly and Eric— insisting "Never cries! Never sick!" and dressing her in the little cotton dress with the faded daisies, surely the best thing they could find among the orphanage tatters—it didn't seem out of the realm of possibility that they might have doused her in air freshener for special effect.

Holly inhaled, and continued to hold her fifteen-year-old baby in her arms. Tatiana didn't pull away, and finally she softened and rested her forehead on her mother's shoulder. They stayed that way for several seconds until Holly heard—vaguely, maybe from underneath a cushion or a pillow somewhere—the sound of her own cell phone playing Bob Dylan's "A Hard Rain's A-Gonna Fall," and she broke the embrace to hurry after it.

❄

IT WAS ERIC on the phone:

"Holly. We're in the car already. Forty-five minutes from home."

"Are your parents okay?" Holly asked. "Was their trip okay?"

"Okay," Eric said, and the tone of it indicated to Holly that something was, actually, not okay, but also that his parents were in the car with him and he couldn't say what it was that was wrong.

"Okay . . . ," Holly said. "Should I be prepared for something unexpected?" She instinctively lowered her voice when she asked it, although she knew that both of Eric's parents were so deaf they'd never be able to hear her through Eric's cell phone even if he had the speaker turned on.

"Maybe," Eric said. "Some confusion. Didn't expect it."

Didn't expect it. Holly inhaled and exhaled with her mouth away from the phone receiver so he wouldn't hear. If it hadn't been so predictable, and so fucking tragic, she would have snorted at him. She would have laughed. She would have said, "You *didn't expect it.* Well, what the hell *did* you expect?" How long was it going to take Eric to realize how elderly and infirm his parents had become?

Instead, Holly said, "Oh dear. Okay. We'll just do our best. Just get them home, Eric."

She punched the end button on her telephone. As usual, the line would not be cut off at first, and Holly had to punch END again and again until the connection was severed. When she put the phone down and turned around, Tatiana was standing on the other side of the kitchen island, smoothing her black hair with one of her elegant hands—long-fingered, nails painted red (to match her dress?). She asked, grimly, "What's wrong, Mom?"

Holly shrugged. "I don't know, Tatty. Daddy's got his parents in the car, and he just said, 'Confusion.' They're getting older, sweetheart. It's hard for them to travel. But they'll be here soon, and we can take care of them. I better take a shower."

Holly smiled at Tatty, who did not return her smile. *Christ.* Was Tatty, like Eric, going to take offense now at any suggestion Holly made that Gin and Gramps were *old*? How long was this denial going to last? Was Holly the only one who could see what was going on here—that this elderly couple should not be traveling alone, should not be *living* on their own? Was she the only one who'd noticed how quickly and completely things had been going downhill for Gin and Gramps in the last couple of years? She turned in the direction of the bathroom. To her back, Tatiana said, "Merry-juana Christmas."

Holly inhaled sharply, but she checked the impulse to turn around. She could not turn around. If she did, she would have to face some expression she didn't want to see on her daughter's face—disapproval, contempt, *dislike*? She didn't want to see it or to acknowledge it—especially not now, with addled family members and unpleasant colleagues (and friends, good friends, don't forget them) on the way. She would never have time to get everything ready before they all arrived for Christmas dinner. She still had a shower to take, and a roast to cook, and a table to set, and a bed to be made, and—

And then it came back to her like a bit of breeze stirred up gently by a few cold fingers:

That *something* she'd wanted so badly to write about when she woke up.

She'd wanted, needed, to write it down because it was the beginning of something she had to understand, or to express, or to unearth, or to face, yet she still hadn't found two seconds to grab a pen and to be alone to write.

Something had followed them home.

And it had been here in the house with them for thirteen years now. Holly had known it was here! But it was only this morning that she'd woken up knowing that she'd known.

If only she hadn't overslept. Certainly, now, there was no time to write. But if she hadn't overslept, would she have had this revelation and this need to write?

In the bathroom, she yanked the shower curtain open. Tatty's tea tree oil shampoo bottle had fallen from the edge of the tub into the bottom of it, and Holly huffed, bent down, picked it up. It was too big, this bottle, to balance with the others in the porcelain corner. She'd told Tatty they needed to buy the smaller bottle, for this very reason, but Tatty had stood in the aisle at Whole Foods with the two shampoo bottles, one in each hand, and said, "Mom. God. The nine-ounce bottle costs *two dollars less* than the thirty ounce. Do you know how much money we're wasting, not to mention *plastic*?"

"Tatty, honey," Holly had said, "we don't always have to buy the economy size of everything. There's a little thing called convenience. It's more *convenient* not to have a gigantic bottle of shampoo in the bathroom, or an industrial-sized jar of peanut butter in the pantry."

"Yeah, Mom, and that's why we're always running out of things, including money."

"What are you talking about?" Holly asked. When had she ever said anything to Tatty about *money*? Whatever money troubles she and Eric had, they were both in agreement that Tatty was never, *never*, to be troubled by them. They'd both been far too aware as children of their parents' financial woes. This would not be their child's burden.

Still, even as Holly stood in the aisle of Whole Foods denying her daughter the enormous sea-foam-green bottle of organic tea tree oil shampoo, she was also taking it out of Tatty's hand and putting it in the cart. This, she knew, was not the hill she wanted to die on, not here at Whole Foods, where, she would have liked to have pointed out to Tatty, no one for whom money was much of an issue shopped. Why did they even bother with economy sizes in a place that charged, unabashedly, eleven dollars for certain tiny loaves of bread?

But what did her daughter know about the economy of any of this? She was fifteen. She was clueless. Plus, she'd been indoctrinated by the school system. Tatty would allow herself to die of thirst in the desert before she'd sip water that had been bottled in plastic. Holly wasn't even sure that she herself had ever even heard the word *sustainability* until a couple of years ago, but Tatiana chanted it like a mantra, along with the name of its evil twin, Waste.

Holly had just shoved the shampoo bottle into the corner again when it rolled, with the heavy solid sound a human head might make, lopped off, back into the bottom of the tub. This time she picked it up and took it to the linen closet. Tatty would have to fetch it and return it there from now on if this was the kind of jumbo bottle it took to make her happy in this world.

Holly hurried back to the shower, where the water rattled against the shower curtain, warming. No time, no time. The tiles were cold on Holly's bare feet. She stepped over to the little lilac bathroom rug and picked her nightgown up off the floor, tossed it into the laundry basket. She thought, as she did nearly every time she opened that wicker basket, of Baby Tatty, who, as a toddler, would crawl into that basket and pull the lid down over herself.

It had been a glorious game, one of those family ritual games that become so much a part of daily life it seems impossible that a time could ever come when it would not be played:

"Where's Tatty? Oh, no, Eric, where's our baby? I can't find her anywhere!"

After five minutes of this, the Jet-Black Rapunzel would leap from the wicker basket and scream, "I'm here!"

❄

BUT, THE FIRST time, it had not been funny at all. Holly had gone that morning into Tatty's bedroom expecting to find her in the Big Girl Bed, with which they'd only a few weeks earlier replaced her crib. Tatiana wasn't in it. Instead, a Barbie doll, with the covers up to her plastic chin, had her head resting on Tatty's pink pillow. Her blank blue eyes stared into Holly's own:

German Barbie, Second Edition, with her absurd blond braids and fixed expression of surprised delight. It was the Barbie Tatty had insisted on when Holly had excitedly pointed out Imperial Russian Princess Barbie to her on the Internet. Although Holly had ended up buying them both, the Imperial Princess never budged from the shoe box in which Tatty kept her at the bottom of the toy box, while the German Barbie slept with Tatty every night.

"Tatty?"

Ridiculously, Holly had spoken her daughter's name to the awful doll. Of course, the doll said nothing, and a wave of horror passed through Holly's body then, a kind of nausea, beginning in her stomach but sliding up her spine and into her brain. Panic.

Had she honestly thought, or only felt, primevally, in her Irish bones:

Changeling?

Holly yanked the covers off German Barbie then to find no three-year-old Tatty under there with her.

"*Tatty?!*" By now, Holly was angry. She thought, she's *punishing* me. Which was also ridiculous! A toddler doesn't *punish* her mother.

The rest was a blur of very precise imagery, as if Holly's horror had been turned into a mental slideshow—fifty very clear slides of herself crashing through the house while holding, inexplicably, German Barbie in her hand by the waist, like a weapon, or like proof of something, or like Tatty herself.

"Please! Tatty! Please! Mommy can't find you!"

It might have been the last place left in the house to look—the laundry basket. Holly had already torn through all the closets. Looked under the beds. She'd stumbled down to the basement. She'd checked the dryer, behind the furnace. She was crying by the time she reached the laundry basket, no longer even calling out her daughter's name. She was feeling the breath of the nurse from the Pokrovka Orphanage #2 who'd whispered into her neck, *Name her American.*

"Sally?" she'd called out, clearly having lost her mind by then. Had she thought that Tatiana might somehow answer to that first name, the one the nurses had given her in Siberia? Tatiana had never even been told about that name. Not even later, when Holly stupidly named their doomed hen Sally, had she or Eric ever told Tatty that Sally had once been her name. So it must have been some primitive, maternal instinct, calling out that infant name in search of her lost daughter.

Still, there was no answer. Time stopped. Holly would never know how long it had taken her to lift the wicker lid of the laundry basket (lifetimes seemed to pass) and to peer into it to find her daughter squatting—froglike, staring up, feigning innocence while attempting, like a much older child or an adult, to suppress a smile, eyes cartoonishly wide with the pleasure of all this, inside the basket.

Holly had staggered backward, leaned against the bathroom wall. She'd wiped German Barbie's alpine apron across her tear-filled eyes while Tatty clambered out of the basket. Tatty knew, of course, that something was wrong. She threw her arms around Holly's legs and started, herself, to cry.

"No, no," Holly had said, kneeling down on the cold tile, taking Tatty fully in her arms. "You didn't mean to scare Mommy. You were being funny. But it scared Mommy because she loves you so, so, so, so much."

But it took an hour to calm Tatty down.

They had to go back to her bedroom and try the whole trick again:

This time they pretended they were Tatty, together, tucking German Barbie into the Big Girl Bed as if German Barbie were Tatiana. Then they pretended that they were sneaking out of the Big Girl Bed into the bathroom, climbing into the basket. They laughed as they did this, but quietly, secretly. Climbing into the basket had been, apparently, quite a feat. Tatty had to make several attempts before she could get it right a second time. And it must have taken truly super-toddler control to stay in that basket, squatting on Eric's T-shirts and socks and a damp green towel at the bottom of the basket, there in the wickery dark with just a bit of light shining through the lid, listening to Mommy call her name.

Holly and Tatty played the game. This time Mommy marched straight into the bathroom, lifted the lid of the laundry basket, and screamed in delight, "Tatty!" And Tatty burst into laughter, sprang up with her small hands above her head, and cried out, "I'm here!" Holly held up German Barbie and said, "I thought the fairies had come and exchanged my pretty Baby Tatty with this doll!"

"No!" Tatty said. "This is me!"

"Brilliant, really," Eric had said that evening when Holly recounted the event of the morning to him as he stood beside their bed, changing out of his traveling clothes into a T-shirt and shorts. "She's a genius," he said. "I mean, that's a level of sophistication that you really wouldn't expect from a three-year-old. Not to mention the self-discipline."

Holly had to agree. It thrilled her that Eric felt that way about it, too. In the morning, she and Tatty reenacted the whole thing for Daddy. And then, for two years afterward, they played the laundry basket game at least once a week—"Where's Tatty? *Tatty?*"—with Mommy's panic and Tatty's stealth being the crucial ingredients to the fun and hilarity. Until finally, surreptitiously, as if in a dream, those years were over, and Tatty had grown too big to hide in the laundry basket.

❄

HOLLY BENT HER head under the stream of shower water, which was too hot—but that was better than too cold, and there was barely enough time left to shower and get ready for the guests, and for Christmas dinner, let alone adjust the temperature of the water. Her hair felt dry and rustically cut. She'd gotten it trimmed a week ago, and it was too short. It felt unfamiliar to her, like a wig, or like a doll's hair. She wouldn't bother to shampoo and condition it. What was the point, since she wouldn't have time to blow it out or use the curling iron? She had far too much to do to fuss with her personal appearance. Now however Holly was going to look when Eric's siblings got here—and Pearl and Thuy, and the awful Coxes—was going to be some compromised vision of what she'd wanted to look like. She'd wanted to look rested and joyful and lovely, but she wouldn't.

Oh, *God* . . .

When Holly remembered the Coxes she also remembered, with the sharpness of a poke of a pencil in the side, that she had to assemble the ingredients for the vegan dish Mindy Cox had suggested Holly make for her horrible son.

Bulgur and sweet potato pilaf.

Jesus.

As if Christmas dinner weren't already hard enough to assemble. Whatever happened to polite people not discussing religion, politics, or money with people outside their own families, and everyone eating, and being grateful for, whatever they were served at a dinner party?

Or, if they couldn't manage that, *staying home*?

Why must everyone be informed of the tastes and requirements and politics of everyone else's diets? Their lactose intolerances. Their tree nut allergies. Their aversion to farm-raised salmon, red meat, gluten. Nearly every night of her entire childhood life Holly had carefully eaten around the things on her plate that horrified her. The soft-boiled carrots. The stringy, deep maroon Mystery Meat. She would dig to the bottom of her salad to find the iceberg lettuce that had remained untouched by the French dressing without ever considering asking her sister to please not drench her salad in French dressing.

She'd even deluded her poor mother into believing that she, her youngest daughter, "ate like a bird," when, in truth, Holly, as a child, had been ravenous, nauseated, polite. And thank God she had been, since how many meals did she ever really even get to eat that had been prepared by her mother before her mother died? And how hard must it have been for that poor woman simply to prepare a meal? What if Holly had decided to announce one night that she would only eat eggs laid by cage-free chickens, or that she was philosophically opposed to Cheez Whiz?

And after Holly's mother could no longer stand in the kitchen long enough to heat up a pot of Campbell's soup, the job of feeding the family had gone to Janet and Melissa—both of them teenagers, clueless, desperate, grief-stricken, and, Holly supposed, resentful, although she could not remember a single word or event that might have indicated that. Somehow they'd managed to keep the family running on Swanson's lasagna, frozen meatballs, and pizzas—and it would never have occurred to anyone to announce that he or she did not eat processed foods.

The shower water continued to run in a burning rivulet down Holly's spine, and she felt as if that heat, that water, might unzip her. She imagined it doing so, the flesh opening at her spine, and how it would feel, then, to step out of her body.

Who would she be then? Where would she go? She recalled the sense she'd had, looking down at her dead mother's blank face, that one might actually do that. Escape her body. That the body was a kind of cage. That the self, the *soul*, was cage-free. That being cage-free was the goal, attained by death.

Ha! *That* had been before she and Eric had themselves owned cage-free chickens! Free-range life hadn't worked out so well for *their* chickens, had it? Some bloody feathers and screeching. They'd called those hens, until the bloody feathers and gang violence, by endearing names. Petunia. Patrice. Sally. But they were not tame, sweet, happy birds. They should have been kept under lock and key.

Holly closed her eyes as the water fell on her face. God, how she would have loved to stuff the plug into the drain and just let the tub fill with scalding water, lie back in it, close her eyes. Why was she so tired? She'd woken up less than an hour earlier, later than she'd slept in years.

WAS IT THE eggnog and rum?

But how cozy that had been, cuddled up on the couch with Eric in the living room, lit up only by the lights of the Christmas tree. Tatiana had gone to bed already, and there was the hush of the house and the snowfall outside and all their memories of that first Christmas—Siberia, Baby Tatty, the ratty blanket, and that baby's enormous eyes. She'd already had lustrous dark hair, but she was not the Jet-Black Rapunzel yet. The nurses weren't calling Tatiana that until Eric and Holly returned, fourteen weeks later, to legally and completely claim her:

How shocked they'd been to find how much their child had changed in those weeks—her hair grown down around her shoulders, and her face narrower, her eyes no longer shockingly large, more in proportion to her changed face.

Was it possible, they'd asked themselves, that Tatiana was even more beautiful fourteen weeks later than she'd been during their first visit?

Of course.

And she'd grown even more beautiful every month since!

Eric had gotten up from the couch and fixed them another rum and eggnog. He brought it back, and they talked some more about that Christmas and their first glimpse of Tatiana. It was what they'd reminisced about every Christmas since then. Their daughter. About how nervous they'd been. About the garlic necklaces. About the vicious dog that had chased them down the street the first time they'd left the hostel to go to the Pokrovka Orphanage #2, and how they'd arrived sweating in their down coats and must have looked to the nurses like crazy people.

Until after midnight, Holly and Eric had sat with their drinks in the light of the Christmas tree, long after Tatiana had gone to her room to sleep. So many years having passed in what had seemed like an instant, they laughed again about how no one had seemed to know where, or if, the Pokrovka Orphanage #1 existed, and how distinctly Russian that seemed. How everything in the country was referred to by its number, but the number seemed never to correspond to any order or sequence. If there was a bus #37, it was sure to arrive at bus stop #4 long before bus #1.

What they hadn't talked about was that they'd forgotten, then, that it was even Christmas that day. They'd arrived at the Pokrovka Orphanage #2 on December 25 to see the baby who would be theirs, and they'd failed to bring a single gift.

No gifts! Not for their child, and not for her caretakers, and although the day was not their Russian Orthodox Christmas, those nurses must have been only too aware of the tradition of gifts on December 25 after so many hundreds of other American families had passed through the orphanage at the end of December bearing them.

And the other American couple who were staying at the hostel had brought Christmas gifts! *They* hadn't forgotten, arriving at the orphanage with the kinds of things that young Siberian women could never be able to buy for themselves—perfume, complexion soap, leather gloves. And for the child they wanted to adopt, those parents had brought bibs and booties and a hand-knitted sweater.

"Oh, my God," Holly had said, fingering the delicate, tiny sweater the woman from Nebraska had brought with her—into the sleeves of which she was just then stuffing the rosy, pudgy arms of the son she desperately wanted. What was that sweater knitted from? Angora? Cashmere? Mohair? Holly knew nothing about yarn, about knitting, about what kind of animals offered up such a softness. Were they baby camels, some sort of special llama? Were the animals sheared, or skinned? And how was it that this yarn was like dental floss, unbreakable, while also seeming to be made of cloud?

"This is exquisite," Holly had said, fingering that sweater, and she'd meant it. "What in the world is it made of?"

But the Nebraskan woman had never really told her. Instead, she'd said, as if Holly herself must be a knitter and would know what this meant, "Little billions."

Little billions?

Was that some kind of knitting strategy, or a brand, or a pattern?

"Well, it's incredible," Holly said, neither wanting to reveal that she did not know what "little billions" were, or to hear a long explanation of what they might be.

"Thank you," the Nebraskan had said, then pulled her ruddy Russian baby away from Holly and turned her back. Over the woman's shoulder, that little boy looked teary-eyed with joy, as if he'd finally found the great love of his life, and the sweater he'd been born to wear, and the mother in whose arms he'd been born to be held. The woman from Nebraska was sexless and ageless and humorless, Holly thought—but she had a passionate soul, which Holly saw fully, shining brightly, the next morning when the woman and her small, quiet husband got the news that the boy in the sweater had been given, the night before, to the sister of the biological father. Apparently that had been the plan all along, but the sister had procrastinated on the paperwork until she was told that an American couple was there, ready to take the baby home with them.

It was the Nebraskans' second trip to Siberia (as required by Russian law) in their quest to take possession of this boy. Until this, they'd never heard a word about a sister, and this was the very day they thought they would fly home with him, bringing him to the nursery it took Holly almost no imagination to picture: filled with stuffed animals, decorated with stenciled airplanes, a crib made up with pale blue sheets.

Instead, that morning, the Nebraskan woman went to the boy's empty crib at the Pokrovka Orphanage #2, took the mattress out of it, held it in her arms (nothing but a plastic-covered mattress, not even a sheet left on it), and walked straight out the door of the orphanage into the snow, without stopping for her coat. As far as Eric and Holly knew, she had never come back.

Though of course, she had to have come back. Her husband had stayed behind, standing speechless at a window for a long time before he turned on the nurses, demanding answers:

"Where is our boy? Who is this 'sister'?!"

But the nurses would tell him nothing. The nurses in the Pokrovka Orphanage #2 had, it seemed, taken vows of silence. You could not have tortured information out of them about anything—not the other adoptive parents, not the other babies, not the biological parents of the babies, not what was behind "that door"—the one that was always kept closed (and which Holly would regret opening, later)—or what would happen to all the babies who were not adopted:

Nothing.

It was *all* a secret. The entire country was a secret, and Siberia was the vast white secret at the center of it. At the Pokrovka Orphanage #2, all Eric and Holly could be sure of was what they could see before them, that which they could weigh in their arms, that which they could explore with their senses. Otherwise, there was only an inscrutable expanse beyond the rattling institutional windows and the paperwork—the reams and reams of paperwork, which, despite its meticulous detail, revealed nothing about anything at all.

Later, when Holly thought of that woman from Nebraska (although she tried not to), she imagined her still walking. That woman could have made a circuit of Asia several times by now, cradling that mattress in her arms.

And what *of* the Russian aunt, cradling the boy in his soft and delicate sweater? Where were *they* now, these many years later? Holly imagined a boy standing at the center of a long line. He would have a thin mustache, acne, maybe a facial twitch. And the sweater that his Nebraskan mother had knitted for him would either have unraveled long ago or been sold. Holly tried not to think of him, either, because when she did she could not help but think of Tatiana in that line behind him—her hair cropped short, and her shoes comfortable, practical, caked with mud.

"Tragic," Eric had called it.

"Well, they could have adopted another baby," Holly pointed out. "There were a billion of them."

"Well, they wanted *that* baby," Eric had said, angrily. "Just like we wanted Tatiana. They'd already bonded. They'd imagined a whole life with him."

"It was time to start imagining again, I guess," Holly had said, feeling that she would somehow be betraying her own good luck, the fate that had brought Tatiana so effortlessly into her arms, if she admitted that what had happened to the Nebraskans could have happened to anyone. Eric had simply looked at her with what she felt was disapproval, and they never spoke of the Nebraskans again after that.

❄

HOLLY STEPPED OUT of the shower. The drain made the heaving sucking sounds it always made as it emptied the tub. She stepped onto the lilac rug, wrapped herself in her towel, stepped over to the bathroom window, and looked out.

Snowy day. A surprisingly white one. Usually in this part of the state, with the wind blowing off Lake Erie and then over the decaying auto factories before it fell into their yard, the snow was gray, nothing like the Bing Crosby snowfalls of her youth. Usually that gray snow didn't shine in the branches, but, instead, just fuzzed up the landscape, which was mostly flatness and emptiness at this time of year, although some dead leaves still held on to the tree branches and here and there a stubborn evergreen would point its arrow at the gray sky.

But this was a *lot* of snow. And it was Christmas-white. This could almost be called a blizzard, Holly supposed, and she thought of Eric on the road home with his parents. She pictured his windshield and the wipers barely keeping up with the white piling up on him. It made for a prettied-up landscape, but the driving would be treacherous.

Again, she thought of her dream, and waking from it, and the need to write something, to make or create or weave something from the materials of her psyche.

But what was the hurry?

Jesus, she'd had plenty of time to write in the last twenty years, and she hadn't written *then*. She'd had one whole summer off—the summer before they'd adopted Tatty, and what had she done with all that time? Instead of writing she'd rented herself a booth in a local antiques mall and filled it with junk she bought at garage sales, which no one but she herself would ever want. She'd completely wasted the months of June, July, and August—the months for which she'd been awarded a nice little grant from the Virginia Woolf Foundation for a manuscript of fifteen poems she'd submitted to them along with a page detailing how she'd use the money to "take time off from my job to finish my first poetry collection, the title of which will be *Ghost Country*, from the title poem of the collection—an ode to my lost ovaries."

She'd written not a single line of poetry. Instead, there was not a mote of dust on a single item in Holly's booth at the antiques mall that summer. She put a thousand miles on the car driving from one estate sale to the next, thrilling herself with surprises:

A ceramic doll she found at a multifamily sale at a trailer park, with ruby flecks for eyes. A last rites box, with a half-empty bottle of holy water tucked into it from an estate sale across the street from a Catholic church. She bought doilies and doorknobs and tiny primitive paintings in tarnished silver frames. But the only thing she sold that summer was the one thing she hadn't wanted to sell—a wreath woven by some bereaved Victorian mother out of her little boy's flaxen hair.

The wreath was glued to a portrait of the boy, who looked like an ugly girl in his lacy dress. Under his chin, in a woman's ink-blotched script, was written *Our Beloved Boy Charles*.

Holly had been stunned one day to come into the antiques mall and find that wreath gone. She'd asked the owner of the antiques booth (Frank, of the handlebar mustache, who worked the register there ten hours a day, six days a week) who'd purchased it, but Frank couldn't remember his customers, ever. And the buyer hadn't written a check or used a credit card, apparently. There was nothing left but the price tag, which Holly had written out herself, plucked from it, and placed in the cash register to prove the mourning wreath had been bought, not stolen. The $325 had been credited to the rent Holly paid to Frank for the booth.

It was during the period of this grant that Holly realized that it wasn't *time* she'd needed in order to write the poems that would finish the collection. What she needed, she decided, was a child. She emptied the antiques booth and began to order books off Amazon about overseas adoption.

THE STEAM FROM inside the bathroom was sucked out into the hallway when Holly opened the door. Once it had escaped, it disappeared so quickly it was as if it had a will of its own, as if it had been a caged animal waiting for this opportunity to escape.

She had taken a longer shower than she'd meant to. In the mirror in the bedroom, she could see that her face and neck and chest were brightly flushed. She was burning brightly, but softly, as if her skin had been sealed—shiny, poreless. Holly stepped away from her reflection. Now that she had showered, the rest of the day, the *real* rest of the day, had to begin.

What should she wear? Tatiana had gone for festive and sentimental with that hideous velvet dress. Eric had left the house in jeans and a sweatshirt, in which he would probably stay for the rest of the day. Ginny and Gramps would be in black. Whenever there was an occasion to travel or to attend a gathering of any sort, Eric's parents dressed like Italian peasants at a funeral. Ginny might even be wearing that black shawl of hers. Gramps's black would be rumpled, threadbare. The two of them would look as if they'd been on a very long journey by ship across the Atlantic, not on a jet from Newark to Detroit.

Once, Holly had suggested to Eric that his parents dressed this way in public in order to be mistaken for poor people.

"Well, they're *not* rich," Eric had said. "I have no idea why you would say that." These words were Eric's roadblock—his refrain whenever Holly suggested that his parents might have (as she knew for a fact, from snooping, that they did) considerable sums tucked away in a bank in Pennsylvania (a bank chosen, Holly felt sure, so that none of their neighbors would hear any gossip of those vast sums).

So why, then, did this couple in their eighties dress in public like a couple two generations more ancient than they were—as if they were the ones who'd come over on that ship, rather than their parents? Gin and Gramps owned plenty of brightly colored polyester sweaters, which they wore around their condominium. Gramps was a retired high school teacher. Gin had once sold Avon door-to-door. She had a huge collection of poodle pins, most of them garish and pink, many of them plastic, and she was never without one in her own home. So, why, then, did they pretend to be Old World olive farmers whenever they needed to board a bus or show up at a graduation? And what should *Holly* wear, given that she knew what the guests of honor would be wearing, if not why?

Eric's brothers and their wives—well, it would be a mix of formal and casual, but there would be tremendous effort put into everything, and very careful consideration:

The nieces and nephews would be scrubbed down to the bones. Eric's three brothers would be in denim mostly, but at least one of them would be wearing a suit coat. Their wives would have flowing sweaters, silk pants. There might even be a cape of some sort. Whatever Holly wore would seem plain in comparison, but she was certainly not going to totter around her own house in high heels. She owned no pretty slippers. She would just have to feel dowdy and flat-footed in her stocking feet.

Holly scanned her closet. Wraparound dresses and dark skirts. Long-sleeved blouses and sleeveless ones. Nothing looked right for Christmas. The Coxes, she knew, would overdo it—a suit for him, a lacy top and Victorian-inspired earrings for her. Their son would be in a button-down with khaki pants.

Pearl and Thuy would be organic—loose, clean, bland in subdued colors—although they'd have Patty dressed up like a Disney princess. Patty was, admittedly, all about princesses, but considering the number of tiaras the child owned (far more than could be reasonably demanded by a four-year-old) Holly wondered if it might be the gender-indifferent Pearl and Thuy who wanted their daughter to be Cinderella. Bless their generous hearts.

Holly pulled a busy jersey dress off a hanger and tossed it on the bed. She'd worn it the other day to Tatty's choir concert, so she knew it fit nicely.

"Mom?"

Tatty's voice startled Holly, but she was also relieved to hear it. Tatty wasn't sulking in her room. There was for-giveness implicit in that.

"Come in, hon," Holly said.

Tatty opened the bedroom door a crack, and then stood with her toes on the threshold, peering in.

"Your phone rang while you were in the shower, Mom."

"Who was it?"

"I don't know," Tatiana said. "I didn't answer. It said 'unavailable.'"

Holly stepped behind the closet door to slip off her robe and put on her bra. She didn't need a bra, of course. She had the kind of breasts that would still be pointing at the sky when she was in a nursing home, or in her coffin (fake ones). But wearing a bra made her feel more "pulled together"—a phrase her mother used to use, complimenting women who were nicely dressed, whose hair had been styled stiffly, and who were not, like Holly's mother, terminally ill.

"Well," Holly said to Tatty. "Can't be too important then. Some robot calling with a credit card offer or something." She stepped into the dress and pulled the tie around her waist.

"On Christmas Day?" Tatiana asked.

"Well, robots don't celebrate Christmas," Holly said. "They don't have souls, remember?"

Tatiana didn't smile, although Holly knew her daughter knew what she was joking about. There'd been a period, around third grade, when Tatiana had become obsessed with what *had a soul*, and what did not. Holly had tried to explain the concept of the soul to Tatiana, impressing upon her that it wasn't science, so there was no real answer to Tatiana's question, unless Tatiana herself had some working definition of what she meant by *soul*.

And, actually, much to Holly's surprise, Tatiana had such a definition:

The soul was the thing hidden inside the thing, and made it what it was. You could not be, say, an actual parrot without a parrot soul.

"So a soul is inside a body?" Holly had asked.

Well, Tatiana had explained, sometimes the soul could be *behind* the body, maybe, and sometimes it could be *beside* or *beneath* or *above*, but, yes, usually it was inside. A book, for instance, had its soul in the crack between the two middlemost pages. This was typical of foldable things. Like butterflies, who had their souls where their two wings came together.

"So, like, the telephone book has a soul then?" Holly had asked, trying not to look too amused. Her daughter hated to be condescended to. She preferred to be argued with outright.

"Well, that's what I'm asking," Tatiana said. "That's why I'm asking you. *I* don't *know. I'm* only nine years old."

"Well, sweetheart," Holly had said, "I'm forty, and I don't know either, so don't feel too bad."

But Tatiana rarely just let a subject go with an *I don't know.* Often, it seemed purely willful to Holly. The pleasure and curiosity would have already gone out of the asking, but the asking would go on. A matter of stubborn pride would take over. A combative insincerity would be at the center of the discussion at that point.

"So do our chickens have souls?" Tatiana asked Holly.

"Well, if books and butterflies do, I—"

"I didn't say they *all* do! I didn't say all books and all butterflies have souls! I don't know! I'm asking *you.*"

By then, Holly was exasperated. Tatiana was very young, but she was too old for this kind of illogic. She must have read something somewhere, or seen some inane kid's comedy drama and was lifting the crappy, bombastic dialogue from it.

"Okay then," Holly had said, tilting her head, rolling her eyes to let Tatty know that she was onto her. "Here's a list of things that have souls: People, cats, chickens, and all other mammals. Fish and insects have souls, and lilac bushes, but no other plant life. Some very nice cars, like BMWs and Subaru Outbacks, but nothing made by General Motors. Also, rocks don't have souls, and robots don't. How's that?"

"That's all I wanted to know," Tatty had said, and shrugged. "I just wanted to know about robots. Thanks, Mom."

There was no sarcasm in it. Holly had shaken her head at her daughter's back, not at all sure if she'd won or lost this game. Eric, of course, when he heard about the exchange, had expostulated about how precocious their daughter was, so Holly hadn't bothered to explain to him that the whole thing had been, actually, not precocious but derivative. Tatty had understood from Holly's reaction that she was making a little juvenile fool of herself with the questions, so she'd played the only card she had left, which was to shut the whole thing down with a shrug of the shoulders and a pat little answer. *That's all I wanted to know.* But what would have been the point of trying to tell the doting daddy *that*? That his perfect daughter could occasionally be unoriginal, or manipulative? Unthinkable!

Now, however, whenever Tatty tried to start some imitative argument ("All the *other* kids are going . . . !") Holly would say, "And robots don't have souls," and Tatiana's nostrils would flare, and there would appear that little muscle pulsing at her jaw, and her bluish lids would draw halfway down over her dark eyes, and Holly would just smile, ending the argument, knowing that her daughter knew exactly what she meant:

You're faking, you heard this somewhere else, you're just mouthing these words, and I know it.

❄

"I JUST THOUGHT you'd want me to tell you that your phone was ringing," Tatiana said. "It might have been important, even if it was Unavailable, even on Christmas Day."

"Honey, my cell phone gets a call from Mr. Unavailable *every* day. Mr. Unavailable has been trying to get in touch with me ever since caller ID was invented. Sometimes I even get a call from Mrs. Name Withheld."

"You're funny, Mom. I mean, you are so, so funny."

Holly felt stung, but not surprised, that the conversation had gone from sarcastic to nasty so fast. She tried not to rise to the bait. She tried to sound genuine, asking, "Well, Tatiana, who do you think might be trying to call?"

Her daughter said nothing. Holly sighed, and looked away from her to the window. She was surprised to see that the curtains were parted. She didn't remember doing that. Perhaps it had been Eric, before he left, and Holly hadn't noticed it until now because the heavy snow that was falling out there was like a second layer of curtains—but made of movement. Chaotic particles. Electrical sparking.

She went to her dresser to find a pair of black tights, and said to Tatty, "Why didn't you answer my phone, sweetheart, if you're curious? I never said you couldn't answer my phone. Answer my phone anytime you want."

Still, Tatiana said nothing. She was looking up at the ceiling, unblinking, so Holly took the moment to peruse her, and noticed that Tatty was wearing the tiny opals that Pearl and Thuy had given her for her thirteenth birthday. She was going all out, wasn't she? The opals for Pearl and Thuy, the velvet dress for Gin. It was sweet. Tatiana had always been a thoughtful child—the first on the playground to run to a fight and try to stop it, the first to comfort a crying baby or a whining puppy—but she was growing into a genuinely considerate young woman.

"That's so nice," Holly said, looking at her daughter's earlobes, "that you're wearing the opals Pearl and Thuy gave you."

Tatiana immediately touched, as every woman does, whatever part of her was under discussion. Her earrings, her scarf, the necklace at her collarbone. Eric used to swat Holly away from her hair, saying that every time he told her it looked nice she put her hands into it and mussed it all up. But it was hard, if you weren't facing a mirror, to be sure what was being observed about you if you couldn't see it yourself. It was natural to try to *feel* it.

"I wasn't trying to be nice," Tatiana said. "I like the earrings."

Holly deflated again. "I wasn't trying to pick a fight," she said. "I like that you thought to wear earrings that were given to you by guests we're having over today. I know there are other earrings you own that you like, and I was trying to point out that it was a nice thing to do to choose those. But, Tatty, I'm sorry if I misunderstood."

Tatty turned quickly on the heel of her black ballet slipper then, and she was over the threshold before she saw Holly grit her teeth at her daughter's back.

Holly sat on the edge of the bed, and rolled one leg of the black tights up her leg. She would, she supposed, be punished all day for sleeping in on Christmas morning. Not only would her daughter be in a continuous state of disapproval, Eric's brothers and their wives would soon be here, full of concern about their parents, which would hold the subtext of blame directed toward Holly that Eric had overslept (which would be Holly's fault somehow) and been late to pick them up at the airport.

Why must Christmas always be at *their* house? Holly

would have happily traveled to New Jersey or Pennsylvania or upstate New York for the holiday. She'd love to spend Christmas Day walking around Tony and Gretchen's house—inspecting Gretchen's silverware for sticky remains of some previous meal, holding her crystal up to the light to see if it was greasy. She'd have happily accompanied Eric to his parents' condominium, for that matter, and cooked dinner there! She'd have happily made arrangements for all of them to meet at a resort in Florida! Or Cancún! Or Bend, Oregon!

But, it seemed, having had Christmas at Eric and Holly's the first year they were married meant that Eric's family would have Christmas at Holly and Eric's forever, even if Holly was so disrespectful and irresponsible that she hadn't even woken her husband up on Christmas morning.

Holly didn't put shoes on, or her perfume, or her earrings, or even her watch. She went straight out to the kitchen in her stocking feet, where she found Tatty holding, and peering into, the iPhone Holly had left on the counter. A cool blue glow rose from the screen of it, and it turned Tatty's skin to a color Holly didn't like—the color of a sick girl, or a drowned girl.

Tatty had a beautiful complexion, which could have been called porcelain. Except that porcelain was whiter than the color of Tatty's skin, which was more the color of crayfish bisque—or at least the crayfish bisque Holly's mother used to make before she grew too ill to cook such things. A little grayer than bone. Creamier than ivory. Cream with a drop of violet mixed into it. In certain light, and in certain photographs, there was a tint of pale blue to Tatiana's face—a little deeper near the temples, under her eyes. Sometimes her lips looked as if she'd just come in from the cold, deep end of the pool.

It was the most beautiful complexion Holly had ever seen. Elegant. Mildly exotic. But institutional light didn't suit it, nor did the glow of the iPhone. "Put that down," Holly said.

Tatty looked up, opened her mouth, unhinging her jaw slightly, and huffed. She put the cell phone down on the marble top of the kitchen island, and then gestured to it, and said, "I *knew* you'd be pissed. You always say, 'Go ahead and answer my cell phone,' but I so much as *pick up* your cell phone and you're *all over me.*"

Holly shook her head. She was so tired of this teenage tone of voice, these reflexive accusations. How long was this phase of Tatiana's existence going to last? "Jesus, Tatiana," she said. "Take it down a notch, would you? I wasn't *all over you*. I just—"

"No. You just reflexively reprimand me these days, that's what! I can't do anything right."

"Look," Holly said, picking up the cell phone between them. "We don't have time for this. Did Unavailable call back?"

"No."

"Well, if and when that happens, just answer the phone. That's that. If the phone rings, answer the phone. Until then, you have your own phone, and please leave mine on the counter where I can find it if Daddy calls."

"I was *at* the counter while I was looking at it."

"Fine, okay, sweetheart. You win. I'm sorry. We truly do not have time for this. I need to start cooking, or we won't have anything to eat."

"God, Mom. You should've started cooking two hours ago," Tatty said. "Every year you start cooking at, like, eight o'clock in the morning."

"Well this year I overslept! Okay? This year I slept in! Shoot me, Tatty! Just put me out of my misery! Please!" Holly turned, and forced a laugh out of her lungs to try to dilute the sound of her rage, and also to spare herself the indignity of having lost her temper, but her heart was pounding hard in the soft spot at the base of her neck, which made her feel like some sort of underwater creature. As if she had some panicky gill there. She could hardly swallow. She was about to instruct Tatty in what she could do to help hurry the Christmas dinner preparations along, instead of complaining, when, on the counter where it lay, her cell phone began to sing "A Hard Rain's A-Gonna Fall."

Holly turned. Tatiana was looking at the phone without touching it. "Is it Daddy?" Holly asked.

"No. It's Unavailable," Tatty said.

"Well go ahead and answer it if you want to, sweetheart."

But Tatiana just stood and stared into the phone. She'd sat down on the stool next to the kitchen island, so that now her feet dangled four inches from the floor in their little black slippers, exactly the way they used to when Tatty was three and a half feet tall and sat behind Holly in her car seat as Holly drove her to day care.

Christ. Holly felt so sad. She'd chastised her daughter, who was now afraid to touch her cell phone. And poor Tatty looked worried. Her eyebrows were arched so that they formed an upside-down V on her forehead. They were dark, a little bushy, Tatty's eyebrows—but that was fashionable now, and Tatty's facial features were so elegant that no eyebrows could have taken away from that. Still, someday Tatty would probably want to pluck them, and the idea of that also made Holly feel sad. Being female was so hard. Always having to rearrange yourself, to pluck yourself and whittle yourself and deprive yourself and inspect yourself in order to feel comfortable in this world. Bob Dylan continued to rasp out the lyrics— *And where have you been, my darling young one?*—and her daughter just kept looking into the phone. Again, Tatiana's face took on that awful hue—the silvery blue of a fish tossed up on a pier—and she made no move whatsoever to answer Holly's phone.

"Oh, come on," Holly said, and picked it up, hit the green answer bar with her thumb. "Hello?"

But the call had already gone to voice mail, and if there was a way to interrupt voice mail and answer the call at this point, Holly hadn't learned it. She'd only learned how to use about half the features of this phone. It was like the brain, the way the experts claimed a human being only used about 10 percent of what was available up there. Steve Jobs, like God, had given her much more to work with than she would ever be able to make use of.

She put the phone on the counter again and cocked her head at Tatty, determining that she was not going to ask her why she hadn't answered. It was, obviously, punishment for Holly's having told her to put down the phone a few minutes earlier. Holly did not want to get into a defensive position again, especially since it *had* been irrational, which Tatiana knew full well and could call her on in a flash. Holly had asked her daughter to put down the phone because she didn't like the color it was turning her daughter's skin as she peered into it. There was certainly no explaining *that.*

"No one's going to leave a message," Tatty said. "They never do."

"No," Holly said. "They don't. They never do. They're robots who want to sell things to people. They don't like to talk to other robots."

Tatiana jumped down from the stool so quickly then

that for a second Holly thought she'd fallen, so she hurried instinctively toward her daughter. But Tatiana held up a hand as if she had to hold her mother back, as if Holly had planned to strike her, not help her.

"You don't know," Tatty said, shaking her head. "You have no idea who's calling."

"I realize that," Holly said. "I don't *know*, because you didn't *answer*. If you'd answered the phone, I would now know who it was who called."

"You told me not to answer!"

Holly took a step back and threw her hands in the air. "I *what?*"

Tatiana muttered something.

"What? What are you talking about, Tatiana?"

Tatty's dark eyes searched the space just to the right of Holly's shoulder, not looking at her directly, but not looking away from her, either. Her profile looked like a marble sculpture. Pale and polished and a little cold.

"I'm not going to continue this absurd argument, Tatty," Holly said. "You didn't answer the cell phone to spite me. Either that or you didn't want to be bothered to talk to the robot, either."

Tatiana turned and began to walk from the kitchen island to the family room, to the Christmas tree in the corner—its branches drooping under the weight of all the ornaments and the strings of lights. The whole scene— the tree, the lights, her daughter in her Christmas dress—

looked wan to Holly in the glare pouring through the picture window, which was now just a scrim of snow outdoors. Who knew how long it might take Eric to get back from the airport, or where his brothers and their families were by now as they attempted to converge on the house from the various hotels they'd spent their nights in? God help her if she had to entertain the Coxes very long without any help. At least Thuy and Pearl and Patty lived only a few miles away. Surely they would have no reason to be late, no matter how much snow was falling.

The Christmas lights drowned themselves in their own dull brilliance as Tatty peered into them, looking curious, the way she'd peered into Holly's cell phone, as if something either wonderful or terrible might be hiding in there.

"What's wrong, sweetheart? Let's not fight. I love you so much. It's Christmas, and we have a *lot* to do."

She waited for her daughter to turn around. When she did, Holly thought, she would take Tatiana in her arms. She would hold her until she warmed and softened in her embrace. They would start the day again.

But Tatty didn't turn around. Instead, she said something under her breath, which Holly chose to ignore, and as it became clear that she could stand there all day waiting, and Tatiana was not going to turn around, Holly herself turned around, went to the refrigerator, and opened the door.

The refrigerator was so crammed full from her shopping trip the day before that Holly had to step backward to see the contents fully. The roast was what she was looking for, but in order to get to it she would have to swim through eggnog and sparkling juice (Eric's brother Tony didn't drink) and champagne bottles (his wife most certainly did) and whipping cream and fruit salad. The roast was at the very back, still wrapped in the plastic bag in which she'd brought it home from the grocery store the day before.

As she always did, Tatty had grimaced at the plastic bag ("They aren't biodegradable! They *never* leave the earth!") as the bag boy slid the roast (sixty dollars' worth of prime) into it.

But Holly had given her a look, and said, "We need it in plastic, Tatty. So it doesn't bleed all over the refrigerator," to which her daughter had made an even more dramatic expression of revulsion and then hurried away from the checkout line to stare into the glass cage of stuffed animals near the automatic doors:

How many dollars, over the years, had Holly stuffed into that machine so that Tatty could try to snag a miniature teddy bear or pink cat? Something cheap and synthetic, probably made in China, stuffed with some kind of formaldehyde-soaked substance that had been outlawed in this country for years? It had been remarkable, really, how many times Tatty, as a little girl, had snagged one of those prizes with the machine's mechanical claw. The cashiers used to comment on it, saying they'd never seen anyone outsmart that game as often as Tatty had.

At the car Tatty had helped her unload the groceries into the trunk from the cart, steering clear of the roast in the plastic bag, which Holly tossed into the backseat (was she trying to rile her daughter?), where it landed with a ridiculous, decapitated *thunk*. Tatty sat beside her in silence as Holly maneuvered them out of the parking lot, but when they were in the road and had reached the speed limit, Tatty said, "Before plastic bags there must have been ways to keep meat from *bleeding* all over the refrigerator, Mom." She said *bleeding* in such a way that Holly anticipated that soon Tatiana would be announcing her vegetarianism.

"That's right," Holly had said. "I bet there were, but I bet they didn't work as well as a plastic bag," and then she turned the radio on to NPR, where some popular musician Holly had never heard of was being interviewed at length about his influences, which included, but were not limited to, the sound of ticking clocks and flushing toilets. She turned it down so the voices were just a whispering background and tried to engage Tatiana in a bit of conversation by asking her if she knew who the musician was, but Tatty just said, "No." And then, as if to pound a nail in Holly's coffin, they passed the town's largest tree—a white pine that towered over the church next to which it grew, even over its steeple—and, snagged practically at the very top like a mocking Christmas star, a white plastic bag fluttered around in the wind.

❄

HOLLY LIFTED THE meat out of the refrigerator with both hands, as if it were a sleeping baby, and put it, in its white plastic bag, down on the kitchen counter.

As she'd known she would, she found the bottom of the plastic bag pooled with blood, but she resisted the urge to call Tatty over to show her what the point was of that evil plastic bagging. She wondered about those many public school teachers who'd driven home their lessons about sustainability and biodegradability and migrating birds with their feet tangled in plastic grocery bags over the years—what did *they* bring their meat home in? A little rivulet of blood made its way down the side of the granite countertop and onto the tiles near her stocking feet.

Holly glanced at it, and chose to ignore it. She'd clean it up later. The tiles were red, and the blood—dark as menstrual blood or cherry syrup—was camouflaged there. No one would know it was there but her. She opened the plastic bag, slit open the cellophane wrapper around the meat, lifted the roast off the Styrofoam it rested on, and peeled off the Kotex-like bandage from the bottom. She then lifted and placed the meat gently (again a sleeping baby came to mind) in the roasting pan she'd left on the counter the night before.

It looked, of course, unappetizing. It looked like an accident, Holly thought. It looked like what it was—an animal, uncovered, like what any one of them would look like, she supposed, stripped of all exteriors. Some mushrooms, onions, and potatoes would help, and pepper, and as Holly began to grind the pepper mill over the top of the meat she called over her shoulder to Tatty, "Could you get the mushrooms out of the crisper and wash them?"

There was no response. Holly turned and looked at her daughter, sharply, to which Tatty responded with an expression of such infinite weariness that it made Holly want to laugh.

This was the expression Tatty gave the world whenever she was asked to do some chore she didn't want to do—a sad deflation, the expression that might be worn by a princess slave as she was being taken in chains to the dungeons.

Holly remembered, then, her own teenage years, and a few friends she'd had like this. Girls who rolled their eyes so languidly and so often it seemed their eyeballs could have permanently disappeared somewhere above their brows. She recalled lying on the floor of Cindy Martin's bedroom, listening to Billy Joel on a transistor radio propped up between them, and the way Cindy had parted her lips at the ceiling in a kind of silent scream, squeezing her eyes shut and letting her shoulders sink deeper into the white shag carpeting when her mother called from below, "Cindy? You need to feed the dog!"

Holly herself had been envious. The mother. The chore. The dog. These normal trappings of a normal childhood. She herself was never asked to do anything at home, because she had two older sisters, each of whom had made it her goal in life to let Holly have a "normal childhood" despite their mother's death and their father's "secret" alcoholism. It was why Holly did not chastise Tatty for her resentful reactions to being asked to empty the dishwasher or take out the garbage. These were luxuries, these small burdens. It was a luxury to be able to dole out such burdens. As Tatiana made her way to the refrigerator, to the crisper, Holly said, cheerfully, "Thanks, Tat," trying to let her daughter know that she recognized that this was an effort for her, this indignity, but also that it was ridiculous, and charming, that it was such an effort.

Outside, a snowplow growled by, and Holly heard the sound of its blades scraping against the pavement. It really *was* a blizzard, then, wasn't it? These days it seemed that the snowplows only came out during emergencies. Cutbacks. And this was Christmas! Imagine the overtime the city had to pay a snowplow driver on Christmas Day. Like the U.S. Postal Service, snowplowing had been a service Holly used to take for granted. There was a time (only ten years ago?) when the snowplows came out just, it seemed, for the show of it:

Give us a flurry, a dusting, a glaze, it had seemed, *and we'll make it rue the day!*

But those days seemed like longer ago than a decade now—like those old-fashioned days when they used to serve you dinner on airplanes, or pump your gas for you, or carry your groceries out to the car. And now, of course, they were talking about shutting the post office down.

How much snow must have fallen for them to be willing to pay overtime to the snowplowers on Christmas Day?

Holly glanced over at Tatty, who was staring at the carton of mushrooms in her hands as if completely baffled by them.

"Did you hear that?" Holly asked.

"Hear what?" Tatty said, under her breath, still looking down at the mushrooms.

That profile:

The lowered eyes. The fixed stare. An ancient beauty carved by someone whose identity was lost to time. And the ancient message of it, which seemed to be, *Gaze upon me, I'm here and also not here, of you and apart from you.*

Tatiana's cold marble profile unnerved Holly. She said, "Just put those down, Tatiana. I'll do it."

Tatiana continued to stare into the carton of mushrooms.

Holly said, too loudly, "Did you hear me?"

Tatiana seemed, then, to hear her, but it was as if she'd picked Holly's voice up on a walkie-talkie from miles away. She shook her head a little, placed the carton of mushrooms carefully in the sink, looked over at Holly—and then Holly realized that the attitude she'd taken to be Tatiana's annoyance at having been asked to do a chore was not that.

Tatiana had been crying!

"Honey!" Holly said, turning from the meat to her daughter, wiping her bloody hands on her dress—because who cared? There were more important things, and the dress was so busily floral a bit of blood would simply look like part of the ridiculous pattern. "Oh my God, what's wrong?"

She took her daughter by her shoulders so quickly that she almost knocked Tatiana over—so thin, that frame, so frail!—and she pulled her to her hard, cupping the back of Tatiana's skull in a hand just as she had when Baby Tatty had been small enough to carry on her hip from room to room, from crib to bath, from car to playground. "What's wrong, my sweetheart?" she asked again.

Tatiana let her forehead rest on her mother's shoulder, but she said nothing and didn't raise her arms to return Holly's embrace. It was like holding a mannequin, except that Tatiana smelled like tea tree oil and citrus fruit and fields full of unearthly flowers—flowers that had been raised in factories and tinkered with until their scents conformed to some inventor's idea of the scent of the perfect flower.

And something else. Something not quite right. A bit of rotten fruit, again. Just a whiff. And then Holly felt that urgency return.

Something had followed them home from Russia!

There was *something* in all of this. Something *about* it that, without time to sit at a desk and puzzle it out in words with a pen, Holly feared she would never understand! And, yet, the very thing she was doing—embracing her child—made it impossible to slip away, to find the pen and paper or to boot up the computer.

And even if she'd had the time—then what? What would she write? Something had followed them home from Russia? It was meaningless! It explained nothing! And Holly was no longer a writer, had not been one for years and years, had not written a decent sentence or a real line of poetry since way back then, back in those days of dinners served on airplanes, back when you could wait at the gate for your loved ones to disembark from the plane and the snowplows roared out into the roads at the first few flakes. Holly knew that she could be given all the time in the world, and despite this conviction that she had something to write and no time to write it, there would be nothing. How many *beginnings* had she jotted down in the last eighteen years, and how many of those jottings had led to anything but frustration and an ill-temper that lasted for days? *Hundreds* of beginnings, resulting in nothing. What could possibly have been the point of trying to break her writer's block, and, no less, on Christmas day?

And still she felt the need to push her daughter (gently) away from her. Holding her, asking her what was the matter—it was just more futility, more fruitlessness. Her daughter, even if she knew what was wrong, wasn't going to answer, would never offer any explanation for her tears or her moping or moodiness. If pushed, she would simply start up the argument about Holly oversleeping again, or the plastic bag. It would be a waste of both their time.

Holly loosened her grip on her daughter, and Tatiana, who'd remained stiff through the embrace, straightened up, stepped away, and headed silently back to her bedroom. Holly heard the door close with an efficient little click, and then (surely not) could she have heard Tatiana slip the hook into the lock's eye? That hook and eye she had refused even to *acknowledge* since Holly had installed it for her? Was *that* the kind of day this was going to end up being? Was Holly *never* going to be forgiven for having overslept?

She shook her head at the place where her beautiful, impossible, impossibly beautiful daughter had vanished from the hallway, and continued to stand and stare at that emptiness until the oven behind her beeped that it was preheated sufficiently to slip the roast into it. Holly picked up the mushroom carton, ripped the plastic off of it, ran cold water over the fleshy nubs, and dumped them into the pan with the meat. She still had at least, she wagered, an hour to deal with potatoes and onions, and almost everything else—the mashed sweet potatoes and fruit salad and the dinner rolls—had been purchased premade at the store. This was not going to be one of her more impressive Christmas feasts. But what difference did it make? She couldn't care less what the Coxes thought of her, and Eric's family—well, how many impressive Christmas feasts was she really obligated to prepare for them in a single lifetime?—and Thuy and Pearl and Patty would have been pleased with nothing but a couple of beers (Thuy), sweet potatoes (Pearl), and fruit salad (Patty).

Holly turned her back on the kitchen and went to the window to assess the snowfall. As she'd expected from the snowplow action, the accumulation since she'd last looked outside was truly surprising. The wind was blowing the flakes sideways as they fell, yet there was still a kind of organization to the mass of it on the ground, as if someone were taking great pains to distribute the snowfall evenly over the lawn. The birdbath—which was a cement angel bearing a water dish in her hands—was completely cloaked. Holly realized that the snow must be sticky and damp, because it clung to every bit of the angel, even the bottom of her wings, and her whole face was swathed as if in bandages. Because that angel was only slightly smaller than life-sized, she looked, disguised like this, as if she could have been a child or a little adult, frozen out there in the backyard, still holding out that plate imploringly, as if begging for something from the picture window and the cozy comfortable interior beyond it. *Please?*

❄

WHEN THEY'D ARRIVED in Siberia on their first trip there, Eric and Holly were picked up by a driver at the airport for a three-hour trip to the hostel run by this orphanage— this, after having traveled by plane and train and bus and again by plane for nearly twenty-four hours. In the car, in the backseat, Eric had immediately fallen asleep, but Holly had been unable even to close her eyes. Never in her life had she been more awake. She'd stared out at the snow and the landscape, and the landscape and the snow, as they became one and the same passing by. The people and their houses and their vehicles and their farm animals—all of them were buried, blurred. Snow ghosts, all of them, everything, for two hundred miles. Holly could not make out a single detail, and early on she gave up trying, yet never felt the slightest desire to close her eyes. It was a kind of comfort, really, to look out at this country and find it to be populated by nothing but apparitions.

❄

NOW SHE PUT a hand to the picture window and watched as the space between her warm fingers filled with fog against the cold glass. It was like that landscape out there. The angel birdbath was an impression, not a figure, and the rest was obliteration. Then she snapped out of it, remembering the roast and the guests and the chores left to be done, and she took her hand away from the window, looked at her watch, gasped at the time. The guests should be here within an hour. Or less. Although she realized it had been nearly an hour already since she'd last heard from Eric. And the airport was only an hour away. Unless they'd closed down the freeway, he should have been home with his parents by now. Surely, he would be here with them any minute. And the brothers and their families would be next. Holly had given the Coxes a slightly later arrival time than the others, so as not to risk their getting there before Gin had been given time to embrace her sons and grandchildren, and to weep for a little while, as she always did.

Thuy, Pearl, and Patty were going to a church service that wouldn't be over until 1:30, and then they needed to stop back at the house and pick up the presents and the bread pudding Pearl had made. So, they would be the last, but, for Holly, the most welcome, of all the guests. Holly knew that Thuy would bring a six-pack of some kind of imported beer, and that she would proceed to drink each one steadily over the course of the afternoon into the evening until she was goofily drunk. Pearl would fawn all over Tatiana—beg to hear her sing her latest madrigal tune and to see every photograph on her iMac and to peruse every song she'd downloaded onto iTunes. Surely this attention from her dearest "aunt" would jog Tatty out of her bad mood.

And Patty! Patty would be a sugarplum, a fairy princess, a little beauty queen! She would hold Holly's hand and chatter about something girly and nonsensical and silly. And all the stories that Pearl and Thuy were sick of hearing, Holly would happily listen to a million times. Except for Tatiana, there was no one on earth whom Holly loved more than her goddaughter, and although she fervently hoped that Thuy and Pearl lived long and healthy lives, she also couldn't help fantasizing that they might die (painlessly!) so that she could take custody of Patty. Holly joked about this with Thuy and Pearl, who forgave her the ill-will, being pathetically grateful to her for loving their only daughter so much, but Holly did not exactly tell them that, not infrequently, she stood in the doorway of the guest room and thought about how, if her dear friends died, she would rip the built-in bookcases out of it and paint the walls sea-foam green for their daughter, who would then be *her* daughter, and give the room a mermaid motif. She'd think about how, as sisters, Patty and Tatiana would make such a pretty portrait between herself and Eric:

One dark and elegant and chiseled from marble, and one soft, with a crooked smile, and full of light.

Although Patty was not, Holly felt, the most intelligent child she'd ever known (for one thing, she was never quiet or still long enough to *think*), she was easily the most pleasant. She was a purely American child. She expected everything to be fine, because everything always *had* been fine. How wonderful it was to be in the presence of such an untroubled human being!

Holly turned from the picture window and crossed the living room to Tatiana's room, where she stood as quietly as she could outside the door, holding her breath to see if she could hear anything coming from the other side. The light tapping of her keyboard, the opening and closing of drawers?

No. All Holly could hear, even with her breath held, was the snow falling outside—on the roof, on the lawn, against the window glass. It did not sound damp to her, as she'd supposed it was from the sticky coating it had bestowed on the birdbath angel. It sounded, instead, sandy. Crisp. Holly breathed in, rubbed her eyes, went back to the living room, back to the picture window, and looked more closely at the backyard beyond it.

Yes, the snow was pebblish now. Grainy. It was unrelenting, this snowfall. Now she could no longer see that angel at all.

She went back to the kitchen, to the oven, and looked in.

The roast, just beginning to sizzle in there, had begun to smell like food instead of flesh. Most of the time, Holly avoided red meat, for health reasons she'd read about in women's magazines, but whenever she smelled meat roasting, she recognized that she was, at heart, a carnivore. Across from the dry cleaners downtown there was a bad diner, the Fernwood, which had been cited several times in the last few years for sanitation violations—but the Fernwood vented its kitchen onto the sidewalk, and every time Holly went to pick up the dry-cleaned clothes she smelled the frying burgers, and could easily imagine herself in a forest, wearing animal fur, ripping a hunk of meat off a bone with her teeth, and the incredible pleasure her ancestors must have found in that.

Holly took a look at her iPhone, which was still at rest on the kitchen counter. Apparently only Unavailable had called (twice) since Eric's call. If Eric didn't arrive home soon, she would call him. Though she hoped she didn't have to. She feared that if he was on the freeway with his addled parents the distraction of a phone call wouldn't help, especially in this weather. Holly wasn't the kind of person prone to imagining fatal car accidents, sudden disasters. In her experience, tragedy struck with a lot of warning—centuries' worth, really—and, in the end, it surprised you mostly with how much forewarning it had given you, how much room for suffering beforehand. No. Eric would not be killed in a car accident on Christmas. At worst, he would be stuck in a snowbank.

Holly left the kitchen island and went to the buffet,

where she kept her mother's wedding china, and the crystal—or what was left of it since three of her mother's iridescent water glasses had been smashed. She opened the glass doors. Little pink rosebuds were painted onto the creamy white plates and cups and saucers in there, rimmed with gold. Janet, her oldest sister, had been given the dinnerware when their mother died, and then she'd passed it on to Melissa, the middle sister, when it was certain that she would, herself, die. But Melissa couldn't stand it, she said, that reminder of their mother and their sister, all that hopeful dinnerware, and she'd dumped it on Holly's doorstep in bubble wrap, in boxes.

Originally Holly had thought that she, too, would not be able to stand it, and she'd left it boxed in the basement for years.

Until they'd brought Tatiana home.

It was then that Holly had felt the tug of the past, and she'd gone to the basement, opened the boxes, and found that, miraculously, the dinnerware had been purged of its association with her mother and her sisters by its long years in those boxes in the basement. She and Eric bought a cabinet specifically in which to store it, and, now, for every special occasion, Holly brought it out and felt pleased with herself for owning it, for being alive to enjoy it after the other women, whose enjoyment had been cut short by a damaged gene, were gone. They did not begrudge her, and they didn't haunt that cabinet, but sometimes, particularly holidays like Christmas, Holly could feel her *own* ghost standing just beside her, wishing that she, too, could reach into the china cabinet and touch something as solid and delicate as a plate, hold it in her hands:

But Holly's ghost couldn't, made of destiny, as she was—whereas the flesh-and-blood Holly, thanks to modern medicine, had been able to shrug her destiny off like a coat.

❄

WELL, OF COURSE, it hadn't been *that* easy.

There had been, for instance, the cold recovery room in which Holly had woken up alone, slowly blinking back into the world, understanding that she had no ovaries, no breasts, no nipples under all her bandages. That her most personal parts had been removed, and who knew where they were now, without her?

And, for the first few months after her surgeries, Holly had felt, horribly, as if she'd been turned into a machine, an unkillable robot. She had terrible dreams in which she was searching for her body parts on shelves lined with thousands of other body parts, floating in thousands of jars. In the dreams, Holly was convinced that her soul had been located in one of those body parts, and now her soul was trapped for eternity in formaldehyde and glass.

But all this passed with time and with the artistic genius of her plastic surgeon, who had provided her with far more beautiful breasts than she'd had in real life, and with the counsel of the nurse who'd assisted Holly's double mastectomy and oophorectomy (why had that word needed to hold two eggs in its name?), who'd told Holly that she'd had, herself, a kind of out-of-body experience during Holly's surgery, understanding that what they were accomplishing in that surgical theater was the undoing of a chain of fate that had plagued Holly's female forebears for a thousand years. "We were snatching you out of that long line of early female deaths."

That nurse, at Holly's bedside after the surgery, wearing white, had been rubbing Holly's hand as she spoke to her, explaining that there would certainly have been no escape, that even if Holly herself had not died because of the mutation (or killed herself in despair of it, as her middle sister, Melissa, had) she'd have passed it down to children, who would have passed it down. It had to be stopped. All that suffering. They could now actually trace her 185delAG BRCA1 mutation back to what might have been the single Indo-Egyptian woman who first bore it and passed it down to Holly.

"Think of that woman," the nurse had said, her dark green eyes filling with tears. "Thank God that you were born in America at the end of the twentieth century. These are remarkable times."

And, thank God, Tatiana could have no such gene, surely. Holly would pass on the uncontaminated dinnerware to Tatiana, who would pass down the dinnerware to her own mutation-free daughter someday.

❄

CAREFULLY, HOLLY LIFTED the saucers off the stack and set them down on the dining room table behind her. She and Eric had put the leaf into the center of the table before they'd gone to bed, and Holly had thrown the tablecloth over it.

"Tatty?" she called. "Time to set the table, Tatty!"

There was no answer. Tatiana was still in her room with the door closed.

(But, surely, not locked?)

"Tatty?" Holly called out more loudly—so loudly that only if Tatiana had headphones and was blaring the kind of music she never listened to would she not have been able to hear. "Tatty? Hey! I need you to help, hon! Dad will be here with Gin and Gramps any second! We need to set the table!"

Holly lifted the salad plates out. Then she stopped to see if she could hear the sounds of Tatty headed out of her room. The scraping of the chair legs on the wood floor. But there was no sound. Holly felt a familiar sense of dejection, rising up from her stomach into her throat. It was a kind of unhappiness that reminded her, sickeningly, of her own high school days—of being ditched by friends or being jilted by a boy. She'd nearly forgotten that kind of despair—how it was physical, absolute—and she had to steady herself with a hand on the back of a dining room chair, truly feeling that silly-weak with it.

What was wrong with her? This was ridiculous, this abject sorrow over *nothing*, so much worse today than the ordinary aggravation she felt, and had gotten used to feeling, when Tatty took her time answering a question or responding to a call for assistance. *That* feeling, Holly had fully expected of motherhood. She remembered, acutely, the exasperated expressions her mother, before she died, had directed at her when she was rude, or late, or begrudging. But to feel so wounded, so *grieved*, by her daughter and by behavior that was, of course, completely normal teenage behavior? This was inappropriate, really, and she needed to shake it off before Tatty saw it on her face.

"Darn it, Tatty!" Holly inhaled, stepped away from the buffet, and headed for Tatty's closed bedroom door. There she knocked with her knuckles, hard, and then stepped back to listen.

Still nothing.

"Tatty. What are you *doing*? Didn't you hear me say I needed your help with the table?"

This time Holly heard what sounded like a sigh, and found it reassuring. At least her daughter was—

What? Still willing to acknowledge the sound of her mother's voice, even if it caused her nothing but vexation?

Still, if Tatty was lying in her bed behind that door, she

didn't budge, didn't even roll over. After all these years in a small house together, Holly well knew the sound and meaning of every squeak of her daughter's bedsprings. And her daughter was not moving in there.

"Tatiana."

This time Holly tried to make it sound patient. She was going to give her daughter the benefit of the doubt. Maybe Tatiana had fallen deeply asleep. Maybe she had menstrual cramps. Holly knew her daughter's cycle well, and although it seemed too early for PMS, the body wasn't a computer, perfectly programmed. Holly hadn't, herself, had a period since she was twenty-four, but she'd never forgotten the ones she'd had. The blank ache that preceded the blood, as if all that soft pottery held in the triangle between her hips were hardening. The vague nausea, too—and always an electrode-like prickling at the temples, around the eyes and sinuses, as if she had inhaled salt water. It had never been enough pain to cry out, but it had always been enough to leave Holly feeling like a captive in her body, like a slave wrapped in chains. Now, seeing the expression on her daughter's face when she was having cramps of her own could bring it all back to Holly in waves of ghost-pain where her ovaries used to be.

"Tatiana."

Holly put her hand on the doorknob. She was going to have to do the very thing she'd told Tatiana she wouldn't do—enter her room without permission. But she'd given

Tatiana fair warning. This was ridiculous. She could not be allowed to hide out and mope in her room all day. As Holly spoke her daughter's name, she turned the door-knob (*"Tat—"*), but the syllable caught in her mouth and the door wouldn't open, and Holly realized that the hook and eye were latched on the other side.

She let go of the doorknob and stepped back. *Jesus Christ.* Holly sighed so deeply that it sounded, in her throat, like a growl as the air passed out of her, out of the depths of her and over her tonsils and back into the world. Jesus. Christ. Okay. So, Tatiana *was*, apparently, going to punish Holly *all day* for having overslept on Christmas. *Go to hell*, Holly felt like saying, but instead she stepped away from the door and said to it, as steadily as she could, "When you decide to grow up, please feel free to join us."

Please feel free to join *us*.

Of course, there was no one else in the house at the moment, and Holly felt the weakness of that. For the first time that day, Holly felt a cool wash of relief about the company on the way, even the Coxes. There wasn't the slightest possibility that Tatty, being the kind of girl she was, would behave this way around guests. She'd be polite to everyone, and happy to see them, and she'd interact politely with Holly because of this, and by the time the day was over the fake Holly and the fake Tatty ("Sweetheart, can you whip the cream?" "Sure, Mom") would have metamorphosed into the real Holly and Tatty.

She glanced at her watch again.

She was going to have to set the fucking table herself.

❅

SETTING THE TABLE for a big dinner had always been something Holly and Tatiana had done together. Even back when Tatty was too little to touch the china or the crystal, she would reach up and slap the silverware onto the table beside the plates. There'd only ever been that one mishap, when Tatty was about six years old and had too excitedly reached into the buffet for the gravy boat. The gravy boat (a white ceramic swan with a hole in its face out of which the gravy poured) had survived, but three of Holly's mother's iridescent water glasses hadn't. It was never clear to Holly what had happened. Tatty was too hysterical—both wildly defensive and tearfully apologetic—ever to tell the whole story, but when Holly turned around the glasses were on the hardwood floor in front of the buffet, and the globe of each was so perfectly cracked away from the stem that it looked more like a surgical amputation than an accident.

"It doesn't matter," she'd said to Tatty. "I have nine more of those. Things break."

"You didn't *watch* me," Tatty had screamed. "You should have *told* me."

Holly had tried not to be annoyed by the injury of this. Not only had Tatty broken her water glasses, but she was now blaming it on Holly, when Holly was simply trying to forgive her. To comfort her daughter, Holly tried to come up with some anecdote about breaking something precious, herself, but she couldn't recall any such incidents. Until she was an adult, Holly hadn't been around anything breakable long enough to break it. Still, one time she'd apparently grabbed a blue crayon and scribbled all over a wall, and that had become a family joke, although Holly had no recollection of it whatsoever. When she'd announced her plans to go to graduate school in order to become a writer, Janet had laughed and said, "You always wanted to be a scribbler!"

Ha-ha.

So Holly had told Tatty that story to comfort her, to show her how things could be damaged both purposely and by accident. Told her how her mother had managed to scrub the crayon off the wall before her father saw it, and had waited weeks before telling him. It wasn't until she was halfway through the telling of it (as she discarded the water glasses and Tatiana sniffled with her face in her hands at the dining room table) that Holly remembered that she'd already told her daughter this story, back in the summer, when she was trying to get her to admit that she'd scratched up all of her and Eric's CDs. Scribbling with a safety pin perhaps? What other explanation was there?

But the anecdote hadn't helped—neither to get Tatiana to admit to scratching the CDs in the summer, nor to make her feel better for having broken (with such precision it seemed frankly willful) the three water glasses on Christmas. Instead, Tatty had narrowed her eyes as if the story of her mother's naughtiness confused and, perhaps, disgusted her:

And this would be the case over the years with nearly every attempt Holly made to make Tatty feel better about something she'd done by describing how she had, herself, once done something equally clumsy, or wrong, or shortsighted. The worst had been when, after Tatty and Tommy had been dating six months and Tommy had turned seventeen, Holly suggested to Tatiana that she keep a condom in her purse, just in case.

"*What?*" Tatiana had said. Her ruby-blue lips had parted in an expression of true horror.

Holly had repeated herself. The condom. She said she thought it best that Tatiana and Tommy wait, of course, but that she knew that sometimes teenagers—

"*Oh my God*, Mom," Tatiana had said. Her dark eyes were wide, her mouth an astonished zero. Holly could see her teeth in there. A perfectly white mountain range. Tatiana had never even needed braces, those teeth were so perfect. Choking back tears, it seemed, Tatiana said, "I have no idea what you were doing when you were my age, but that's not what Tommy and I are doing."

"Well, Tatiana," Holly had said, and she'd gone on to

explain that, at Tatty's age, Holly and her boyfriend also hadn't planned to have sex, but, since no one had been open enough with Holly to tell her about contraception, she'd been unprepared, and she'd gotten pregnant, and had an abortion. It had been a terrible experience. Thank God, she'd told Tatty, it was possible to get an abortion at Planned Parenthood at fifteen without your parents' permission, because if her father had found out—

Tatiana, then, had collapsed onto her bed and burst into tears and refused to be comforted until Holly had promised never to raise the subject again. Holly agreed, but she insisted that Tatiana know that she could come to Holly whenever she needed—

"I know! I know! Stop talking! I don't want to hear about you! I don't want to know about your mistakes! I'm nothing like you!"

For a terrible second Holly was sure that Tatiana would say the words she'd dreaded and expected all those years:

You're not my mother.

But she didn't. Not then. Not ever. Only once, when she was four years old, Tatiana had asked, tentatively, "Mom, do you know who my real mother was?"

To hear those two words together, *real* and *mother*, had made Holly's eyes fill instantly with tears, the physical response happening before she'd even processed those two words in her consciousness.

But, as she'd always planned to do, Holly told Tatiana

the truth—that she didn't know anything about her biological mother. That, given the conditions in the town that Tatiana was born in, it was likely that her mother had been a teenager, maybe an orphan herself, probably very poor, very uneducated:

The whole area had been teeming with abandoned children. The orphanages, of course, were full of them, but there were also older abandoned children everywhere, who'd either never been institutionalized or who'd been released, and they rushed at the passersby at every bus stop and crosswalk, asking for money, or for something—your watch, your candy bar, your scarf—and running alongside you with their hands cupped, shouting into your face. Holly and Eric had been warned not to talk to these street children, and not, under any circumstances, to stop or give them money, that if you did so these children would steal your purse while you were fishing through it. Or worse. There was a story of one couple who'd gone to Siberia to adopt a baby and had been badly beaten by a pack of children in an alley after stopping to offer them food. The prospective mother had been permanently blinded by a blow to her head. The question Holly had wanted answered—did they still adopt the baby?—could, apparently, not be answered.

When they were still back in the States, being given these dire warnings by the adoption agency's overseas travel director, Holly could not imagine hurrying past an abandoned child at a bus stop. But, as it turned out, it was easy. There were *so many* of them, so badly dressed, so filthy, so rude, that they did not seem like children. And this, it turned out, was the attitude of the Russians themselves toward these children—that they were not, exactly, children, that they were tainted by bad genes, even the youngest of them. It was an attitude that was held even toward *infants*, and it was the reason, Holly and Eric had been told, that there were so many available babies to adopt in Russia. Russians did not want these castoffs. Even childless, desperate Russians did not want to adopt these children.

"Russians are exactly like Americans," the overseas director (who was Bolivian, herself) had told Holly and Eric, "except that they've been through centuries of pure hell. Like Americans, they're affectionate and sentimental and egotistical"—at this, Holly and Eric had looked at one another, amused by this description of themselves, which was clearly an insult—"but not nearly as naïve. This is why it's so easy for Russians to take advantage of Americans. They understand Americans because they are like them, but they believe that Americans will always choose not to see basic truths that Russians are born understanding."

Of course, she did not tell Tatiana this, but Holly imagined that Tatiana's mother and father could have been among those Siberian street children. Abortions were so common and so readily available as a form of birth control in Russia (there was, it seemed, no taboo against them, and they were offered so far into a woman's pregnancy that, Holly had been told, some of the babies one found in orphanages were actually the result of abortions that didn't "take") that unless the mother was too strung-out on drugs or vodka to obtain the procedure, she might simply have been too young even to understand that she was pregnant until her baby was being born. And, since they'd been assured by the Pokrovka Orphanage #2 that Tatiana had no drugs in her system at birth, and clearly did not have fetal alcohol syndrome, it seemed that she could easily have been the abandoned child of one, or two, of those thousands of other abandoned children.

"We'll never know," Holly had told Tatiana of her birth mother. "But I'd be honored to always-always-always-always be your real-real-real-real mother." She'd taken her daughter in her arms, and they'd stayed like that, with their faces pressed together, mixing their tears, and it had been, and would always be, the sweetest moment of Holly's entire life.

AFTER THE DISHES and the glasses and silverware were set on the tablecloth (Holly still planned to leave the arranging to Tatiana), she glanced again at the picture window.

Now absolutely everything out there except the snow itself had been erased by the blowing snow. Christ, Holly thought, this isn't a *snowfall* any longer. This is a blizzard. There'd been no word about a *blizzard* on Christmas Day that Holly had heard. No weather warnings on the radio or the television at all. Until yesterday, when flurries had been predicted, they'd actually been suggesting that this year it might not even be a white Christmas.

Holly went to the kitchen island to pick up her iPhone and, just as she did, Dylan started singing his haughty warning again, *it's a hard, it's a hard, it's a hard, it's a hard, it's a hard rain*—all that foreboding captured somehow in a space as small as the palm of a child's hand—and the screen lit up the name Thuy.

"Thuy," Holly said into the phone.

"Holly," her friend said. "Merry Christmas. But, Jesus, have you looked outside?"

"I know, I know," Holly said. "I can't believe it. Eric's still on his way back from the airport with his parents. And I expected his brothers and their families to start showing up one carload at a time by now, but no one's here except me and Tatty."

"Sweetheart, they've closed down the freeway. If your relatives aren't already in town, they won't be showing up for *hours*. You'd better start making some phone calls. And don't leave the house! Patty, Pearl, and I barely made it home from church. It took us an hour to drive ten miles. Pearl's on her back on the floor right now, re-covering. She was driving."

Holly heard Pearl call out from some space beyond Thuy and her cell phone, "Tell her it's one for the books."

"Seriously?" Holly said to Thuy, not ready to fully believe this account of things. "I mean, where did this come from? I thought it wasn't supposed to snow today."

"Well, they started the dire warnings about six o'clock this morning, but it was still barely snowing when we left for church at eleven, and we thought, yeah, right, I mean, how much snow can fall during the span of an hour and a half? Well, let me tell you. A lot. And a lot more is on the way. You better turn on your radio."

"Oh, God." Holly suddenly understood what the implications of this were. She put a hand to her forehead and said, "Thuy, you're not calling to say you're *not coming*, are you?"

There was a silence, and into it Holly made whiny-puppy noises.

"Holly, there's no—"

"Oh my God, you're going to abandon me on Christmas Day! Rent a sleigh! I'll come get you! I need my Thuy and my Pearl and my sugarplum fairy."

Thuy laughed a little, but not much. They both knew it was only partly a joke, that not coming over for Christmas Day broke a tradition that mattered more to Holly than it did to them. Holly was trying, with the melodrama, to sound less desperate than she felt.

"Holly, there's no way. Even if it stops snowing right

this second, which it's not going to do, the roads won't be clear enough to—"

"I heard a plow!" Holly said. "Just, maybe, thirty minutes ago. I bet our road is clear!"

"Hon, that plow is a finger in the dike. No pun intended. And, besides, I couldn't get Pearl off the floor and back into the car today if our lives depended on it."

Holly heard Pearl call out, "Tell Holly we're so sorry! We'll bring over our presents and our sugarplum fairy tomorrow or the next!"

Pearl, Holly knew, was trying to get Thuy off the hook, and off the phone. She knew that they would have liked to come for Christmas, but it wouldn't ruin their day now that they couldn't. They were probably planning to make a fire in their woodstove, cuddle up on the couch with Patty. They'd probably stocked the fridge and freezer with things they could make a Christmas dinner with, in the event that this would happen. It might even have seemed like a relief to them, staying home, just the three of them, instead of being here, dealing with Holly's in-laws and the Coxes. But Holly couldn't stop herself. She said, "You're sure? This will be the first Christmas in fourteen years you haven't been over here. Tatiana will be heartbroken. She's already in a terrible mood."

"Oh, Holly," Thuy said, and Holly could imagine her making a face at Pearl, maybe pointing at the phone receiver, shaking her head. "It's impossible. Really. Or we'd be there, hon. It's truly not possible." She enunciated and emphasized each of her last three words, as if Holly, not Thuy, were the nonnative English speaker.

"Bleh," Holly said. "I hate you. I love you. You're ruining my life."

Thuy laughed then, recognizing the humor as permission to get off the phone and get on with her own life, with her own family, with her own Christmas. "Well, tell Tatiana we love her," she said.

"I will," Holly said, "if she comes out of her bedroom today." She wanted to tell Thuy about Tatiana. Her bad mood. She'd locked Holly out of her room! Although Thuy had been a mother half as long as Holly had, Thuy always had the best mothering advice.

"Oh, no," Thuy said. "What's wrong with Tatty?" But the tone didn't invite Holly to go into detail. The conversation was winding down, not up. Holly had known Thuy for two decades and logged hundreds of hours on the telephone with her. She knew when Thuy was standing at the counter, ready to walk out the door, and, conversely, when she was settling into her lounge chair, ready to chat for hours, by the length of the pauses between her sentences (although there'd been less and less of the latter since Pearl had moved in, and almost none now that they had a child together).

"I don't know," Holly said. "She's just grumpy, I guess."

"Everything okay with Tommy?"

"I think so," Holly said, but in truth she hadn't thought about the possibility that there was some problem with Tommy. "That's a good thought, though. I'll ask her."

"Okay, Holly. Merry Christmas, my dear. Call later if you need to vent. But, honestly, I wouldn't get too excited about a big party at your place today. This isn't our grandmothers' white Christmas."

"Hmm," Holly said. "That could be good, or that could be bad. I'll let you know. Bye-bye."

"Bye, babe."

And that was it. The line between them was severed—or, now that there were no telephone lines, the band of energy, the ghost-wave that had carried their voices to one another was—what? Snuffed? How did that work? Holly had never even understood how the *old* system worked—how sound had traveled through wires strung from one pole to the next across the country, let alone got transported across oceans. But at least that system had made an intuitive kind of sense. The sound was in the wires, and if you had to call overseas the system became more complicated, and astonishingly expensive, so you didn't do it very often, and when you did the voices you heard sounded very far away—echoes and buzzings accompanying the voices—and sometimes you used to be able to hear the murmurs of other conversations taking place under the conversation you were having, and all of this had made the process of speaking to a disembodied person over a great distance seem possible, physical.

But, now, the voice of someone in Siberia would sound as close or as far as someone down the block. Often, Tatiana, just calling home from Tommy's house two blocks away, sounded on her cell phone as if she were calling from Siberia. Conversely, when Eric had called on his cell phone from Tokyo two summers ago, it had sounded as if he were standing just outside the closed front door.

❄

ERIC.

Christ, in all this melodrama with Tatiana, Holly had managed to forget all about Eric and his parents in the car, trying to get home from the airport in a snowstorm. She looked at her watch again. What if Eric had gotten stuck in a snowbank, or gotten into a fender bender? That's as far as her imagination would take her, but it chilled her. Why hadn't he phoned to let her know where he was?

"Tatiana?" Holly called out. She needed to break the news about Pearl and Thuy and Patty to her daughter, but she also just needed company now. She needed someone with whom to discuss the day's changed plans. Should she bother with the mashed potatoes now? Was anyone going to make it here for Christmas dinner? Should she start making phone calls, and to whom? "Tatty?"

Still, nothing.

God damn her. That little bitch. Holly decided just to let herself feel that anger. Usually, she tried to stuff it down, to remind herself that Tatty was still a child, and that she herself had been no picnic when she was a teenager. When she felt this angry at Tatty she always tried to remind herself how badly she'd wanted a child. What about that? Had she thought it would all be rainbows and gumdrops?

Well, she and Eric had gotten nearly fourteen years of rainbows and gumdrops and kisses every day and love cards every holiday and birthday, construction paper cards carefully decorated with crayons: *I love you so much, Mommy. Daddy I love you to the moon!* Holly would tell herself that she would just have to focus on those memories as Tatty passed through these few years during which she did what teenagers are supposed to do: separate themselves as best they can from their parents so that they can go out into the world on their own.

Still, Holly could feel angry in her mind, couldn't she? She would allow herself that today. Thoughts were free, right? It wasn't as if she and Tatty were psychically linked. Tatty couldn't hear her thoughts. Holly didn't say it out loud, didn't even move her lips to it, but again she thought it:

God damn Tatiana.

Did she *have* to be a little self-righteous bitch on Christmas Day?

Did everything *have* to be about her?

Was there not even a *shred* of gratitude in her?

Did she *ever* consider what her life might have been like if Eric and Holly hadn't come along? This was something Holly would never, *never*, say to her daughter, but she could think it, couldn't she?

"Tatty?"

This time she shouted her daughter's name loudly enough that there'd be no mistaking that she expected an answer—but she didn't have time to hear whether or not she got one before "A Hard Rain's A-Gonna Fall" started playing in her palm. She glanced down: Unavailable.

Holly smirked, shook her head, called out (not nicely: she knew this wasn't *nice*), "Hey, Tatty. It's Unavailable. I'm answering this one for you!"

She pressed the green icon and held the phone to her ear. "Hello?" she said loudly enough for Tatiana to hear.

"Hello, Mrs. Judge?"

Surprisingly, this was not a robot. This was a young woman. Nonnative speaker of English. Although she hadn't said enough for Holly to determine what her first language would be, there was no pause between "hello" and "Mrs.," and "Judge" was pronounced as if it rhymed with *stooge* not *fudge*.

"Yes, this is Holly Judge," Holly said, pronouncing her last name correctly. Judge was her maiden name. She'd never taken Eric's name—Clare—because, frankly, she thought when she married Eric that she had a career as a published poet ahead of her, and "Holly Clare" sounded to her more like a kind of doughnut than a serious writer.

"Merry Christmas, Holly Judge."

"Thank you. What can I do for you? I'm busy. If you're selling something—"

"No, no, no, ma'am. I'm calling from . . ." The caller said a name that might have been May-um. May-hem. Maim. Maine? The young-sounding woman did not go on. She seemed to expect that Holly would respond to that place-name (whatever it was), as if she'd recognize its significance.

"What? Maine?" Holly asked. It was, she supposed, time to get actively hostile. What corporation or catalog company was in Maine? Garnet Hill? Lands' End? Holly had bought a jacket from a Land's End catalog for Eric for his birthday a couple of months ago. Surely they weren't calling her on Christmas?

But then again, why not? Capitalism was, God knew, running amok these days. With the economy collapsing, why not have people from foreign countries—people you could pay pennies an hour—calling Americans to sell them goods and services on Christmas Day?

"What are you selling?" Holly asked.

"I'm telling you I'm calling from *mayum* for you. I still found your phone number."

The voice sounded unprofessional, Holly thought.

Young and informal and untrained. "Okay. I'm hanging up on you now," she said into her iPhone. "I have no idea what this is about, and you're not telling me, so—"

"I'll call back Mrs. Judge in forty minutes when I find *lab-i-lus*. I am excited to find you home and *lab-i-lus* will speak of it."

"No," Holly said. "Don't call back." She placed her thumb on the red end bar on her phone. However, the seconds continued to tick around its little screen, indicating that the line had not been disconnected. She pressed the button again, and then she held the phone to her ear, listening to the seashell sound of it, and then a gasp followed finally by dead air, and she turned, still with the phone against the side of her face, and screamed—

Holly hadn't even realized she was screaming until she managed to close her mouth on it, almost snapping it back out of the air, when she realized that it was simply Tatiana standing there, only inches away. "My God," Holly said. "Where did you come from? I never heard you." Her heart was still racing, pulsing hard at her temples. "I didn't mean to scream, but you really scared me."

Tatiana's eyes looked both dark and bright, like black, polished stones. When Holly was a child, soon after her mother's diagnosis, her father had bought a rock tumbler and taken up the hobby of rock collecting, and many nights of her childhood Holly had fallen asleep to the sound of that grinding and pummeling. It was a miracle, how he could put a homely gray lump of something into the round barrel, and remove it, a week later, shining, full of colors that must have been there all along, but hidden. Looking into her daughter's eyes Holly thought of how those stones had come out of the tumbler bearing, it seemed, almost no relation to the stones that had gone in.

It wasn't that Holly did not notice, every day, how beautiful her daughter's eyes were, but had they ever really been *this* beautiful? She couldn't look away from them. They were the most beautiful eyes on earth.

❄

HOLLY AND ERIC had both, upon first seeing Tatiana during that Christmas trip to Pokrovka Orphanage #2, been stunned by her eyes. Lying in bed at the hostel that night, they repeated to each other maybe twenty times, "My God, did you see that child's eyes?"

Those eyes!

Everyone had told Holly and Eric before they left for Siberia not to get their hearts set on one particular child, that some adoptive parents had been through this process four or five times. You might be certain, for instance, that you were fated to have a particular child only to find out, after the medical exam, that there was something terribly wrong. And even when the child passed the medical exam, there were risks. Whether the medical examiners were even qualified, or sober, was a question in a country like Russia. Whether they had an interest in hiding the truth about a child from prospective Western parents was another. There had been couples—plenty of them!—who'd come back to Siberia after the required three months to find, to their horror, that defects they'd not noticed—attachment disorder, failure to thrive, lung diseases, heart diseases, autism, muscular atrophies, bone dysplasia, fetal alcohol syndrome—were now undeniable.

And although the orphanage nurses pretended to be dispassionate, they were often very invested in the children and in their own fantasies of those children's American lives. They might refuse to acknowledge these defects, or try to hide them. Sometimes they'd rouge sick children's cheeks or cover their patchy-bald heads with knitted caps, or put makeup on bruises that might have indicated blood disorders. If a couple had already fallen completely in love with a certain child, they would be easy to fool. They would be home in the United States with their child before they noticed that something was horribly wrong.

But Eric and Holly always joked, afterward, that they'd done exactly what they'd been warned not to do. They'd fallen completely and deeply in love with Tatty upon first sight. Those eyes were to blame. Holly had memorized those eyes during their first trip to Siberia, and had kept them in the very forefront of her mind during the long three months before they could go back to take custody of those eyes.

When they'd gone back for their second (and final) visit to the Pokrovka Orphanage #2, it was still a month shy of Easter. This time Holly would not be remiss. She filled two suitcases with nothing but gifts. There were stuffed white rabbits for the orphans—seventeen of them!—chocolates for the nurses, marshmallow eggs, jelly beans, and Reese's Peanut Butter Cups wrapped in their seasonal pastels, as well as less seasonal gifts. Holly had picked out half a dozen of the most expensive little bottles of perfume she could buy at the mall, along with silver necklaces and earrings and panty hose. She and Eric had burst into that orphanage—its smell of sodden towels, urine, bleach—bearing all these gifts, along with three bouquets of flowers they'd bought at the train station.

And there she was!

Their daughter!

She was still in the same crib—fourth from the wall, seventh from the hallway—with her name written in Magic Marker on a piece of cardboard in the Cyrillic alphabet, all swirls and spikes: *Tatiana.* (Holly had very forcefully requested that their daughter be called *Tatiana* for those three months, not Sally.) Although she did not seem to recognize them (how could she?) Tatiana had made no sound of protest—no sound at all, really—when Holly rushed to her and snatched her from the crib.

She had changed, of course. Three months is a long time in the life of a toddler. She was not the same baby she'd been when they left, of course. Now she was an older and more stoic version of the affectionate, enormous-eyed baby they'd left behind. Her hair was longer, lusher. She was no longer puffy-limbed, like a baby, but thinner, like a child.

But she *was* still Tatiana/Sally. Holly breathed her in, shed tears into her daughter's glossy hair, and then pulled back to look into her heart-shaped face.

Of course, it was natural that the eyes were not as startling at twenty-two months old as they had been at nineteen months. Not as long-lashed, perhaps. They did not seem as large. The child's face had grown, of course, along with the rest of her. That's how it was with everyone, wasn't it? Now it was her hair that set her apart from all the orphans: the Jet-Black Rapunzel. And the milk blue of her complexion. Her maturity, too. Three months had changed so many things! Tatiana did not need a bib any longer. She did not even wear a diaper. She was still two months away from being two years old, and she held a fork like an adult at a five-star restaurant. She wiped her mouth with a cloth when she was done eating!

She was gorgeous. She was breathtakingly gorgeous that spring day at the Pokrovka Orphanage #2, just as she was now, standing with one hand on the surface of the kitchen island, twirling an earring in her earlobe with the other, seeming not displeased to have crept up on her mother and scared her enough to make her scream.

"Tatty," Holly said briskly. It wasn't so much that she didn't want to give her daughter the satisfaction of having unnerved her; it was that she felt ashamed at having allowed her daughter to unnerve her. She tried to sound all business: "I've got bad news. Thuy and Patty and Pearl can't come. It's a bad blizzard. That's why everyone else is late. We're going to have to call Daddy and see what's going on."

Tatiana said nothing. She just stared at Holly. There was that hint of satisfaction in the curve of her lips, but her eyes looked—

Had she been crying? Was that why her eyes were so large and—

What?

So sad? She seemed to wear the expression of a child abandoned. Maybe all this emotion *did* have something to do with Tommy. Could they have had an argument? Tatiana always insisted that she and Tommy ("Unlike you and Daddy") never argued, but there was a first time for everything.

Or maybe it *was* her period, arriving early. Holly realized that Tatiana had changed dresses. She was wearing a black one now, lower cut. It made her look thinner and much less festive, but at least it didn't have that awful, choking, lacy neckline Ginny always opted to attach to any female garment she sewed. Holly didn't recognize this black dress, actually, but Tatty owned at least twenty dresses, and it might have been something she'd bought at the mall without Holly, anyway—or maybe at that teenagers' secondhand shop they all liked (Plato's Closet) and to which Holly objected (lice, bed bugs, crabs).

"I'm sorry, Tatty. I know you wanted to see them, and to see Patty."

Tatiana had changed her earrings, too. She was wearing silver studs now instead of Thuy and Patty's opals. It made Holly want, unhelpfully, to sigh or roll her eyes. She couldn't help thinking Tatiana had changed the earrings because Holly had mentioned that it was nice of her to wear them. Apparently the mother of a teenage girl wasn't even allowed to compliment her daughter's thoughtfulness without consequences. But Holly didn't say anything. She and Tatty were, it seemed, back to normal, and she didn't want to disrupt that. Her daughter was out of her bedroom at least.

"Who was that?" Tatiana asked, glancing at the iPhone in Holly's hand.

Holly looked back at her phone. "Thuy," she said. "I told you. They were driving back from church, and—"

"No," Tatty said. "After that. There was another call."

"Oh," Holly said, nodding. "Sorry. That was your friend Unavailable. She said she'd call back in forty minutes or so, after she learned to speak English. It seems that scam artists don't get Christmas Day off after all."

"No rest for the wicked," Tatty said.

Holly blinked and shook her head a little. What? Had she misheard? That wasn't like anything Tatty would ever say. Such a platitude would have sounded more natural on her *own* lips than on her daughter's. Holly shrugged and said, "That's right. I guess."

"Don't answer when she calls back," Tatty said.

"No," Holly said, and nodded again at her daughter's common sense and change of heart. "There's no law that says you need to answer the phone every time it rings. There's voice mail now. And Unavailable is never a good bet."

"That's right," Tatty said. "And it's not Christmas today in Russia anyway."

Holly nodded, but she was surprised that Tatiana knew, or remembered, this fact. When Tatty was very little, Holly had thought it might be fun to celebrate Christmas on the Russian Orthodox holiday as well, in honor of Tatiana's origins—but this had angered and confused Tatiana, who at first pushed the gifts away that Holly gave her and said, "It's not Christmas."

"It is in Russia!" Holly had said, and began to unwrap Tatiana's gifts for her. Eric was at work, so it was just the two of them, and Tatiana wanted nothing to do with the unwrapped presents—a Russian nesting doll, a Russian lacquer box with a brightly smiling Snow Maiden on it, and a pair of black mink mittens. Holly, who'd done some research, tried to explain the concept of Grandfather

Frost to her, but Tatty put her hands over her ears and said, again, "It's not Christmas," and she never, to Holly's knowledge, had looked at those Russian gifts again, although Holly kept them dusted for her on a shelf in her bedroom.

"No, you're right," Holly said. "It's not Christmas in Russia. It is here, though. Would you mind setting the table now? Until we get word that no one's showing up at all, we have to pretend we're having Christmas dinner per usual, right?"

"Right," Tatty said, and although it sounded noncommittal, dispassionate, she headed obediently over to the table.

The roast made the sound of splattering fat inside the oven, and when Holly opened the door, the succulent smells rushed out to her, along with the heat, which turned the silver chain around her neck to a burning trickle of heat conduction. The meat, lit up under the oven bulb, was still bloody, but now it was at least browning a little at both ends. Although the smell flipped that primitive carnivorous switch inside her, the sight of the meat still repulsed Holly. She'd seen roadkill a lot like this— and also photos of carnage, horrible scenes in violent movies with leg stumps, dead babies, human remains.

Still, Holly's stomach rumbled. She was hungry. Neither she nor Tatiana had eaten at all today. As soon as she'd shut the oven, she was thinking about sitting down with a knife and eating that meat. "The roast sure smells good, doesn't it?" Holly said over her shoulder to Tatty.

But there was no answer. Holly looked into the dining room. Tatty wasn't there. The table was not set. Not a single dish or water glass or utensil had been touched, and Tatty was gone.

"Tatty?"

No answer.

It was a small house. If Tatty couldn't hear her mother's voice she was either in the bathroom with the door closed, or she'd gone outdoors or down to the basement, or she had her bedroom door shut again and was purposely not responding. Holly started down the hallway, shaking her head and ready for the argument she'd been trying to suppress all day if that's what Tatty wanted, and saw that the bathroom door was open and the light was on (how many times had she asked Tatty to remember to turn the overhead lights off when she left a room?), and then she continued on to Tatiana's room.

Door closed.

"Tatty?" Holly said to the closed door for—what?—the *thousandth* time today. She raised a hand to knock, and then she thought *to hell with it.* It wasn't as if she couldn't set the table and prepare the Christmas dinner and clean it all up afterward herself. She'd managed it for years, with only that brief stretch of time when Tatty was between nine and fifteen, old enough not to be in the way and actively eager to be helpful. This, Holly thought, was going to be the new normal for a while. Just like they'd all told her: "Try to remember how sweet she was, to sustain you when she's a teenager!"

Holly recalled how other mothers had seemed to delight in saying such things to her when beautiful four-year-old Tatty came running across the park to throw herself into her arms, crying out, "Mommy, I love you!"

So, why should it surprise Holly so much that they'd been right?

NOW THE SNOW beyond the picture window looked like a staticky wall, like something that was being built from the ground up rather than falling from the sky. Now there was either no breeze—and the heavy flakes were simply, in their density, floating—or there were so many flakes falling that they replaced themselves more quickly than the eye could detect. Holly knew, several seconds before the song started up, that her cell phone was about to start playing "A Hard Rain's A-Gonna Fall," but it wasn't precognition. There was a flash of light from the phone, so quick it was nearly subliminal. She looked at the iPhone as Bob Dylan began to sing, and she recognized the local area code. It was the Coxes.

"Holly? This is Tom. Have you looked out the window lately?" Tom Cox laughed as if he'd made a clever joke, maybe at Holly's expense. Surely he knew she didn't like him. He must have assumed, over the years, that she'd been privy to some of Eric's office conflicts. And Tom Cox wasn't a complete idiot. He would know that while a man might choose to remain pals with someone he worked with, and despised, the man's wife didn't have to like him.

"Yeah, actually, I'm looking out the window now, Tom," Holly said. "It's snowing."

"Snowing, ha! That's a good one! Well, oh—just a second here, Mindy's taking the phone, tell Eric, I—"

"Holly, it's Mindy. I'm *so* sorry. I know you've probably been working yourself sick getting Christmas together for all of us, and we were *so* excited to be there, but we just went outside to assess the situation, and, God, we can't even *see* the street from our driveway. I mean, *nothing's* going anywhere."

Mindy Cox made so many apologies and went into so much detail about the blizzard, and the road, and their car, and the impossibility of even shoveling enough snow to walk *out* to the car, that Holly realized something she'd been somehow too myopic to see until then—that Mindy didn't like her or Eric, either. That she hadn't wanted to come over for Christmas. That she had been, perhaps, dreading it for days. That her heart had sunk when Tom had told her they'd been invited, and that maybe they'd even been arguing about it, but what could they do? This was the kind of relationship Tom and Eric had, and all of their livelihoods depended on the continuation of this relationship. Tom would feel he owed it to Eric, who would have felt not only slighted but unnerved if Tom had turned him down, and Mindy Cox had been praying all night for a blizzard, and God had come through for her.

After much reassurance, Holly said good-bye, exhausted by all the pretense, all the false bonhomie. And, yet, after Mindy Cox hung up, Holly continued to hold the iPhone to her ear, feeling inexplicably bereft. She felt even sadder than she'd felt about Thuy and Patty canceling! Ridiculous! What did it say about her that she was this upset to have been rejected by people she had not wanted to be with in the first place?

But suddenly she *did* want to be with them. Suddenly Holly realized that the Coxes had been an intrinsic part of the day, a part of her life, a part of the plan—and that putting up with them had been for herself, and no one else. Wasn't their company—on Christmas but also on earth!—one of the consolations of being a human being? Now she realized, too late, that she'd even actually wanted to feed their tiresome son his vegan salad. That poor, awful child, with a haircut out of *The Great Gatsby* but a face like a tangle of wires.

Still, she reassured herself, Christmas dinner wasn't entirely a dead issue yet. None of Eric's siblings had called yet to say they couldn't be there. The call of the tribe might be strong enough for them to make it through anything to be here with their parents and one another on Christmas Day. They could still begin to arrive, car by car, hungry, complaining, stomping the snow off their boots in her hallway. Holly needed to boil the potatoes!

Setting the iPhone down on the kitchen counter, Holly considered calling out to her daughter again—but that was just out of force of habit. She didn't expect Tatiana to respond, and did she even want Tatty's help now, knowing how begrudging it would be? A better mother, Holly knew, might force the child out of her room in order to interact with her. (Hadn't she read an article about that in *Good Housekeeping*? Hadn't one of the rules been never to let your child isolate herself, to maintain physical proximity even when the two of you were angry at one another?) A better mother would exert whatever energy it took to get the child to confess what was wrong (something with Tommy? or *had* she gotten her period?)—but that was, frankly, far more energy than Holly herself had left after the long, wrangling morning, and her low-grade hangover.

She was also fearful.

Tatiana was in the kind of mood, it seemed, in which she might say anything. She might not say the most hurtful thing (*You're not my real mother!*), but she might hint at it (*I'm nothing like you!*), or she might, as she already had today, without words, taunt Holly for the marijuana smoking.

That was an issue that never failed to put Tatiana squarely in the right and Holly squarely in the wrong—the *one time* Holly had indulged in *one puff* since Tatiana had come home with them from Russia. A huge mistake, no doubt about it, but a small one in the scheme of things, surely? Holly's favorite coworker, Roberta, fourteen years her junior, had been dying to get Holly stoned ("It would be so fucking fun!") ever since the two of them had swapped college stories one day, literally around the office watercooler.

"Maybe you'd be inspired to write some poems again!" Roberta had said.

The suggestion had made Holly cringe and wish she'd never told Roberta that she'd once been a poet. "I don't think clearheadedness is what's standing in the way of my poetic inspiration," Holly had said.

"Well, how do you know unless you get high?"

Roberta had gone on and on about how fun it would be to get stoned together, and eventually the nostalgia of it—silliness, youth, camaraderie—began to intrigue Holly. So one Saturday night when Eric was out of town, and Tatiana was out, Roberta had come over with a joint, and she and Holly had lit it up on the patio—an instantaneous fog of surreal entertainment (Holly had felt that her bare feet had turned to rubber, which instead of being alarming had seemed hilarious) but suddenly at the center of the cloud of sweet smoke, the giggling and Doritos and Roberta's unintelligible story of the first time she'd gone snorkeling, stoned, there were Tatiana and Tommy, home from the high school football game hours early, standing beside them on the patio. Holly really couldn't face *that* condemnation again today, whether she deserved it or not. She would just let her daughter sulk in her room until Eric, his parents, and his siblings finally arrived.

❄

THE CARROTS, WHEN Holly pulled them out of the crisper, looked shaggier than she'd remembered them. Fine little hairs now covered them, and the green tops seemed almost as if they'd grown longer since she'd brought them home two days ago from the grocery store. They looked, now, like they'd be a lot more work to clean and shred for the carrot salad (Gin's overly sweet recipe/tradition) than she'd thought they would be. Like everything else, this was something Holly should have attended to last night instead of finishing that bottle of Sauvignon Blanc with Eric at dinner. And then the eggnog.

She held the carrots in her hands. Was this actually even the same bunch she'd brought home from the store? Was it possible these were an older bunch, some purchase she'd stashed and forgotten about months ago? Holly put them down on the counter, went back to the refrigerator, opened and closed the other crisper. No other carrots.

Well, she supposed, it was natural that carrots might

continue to grow after being closed up in the cold dark of the refrigerator crisper for a couple of days. Didn't they say that the hair and fingernails of a corpse continued to grow in the grave? Carrots were, after all, roots. The cold dark was where they'd thrived before they'd been yanked out of the ground. Why *wouldn't* they mistake the refrigerator for the earth? Holding the whole bunch under the faucet, letting the water from the tap run over them, it was easy to imagine them underground—the way they would be feeling, feeling, *feeling* their way around down there, like long, creeping fingers.

God, how hungry the first person who ever dug up a carrot and ate it must have been! These were nothing like slices of roast beef. Who was the first person to give that dirty thing a taste, and then to call over the rest of the clan and persuade them to try it?

Holly took the chopping block out from under the sink, set it on the cupboard, and pulled a knife out of the drawer. She hated knife work, really. She knew there were special classes one could take just to learn how to hold a knife—something she'd never been able to do. If she ever had the time, maybe she would take such a class, but, in the meantime, she just held a knife clumsily in one hand and a shaggy carrot in the other.

Unlike Tatiana, she'd never helped out her mother in the kitchen—or, if she had, she had no memory of it. Holly had taught herself to cook through trial and error.

By the time Holly would have been old enough to help, or to remember helping, her mother had given up and let Holly's sisters take over the running of the household. So, Holly's memories of the kitchen mostly consisted of being gently pushed out of it by Janet or Melissa while something bricklike unthawed itself in the oven and someone checked a loaf of Wonder Bread to make sure it hadn't gotten moldy. (Something Wonder Bread seemed perversely immune from, but still . . .) "Go watch TV, Holly. We'll call you when it's ready." So that's what Holly had done.

All through the years of her mother's slow death and her sisters' servitude and her father's enslavement by the U.S. Postal Service and her much older brother's boring and inexorable suicide-by-Beefeater-and-tonics (so much more dramatic and prolonged than Melissa idling to death one night in a garage!), Holly had been lying on a floral couch with her dead grandmother's afghan pulled up to her chin while one or another of the family cats slept on her ankles, and watching *Gilligan's Island*.

If only, Holly thought, she could take Tatty back there, to that doomed family (really, like a horrible fairy tale, how they'd started dying one by one as soon as Holly had been born!) and point out the lonely child on the couch who had once been Holly herself. She would say to Tatiana, "*This* is why you should be happy to be asked to help your mother with Christmas dinner. By the time your mother was your age, her own mother, her sister, and her fucking brother were dead. And the rest of them were well on their way."

"Tatty?" she called then (again, force of habit) over her shoulder. Why not give it one more try? Tatty was going to have to come out of there eventually. She'd need to use the bathroom, if nothing else. She'd grow hungry, wouldn't she? And even with a roomful of electronics (and an Internet connection that could attach her to any corner of the globe and any other connected person on that globe in a matter of nanoseconds) surely she'd get bored, wouldn't she? And, anyway, of course, when Gin and Gramps got here, Tatiana would be by their sides. Gin and Gramps had seven other grandchildren, each of them biological, but not one of them was as devoted, as in love, as respectful, as reverential of her grandparents as Tatiana.

Three Christmases earlier, Eric's brother had posed all those grandchildren around Gin and Gramps, and taken a photograph, and then posted it later, of course, on Facebook. In the photograph there were seven freckled, blue-eyed children ranging in age from three to twenty standing in a semicircle around the old couple in their black clothes. Each child bore a cautionary resemblance to one or both of the grandparents—that portrait seeming to whisper *These are your future faces, these black-clothed elders, this is what happens to pretty little freckled people who survive on this planet for eighty years, see how time and the sun and gravity will wither and bend you, beware*—except for Tatiana.

She was the Jet-Black Rapunzel at the center of that portrait. And even though it could not have been more clear that Tatty bore no biological relationship to these grandparents, *she* was the one standing at the center of the photograph with one hand on each of her seated grandparents' shoulders. She was the closest to them, and she was the happiest to be there. Gin had an arm crossed over her chest, and her spotted hand was at rest on Tatiana's wrist. Gramps had his head tilted in Tatiana's direction as if he were trying, lovingly, to listen to his granddaughter's heartbeat. Someday, Holly felt sure, some descendant would unearth (or, in the case of electronic photographs, *download*?) this portrait, and would point out Tatiana and wonder aloud, *Where did this one come from?* But it would also be clear that the story this photograph told was that Tatiana, stranger in a strange land, was the one who loved and *was* loved best.

"Tatty?" Holly called again. Then, speaking as loudly as she could without feeling absurd: "I'm worried about Gin and Gramps and Daddy, aren't you? They should have been here a long time ago."

Holly turned the faucet off and held still, a carrot in one fist and a knife in the other. She listened for the creaking of Tatty's bedsprings, but didn't hear a sound. She placed the carrot and the knife in the bottom of the sink, dried her hands on a dish towel, and stepped over to her iPhone again, checked her messages. No one had called.

And why the hell not? They all had cell phones. Probably each of Eric's siblings' cars held three or four cell phones! They were *all* late, *very* late, by now—and whether it was because they were on the freeway in a blizzard or not, late was late, and people called their hostesses to explain why they were late. Right?

Holly looked for Eric's name in her list of contacts. She'd never figured out how to put him on speed dial, and had never memorized his number since all she had to do was touch his name to reach him (although she did occasionally wonder what would happen if her phone fell into a lake, sank to the bottom, and she needed to call from a pay phone).

Eric picked up on the third ring. "Hello." Not a question. He knew who it was from the name on his own cell phone, and he had clearly been expecting her to call.

"Eric," Holly said. "What's going on? Are you stuck on the freeway?"

"No," he said. "Not anymore. I was going to wait to call you until I had some idea of what to say. We're at the emergency room. St. Joseph's Mercy. Something's wrong with Mom. We're in a room with her now, waiting for the doctor."

"What?"

It was the only word that came to Holly's mind. She wasn't really asking Eric to repeat himself, but when she heard him sigh impatiently she realized that's what he thought she was asking, that she hadn't heard him. He hated cell phones, became irate when a call started to break up or someone hadn't heard what he'd said. He'd go on and on about how bad the phone service had become these days, and how back in the old days you were connected to a cord, yes, but you could carry on a *fucking conversation*. Pointing out to him that now you could be standing in the center of a forest while talking to someone at the top of a mountain did no good. He'd ask what difference it made if you couldn't *communicate*. For his birthday, she'd bought him an iPhone, which he'd returned to the store. He'd apologized, saying that it was a thoughtful gift, but he didn't want to carry a tiny high-powered mainframe on which he could compute astronomical algorithms, or check Facebook. He wanted a phone.

"Well," Holly had said, feeling more hurt than was warranted, since it wasn't a very sentimental gift—still, she'd been excited to give it to him—"it's a phone, too, even if it's more than a phone." She realized, as the words left her mouth, how much like an advertisement they sounded.

"And Steve Jobs is more than a human being," Eric had said. "That's why his Chinese slave workers are happy to throw themselves off the roofs of his factories as a human sacrifice to the iGods." He hated Steve Jobs.

Holly thought she could hear some sort of hospital machine whirring behind Eric.

"You didn't hear me?" Eric asked, and the irritation in his voice was clear. Their connection itself was, actually, crystal clear—one of those connections that made it possible even to hear the clicking of the speaker's teeth in his mouth as he sounded out consonants.

"Yes," Holly said—all business now. "I'm sorry. I heard what you said about Gin and the hospital. I just—I just don't know what to say. Should we come there? Can I—"

Eric laughed with what sounded to Holly like bitter condescension. He said, "You're kidding, right? I guess you haven't looked outside yet today?"

"I know it's snowing, Eric."

" 'Snowing' doesn't exactly describe it, Holly. Don't you two *dare* leave the house."

Holly didn't like his tone, but she also felt touched to hear him express concern for his wife's and daughter's safety, despite his distraction and anxiety and annoyance. His protectiveness was one of the hundreds of things she loved about Eric. On their very first date, strolling from his parked car to the restaurant, he'd switched places with her on the sidewalk, and Holly had understood that it was so that, if a car jumped the curb, it would kill him instead of her.

"Oh, sweetheart," she said, no longer annoyed. "What *happened*? What's wrong with Gin?"

"I can't go into that right now."

"Because Gramps is there?"

"Yes," he said.

"Can you call me back?"

"Later. Wait. I've gotta go. I'll—"

"Eric, no one's here yet. Have you heard from your brothers?"

"My brothers? Of course! No one's coming, Holly. They're wherever they could get a roof over their heads. If they can get anywhere at all, it will be here to the hospital. They certainly won't be making it to Christmas dinner. Just stay home, Holly. I'll call when I have real news. Bye."

Before the connection was cut Holly heard Eric say a grave hello to someone who must have just walked in the door, and then what sounded like a rooster, cut off in mid-crow—but of course that couldn't have been it. It had to have been the legs of a chair scraping against linoleum, or a door with squeaky hinges closing. But it alarmed her. She fought the urge to call back, to ask what that sound in the background had been, but calling him back would only add to Eric's distractions. He'd said that he'd call her. And they were at St. Joseph's Mercy Hospital, he'd said. Even if that sound had been the worst thing Holly could imagine (some sort of agonized cry for help?), they were at a *hospital.* In the emergency room. To call Eric again would be selfish, as if this crisis had anything to do with her. It didn't, and she knew that, and so did he. Although Holly had always been fond of Gin and Gramps, they weren't her parents. She didn't *love* them. She knew that, and they knew that, and they felt the same way about her.

In point of fact, Holly felt she barely knew Eric's parents, really. They'd lived hundreds of miles away from anywhere she'd ever lived since she'd been married to their son. How much time had she spent in the same room with them in all the years she and Eric had been married? Could it have totaled more than a hundred hours? Maybe not even close! And never alone. She'd never been in a room with the two of them that hadn't also been occupied by at least ten other pale and freckled members of the Clare clan.

Still, she knew, it would be terrible for Eric, and it would be terrible for Tatty, if anything happened to either one of them. Especially on Christmas Day.

Then Holly stopped, as if slamming on the brakes before hitting a snowbank, and realized that Christmas was over—truly over. Or, more accurately, that it was not really going to be Christmas in any familiar kind of way this year at all.

Then, as if slamming into that bank of snow despite the brakes, Holly realized that none of Eric's family members had thought to call her, to tell Holly herself that they wouldn't be there for Christmas. They'd all called Eric, not her.

Well, she thought, that made sense, didn't it? She tried to fight off a terrible sense of rejection, and its accompanying sense of failure, by telling herself that perhaps it had been the brothers, not their wives, who'd called. It would be only natural that the brothers would call their brother, Eric, not his wife, to update him on their progress through the blizzard, and lack thereof. They would simply have assumed that Eric would let Holly know (and why he hadn't let her know sooner was something Holly could argue with him about at a much later date, after the crisis with Gin had passed). Eric's brothers didn't even have Holly's cell phone number, she assumed. And who used landlines any longer? Obviously even the robots were calling cell phones these days.

Or (of course!) Eric had called *them* before they'd had a chance to call him—or Holly, or the house. That was it. Eric had called his brothers from the freeway, just as he'd called her, when he and his parents had first left the airport, to tell them about the "confusion." At that point, they'd told Eric that there was no way to make it through the snow to the house for the day. Eric had been in the car, in a blizzard, on the freeway, facing a crisis with Gin, and of course he hadn't thought to call Holly to tell her about the cancellation.

Still, it was hard to shake the feeling that she had been rebuffed. Eric's brothers and their wives would have known that Holly was at home cooking, setting the table, arranging things, expecting them. Wouldn't it have made sense to call her, to apologize, even if they were sure that Eric would let her know? Which he hadn't. There was a cliché in her throat—a lump—and tears, which she blinked back, in her eyes.

Holly glanced down at her feet. They felt cold and cramped without slippers or shoes on the bare tile of the kitchen floor. Through the black nylon of her stockings, Holly could see the intricate bone structure under the skin. They had become, suddenly it seemed, bony feet. This was something new about her body. Something she was only noticing now. These were like an old woman's feet.

On only one occasion in all those years had Holly glimpsed Gin's naked feet—long ago when, during a summer visit from Gin and Gramps, Tatiana, only four or five years old, had begged her grandmother to come into the blow-up pool in the backyard with her.

Poor old Gin would never, of course, have denied such a request. Although she could do no more than remove her orthopedic shoes and her flesh-colored socks (Holly was sure the woman had never owned a bathing suit, even as a child), Gin did manage to step into Tatty's little vinyl pool with her, and that's when Holly saw her mother-in-law's feet.

They looked to Holly like awful, plucked birds. Emaciated, wingless things, prepared for a meager prison meal or a third-world soup. Holly thought she could actually see the blood moving through the veins in those feet, collecting in little lozenge-sized clumps before pumping on. She'd felt sick with pity for those feet. She'd thought *no wonder* the old woman hobbled so badly. How did Gin even manage to walk? And how much longer could someone with feet so damaged, so exhausted, continue to walk this earth at all?

Holly looked down at her feet and recognized that they were not yet like Gin's, but that, if she lived long enough—unlike her mother, her sisters—they would be one day, and then she realized that, all around her feet, there was something dark, or dirty, spilled on the floor.

Dust? Ash? What was this?

Holly lifted a foot and touched the sole of it to see if it was damp, if she could be standing in a puddle of something. It wasn't. This wasn't from the tiny bit of blood that had dripped onto the floor from the roast. That little trickle couldn't account for this darkness spreading around her. She took a sponge out of the sink, got on her knees, and ran the sponge over the floor.

Nothing.

Nothing came off the floor with her sponging, and whatever this darkness was, it wasn't sticky or grimy. She ran her hand around the spot, and found it dry, and realized that there didn't seem to be anything spilled there, recently at least. That circle was simply a darker darkness than the rest of the floor.

Had the ceramic tiles (expensive, baked clay, burgundy,

installed only two years before) begun to discolor? Or had they been discolored all along, and was she only now, in the snow-glare pouring in through the picture window onto the shiny surfaces of the kitchen, noticing it?

Holly pressed harder with the sponge, but nothing happened.

Or, did it?

Was it her imagination, or did the dark circle seem to spread, to bloom, as she moved the sponge over it?

"What are you *doing?*"

Startled, Holly looked up to find Tatiana standing above her, wearing the red velvet dress again, gazing down on Holly with an annoyed expression, as if Holly might have spilled something that Tatiana had wanted to drink, or as if she'd broken a dish that Tatiana had particularly liked and was now ineptly picking up the pieces. It must have been, Holly thought, the expression Tatiana had received from Holly a hundred times in the first five or six years of her life in this house—her mother, looking down at her from her adult height, looking at the broken glasses or the torn book or the spilled juice, saying, "What did you *do?*"

"Jesus," Holly said. "You surprised me. I thought you were still in your room."

"Mom, what are you doing?" Tatiana asked again, still with that expression of annoyed surprise.

"Well, there's something on the tiles, it seems," Holly

said. "I can't sponge it up, though. But see how all of this is darker, this whole circle? It's like a stain, or discoloration, or maybe—"

"It's *you*."

Holly looked up at her daughter.

"It's *you*, Mom."

Holly didn't want to ask Tatiana what she meant. She didn't trust her now. It seemed that she could find something to criticize in *anything* Holly did or said. Who knew what she was going to find ridiculous about Holly this time? What joke at Holly's expense she might make. She didn't ask Tatiana to explain, but continued to regard her.

Holly could see that there was a crease from Tatiana's pillow on her cheek. She was relieved that Tatty had been, apparently, sleeping in her room. A nap. It's why she hadn't answered Holly's calls. She'd been deeply asleep—that sort of deep nap one takes on a snowy midday. Tatiana was simply tired. Very tired. That was why she was so cranky, why she'd been acting the way she had. It was surprising to find that she'd changed out of that black dress and back into Gin's red velvet one—but who knew why she might have changed dresses, and then changed back? Wasn't that something Holly did herself, sometimes two or three times in the morning before she went to work? There was nothing any more wrong here than there was for any mother snowbound on Christmas Day with a teenage daughter, Holly told herself firmly, and then she worked up the nerve to ask Tatty, "What do you mean it's *me?*"

"Mom, can't you see what you're doing?"

Holly shook her head. She looked from Tatiana to the sponge in her hand, and then from the sponge to the dark circle around her on the floor.

"Mom, you're trying to scrub your shadow off the floor."

"What?" Holly asked.

Why were there suddenly tears in her eyes? Why, again, did she have that feeling of complete abandonment, of having been rejected, abandoned, by *everyone?*

Holly dropped the sponge and put her hand to her eyes.

"Stand up, Mom," Tatiana said. Her voice was soft now. It wasn't the voice of the loving little girl she'd been—truly, only yesterday!—but there was kindness, compassion there nonetheless. Tatiana held out a hand to help Holly to her feet (her bony feet!) and she said, "Step over to the other side of the kitchen island, Mom." Holly did, and then Tatiana said, "Look," pointing to the floor, to the ceramic burgundy tiles, which were now their original mono-color. There was nothing on the floor where there'd been—

Where Holly's *shadow* had been.

"Good Lord," Holly said, and then felt an actual tear rolling down the side of her nose, headed toward her lips, which she didn't bother to wipe away. "I must be getting senile, Tatty. I was getting ready to go to the basement for the bleach. I was going to try to bleach my own shadow out from under me, wasn't I?"

Tatiana came over to Holly and put her hand on her back, right between her shoulder blades, and Holly felt herself sag a little under her daughter's gentle touch. Tatty patted her, and laughed a little, and the sound was lovely, like a crystal bell tapped with a silver spoon. Holly laughed, too. Despite her tears, and the sense of shame and desertion she felt, she was also amused at herself. And she was so, so relieved:

Tatty was back.

Tatty had napped, and even if it was only going to be the two of them for Christmas—

Well, maybe that would be wonderful! Mother and child! Maybe this would be the most memorable Christmas of all! While they waited for Eric to get home with Gin and Gramps (because surely Gin would be fine) Holly and Tatiana could play Scrabble, or read. Or, maybe, while Tatiana read, Holly could write for just a little while. If Tatty maybe took another nap, or if she were happily curled up under the afghan on the couch, texting Tommy, Holly could just say, "I'll be back in a few minutes, Tatty. I need to write something down." Tatiana would understand. Although she'd never been told much about it, Tatty knew that her mother used to write, had studied creative writing, and had an MFA, and that there had been a time when she was working on a collection of poems. Holly had even told her the title, *Ghost Country*—although she hadn't told Tatty what the poems had been about. But Tatiana was old enough now that she might actually be proud if her mother took up writing again. She might like to hear her mother say, "I think I'll go into the bedroom and jot a few ideas down . . ." Perhaps this would be the day, the Christmas Day, that Holly would start writing again.

She turned to take Tatiana in her arms then—and although it wasn't the warmest embrace she and her daughter had ever shared, their bodies still came together completely, and still fit together perfectly. Her daughter was several inches shorter than Holly, and she always would be. Holly wasn't tall, herself, but the poor nutrition of Tatiana's prenatal months and her first twenty-two months had surely affected her height. And who knew how tall her biological parents had been? There would never be any way of knowing what genes for height Tatiana carried. Tatty would always feel like a child in Holly's arms. Holly would always be able to lean down and kiss the silky top of her daughter's hair, breathing in that smell of tea tree oil shampoo and L'Occitane eau de toilette. Holding her daughter in her arms, Holly could also smell her sweet breath—mint, milk, and something else. Fruit? Fruit that had softened under a warm lamp?

"Did you eat any breakfast?" Holly asked. "While we were still asleep this morning? Are you hungry?"

"I'm not hungry," Tatiana said, and Holly realized, suddenly, the most obvious thing of all:

That was the problem! Tatiana hadn't had breakfast! She was starving! "Oh my God, Tatiana, you need to eat something *now*."

Holly had tried to make it sound nonjudgmental—teenage Tatiana hated being told that she was hungry and needed to eat, or tired and needed to go to bed, or cold and needed to put on warmer clothes ("I'll put on my mittens if my hands are cold, Mom. Do you think I'm a two-year-old?")—but her daughter stiffened, took a step back, and said, "I told you I'm not hungry," loudly, as if to a deaf woman. She narrowed her eyes.

"Okay, okay! You're not hungry," Holly said, holding up her hands. "But you'd probably be in a better mood if you ate something."

"I'm not in a bad mood!" Tatty dramatically swept her hair away from her face and turned away, and when she did Holly saw that she was wearing the opals again.

"Oh," she said, knowing she ought not to comment on it even as she did. "You're wearing your opal earrings again. What a shame that Thuy and Pearl won't be here." Holly made a sad clown face, sticking out her lower lip. It was a peace offering, being silly.

"What?" Tatiana said, turning back around quickly. "Where are they?"

"I told you, hon—the snow. They left their church service and realized that there was no way they could get here in this blizzard." Holly gestured to the picture window, but when she looked in the direction that she herself had gestured she could see that now the snow was simply a stillness out there, as if it were a painting of snow. It seemed benign, fully penetrable, a kind of banal mirage of snow.

"You never told me that Thuy and Pearl and Patty weren't coming!" Tatiana shouted.

"Of course I did," Holly said.

"No you *didn't*!" Tatty said, and balled her fists, shaking them near her own face, as if she might strike herself. "*Fuck.*"

"Tatiana!" Holly knew she should take a step forward, take those fists in her hands, but instinctively she took a step backward and put a hand to her own mouth, as if the word had come from there.

Tatty shook her head, as if surprised herself to have said it. Her eyebrows were knitted together—this time in genuine distress.

"What in the world is the matter with you, young lady?" Holly asked.

"I just can't believe it!" Tatiana said, her shoulders sagging in despair. "I wanted to see them!" She was on the verge of crying. Holly could see it. Just as when she was a toddler, Tatty's nostrils had begun to flare, and the tip of her perfect nose was turning red. Sometimes, back in the toddler days, if Holly or Eric acted right away, they were able to prevent a meltdown at the grocery store, or just before they dropped Tatty off at the day care, if Tickle Me Elmo were brandished in the nick of time. Or if there happened to be a graham cracker handy, they might interrupt the process before it started—the flaring of the nostrils that would come next, leading to a hiccup, which would be followed by a whimper, before the sobbing began in earnest and went on and on and on, as if in response to mortal injury or unbearable grief.

Holly would never forget the first few times she'd dropped Tatiana off at Wee Ones Preschool (which was just a fancy name for a kind of a daytime orphanage, really, because there was no actual school, "pre" or otherwise, for a two-year-old. Everyone knew this. Wee Ones was just a place where other women—women who were poorer, and who were paid—put your child down to nap and made sure she didn't hit her head on the rail of a playpen).

That first morning Tatiana had been pitifully excited. She'd run into the place and looked around excitedly at the other toddlers—several of whom were crying—and at the toys, most of which were on shelves too high for her to reach. But Tatiana was in wonder at the new place, the new people, the promise that it all held, and she hadn't even looked over her shoulder when Holly left her there.

But by the second morning Tatiana knew what it meant to be dropped off at Wee Ones—that she wouldn't see Holly again for nine hours once she walked out the door—and Tatty's nostrils (perfect, tiny things—her nose being one of the best features of her face full of perfect features) had begun to flare before they'd even crossed the threshold, and then the hiccup, the stifled sob, and then, when Holly, in her high heels, had stepped toward the door, Tatty had let out a scream so piercing it sounded exactly as if the child had been stabbed in the back with a long, thin knife.

"Go!" the day-care director had said, inexplicably smiling and laughing. "She'll be fine once you're gone. But if you prolong it, this will go on forever!"

So Holly, against every instinct she had in her body and soul, had hurried out the door. And then, even worse than hearing another scream like that one was the silence on the other side of it when it closed.

Holly had wept on and off all day. She'd called Eric, who'd told her that the worst thing she could do would be to drive back over there and pick Tatty up. It would reward her for her own misery.

"Maybe day care is a bad idea," Holly had said.

"Well, do you have a better idea?"

"Maybe I should quit my job, stay home with her?"

"Jesus," Eric said. "We'd have had to do a lot better planning than we've done to make *that* happen."

He was right, of course. There were the cars, the mortgage. How did she think they would survive on one salary? And somehow Holly had made it through that day—which had seemed, actually, longer than the ninety-three days they'd had to wait for their adoption to be approved, to return to Tatty in Siberia, and Wee Ones had seemed even farther away from her than the Pokrovka Orphanage #2.

But when Holly had gotten back to Wee Ones that evening, the day-care ladies had all chortled and said that although Tatty had cried for quite a while—cried until she'd finally fallen asleep standing up in the center of the day-care center—she'd been perfectly happy the whole rest of the day. She'd watched *Dora the Explorer*. She'd asked for a second cookie. She hadn't said a word about her mother. And they all loved Tatiana. Her dark hair. The Russian words she still blurted out when she was excited or frustrated or tired. She was loved by the day-care women just as she'd been loved at the Pokrovka Orphanage #2.

❄

NOW, AS HOLLY looked into her nearly grown daughter's stricken and pale blue face, and although it was all out of chronology, out of context (Tatty was sad that Thuy and Pearl and Patty wouldn't be here for Christmas, not that she'd been taken to day care as a toddler!) she thought, *Dear God, do I have to be punished for all of eternity for having left her there, screaming, at Wee Ones? For not having done the "better planning"? For not having had the courage to tell Eric*

*that it didn't matter, that we would have to start planning for
it that very day because I would not be abandoning my daughter
at that place ever again?*

Why *couldn't* she have quit her job?! At least for those
first prekindergarten years? To keep the tiny girl by her
side, to spare her that separation? Holly and Eric had
lived on *nothing* all through their twenties—one crappy
car and a two-bedroom apartment—and their lives had
been completely filled with inexpensive comforts and joys!
Why couldn't they have done it for a few years later in
their lives, too?

But, of course, no one did that. Some of the mothers
who brought their children (even younger than Tatiana)
to Wee Ones arrived in cars that cost the annual salaries
of *two* of the day-care workers who watched their children nine, ten, *eleven hours every day.* She had no idea why
those mothers had done it, but *why had Holly done it?* How
quickly those years had come and gone! And what had
she been doing all those hours and days of her daughter's
earliest years while she watched *Dora the Explorer* in a col-
orful institution surrounded by strangers—her sippy cup
empty, her eyes dry, her little chin pointed upward toward
the television as if to say that she had suffered worse, that
she had suffered before, that she could suffer again?

No. Surely, no. It hadn't been that bad. Tatiana had
made friends (*although, where were those friends now?*) and
she'd grown to love the day-care ladies (*although, where*

were those day-care ladies now?). And after that one terrible morning Tatiana had never again cried upon being left at Wee Ones! The tantrums she threw after that (and she *did* throw tantrums) were not about being left somewhere, but in reaction to others leaving:

Thuy might stop by the house for the briefest or longest of visits, but as soon as she picked her jacket up off a kitchen chair and started to put it on, Tatiana would blanch, stagger over to Thuy, pleading as if she were a child being left alone on the *Titanic*, *Don't go.* Sometimes there were even Russian words—words Holly had assumed her daughter had long since forgotten—uttered, sobbed, or screamed. Sometimes that well-timed Tickle Me Elmo or graham cracker managed to calm her down, but often she just had to be left to sob until she fell asleep, curled on the couch or standing with her head resting against a wall. They were terrible sobs, the sobs of the utterly bereft. But those sobs had nothing to do with Wee Ones.

A SINGLE TEAR slid down Tatiana's cheek. It was turned so silver by the bright blizzard light shining in from the picture window that it looked like a drop of mercury.

"Sweetheart!"

Holly forced her daughter into an embrace again—and this time it was a hard embrace. This embrace was a *de-*

mand. This embrace, Holly knew even as she executed it, was being stolen from Tatiana against her will. Tatiana, in reaction, went even stiffer, and she put her hands to her face so that her forearms and elbows were between her own body and Holly's. She inhaled a ragged breath, and then the silver tears seemed to pour out of her, into her hands, slipping through her fingers and onto her chest. It was as if Tatiana contained inside of her a sudden, tiny waterfall.

"My God," Holly said. "Sweetheart, sweetheart, my darling. We'll have a good Christmas. I promise. And tomorrow Thuy and Patty and Pearl will come over and we'll have our usual Christmas. Look!" Holly said, and she let go of Tatiana and went to the oven, turned the knob to off. "Look! I'll save the roast until the snow melts, for when we can all be together again. You and I will just eat the Coxes' son's vegan salad! I'll make that! How does that sound? You'll like that, right? We'll dig into the dinner rolls and the creamed herring and the sharp cheddar cheese. And when Daddy and Gin and Gramps get here, we'll—"

"What?" Tatiana asked, looking up from her hands, sober now, understanding. "Where are *they?*"

"You didn't hear me on the phone with Daddy?" Holly asked.

"No."

"Well . . ." Carefully, Holly began to lie. "Well, everything's fine. They've stopped, though, because of the snow."

There was certainly no sense in telling Tatty that Gin was having some sort of health issue, was there? That they were at St. Joseph's Mercy Hospital? At the emergency room? If Tatiana had to eventually be told at all (Holly still expected that this would be a false alarm and that they'd walk through the door any minute) it could certainly wait until a little later.

"Even the Coxes aren't coming?" Tatiana asked.

"No," Holly said. "That's the good news."

Ah! Thank you, Jesus! Holly had found the Tickle Me Elmo! The graham cracker! Despite herself, Tatiana was smiling now.

And such a smile! Despite the poor nutrition of her infancy and the fact that Holly (although she knew she should have) had rarely denied Tatty candy or soda, those teeth were brilliantly white. Without whiteners! And perfectly straight, without braces! Strangers would seem to comment on her smile nearly every time they left the house. "Wow," they'd say when Tatty looked at them and bestowed that smile upon them in return for an ice-cream cone or a receipt, "that's a million-dollar smile," or, "Your smile just made my day!" or, "Where did you get that smile?"

Of course, that was the one that pained Holly, for Tatiana did not "get that smile" from Holly, or Eric. The origins of that smile were somewhere east of the Urals and west of Lake Baikal on the Ukok Plateau. It wasn't, in fact, unthinkable that the smile had been carried in the genes of Mongolian warriors or the prostitutes from Moscow and St. Petersburg who'd been pushed over the Urals during the revolution. There'd been some strange bragging that Holly had found on the Internet when they'd first begun to research the Pokrovka Orphanage #2, that the girl children in that area were the most beautiful in Siberia because they were descendants of those prostitutes.

Who knew where Tatiana's smile came from? In the permafrost of that plateau, one of the world's oldest mummies had been exhumed in 1993. She was called the Ice Maiden, and the reconstruction of her face was made into a cast-iron bust that was kept behind glass at the Altai Regional Museum, and although Eric and Holly hadn't visited, they'd bought a postcard of the Ice Maiden bust from a vendor near the bus station. Holly kept that postcard in a file with all of Tatiana's adoption paperwork. That maiden wasn't smiling, but she could easily have been Tatiana's mother—her heart-shaped face and elegant nose—although she'd been born and died in the fifth century BCE.

Of course, the people who asked Tatiana, "Where did you get that smile?" did not mean to question the genetics of it—or did they? Sometimes Holly wondered. Were they asking where the smile came from because they could see that Holly was not Tatiana's biological mother?

"Of course not!" Thuy had said. "Christ, no one does *that*. Not these days, anyway. Half the kids in this town are adopted. Or mixed race! No one means a thing when they say, 'Where'd you get all those blond curls,' to Patty! And they say it all the time! They know perfectly well that I'm her mother and that she didn't get them from me!"

Holly had nodded, and pretended to take Thuy's assessment as the final word on the subject, but she knew that it was different with Thuy and Patty. In the case of Thuy and Patty, they would not be implying anything like that—but Thuy was Vietnamese, and she was a woman married to a woman. It was clear that she had not created her daughter with her own DNA, and it would have been political incorrectness of the highest order to *mean* such a thing in such a situation. But Tatiana and Holly, out in the world, were not such an easy target to miss. They were white, and although Holly was tall and blond with a short nose, blue eyes, and pale and freckled skin, there *could* be other explanations for the differences between a daughter and her mother. A dark father with a fabulous smile? A man to whom this blond mother might be married? When the bicycle repairman said, "Wow. Where'd you get that smile?" might he not have been genuinely and innocently wondering about Tatiana's genetic material? Tatiana would always just shrug modestly and cast her eyes downward, saying, "I don't know," while still smiling. She didn't betray it if any of this crossed her mind as well.

"Well your dentist must love you," one old volunteer at the library had said once. At that Holly had pulled Tatty along before anything else could be said. In fact, Holly had only taken Tatiana to a dentist one time in her life. When they'd refused to let Tatty come a second time for a cleaning without dental X-rays, Holly wouldn't bring her back. There was no way Holly was going to let her daughter be exposed to that kind of radiation, aimed at her face, for nothing. Anyone could see that her teeth were healthy, perfect. Holly's teeth were perfectly fine, too, and she hadn't been to a dentist herself in two decades. She simply took good care of her teeth—and now of Tatty's teeth, too. It took no more than a quick glance inside her daughter's mouth to see that she had no cavities, that her teeth were pristine.

Eric, of course, wouldn't have approved if he knew, but Holly let the name of a dentist in a neighboring town (not the dentist Eric went to) roll off her tongue often enough that he must have assumed they were getting themselves to that dentist every six months or so. Which would have been completely unnecessary.

The proof was in the smile.

❄

NOW, IN RESPONSE to Holly's joke about the Coxes, Tatiana was smiling that smile—and Holly felt wildly grateful for it, as if she'd been granted a pardon while on death row. She still felt under that mantle of guilt and suspicion for having overslept, but she was overjoyed to think that, despite everything, the day might not be a disaster. That her daughter didn't hate her, would not hide in her room (with the door locked!) all day. That, instead, they would play some board game at the table—there being no reason any longer to set the table—and then that other little fantasy, that maybe Holly could slip away to the bedroom with a pen at some point, excavate her notebook from the bottom of her dresser drawer, and write.

Not unexpectedly, "A Hard Rain's A-Gonna Fall" started up on Holly's iPhone then. It would be Eric, she thought. Or one of his brothers. Or one of their wives. Selfishly, Holly felt no urgency to speak to any of them now that Tatiana was smiling, and it seemed that their Christmas together might progress happily enough without anyone's company. Of course, if she could have helped Eric with his parents, she would have, but, since she was snowbound here anyway, what could she say to her husband on the telephone that would help?

Holly glanced at the iPhone on the kitchen counter but made no move to pick it up. "Maybe I just won't answer," Holly said. "Like you told me."

"What?" Tatiana asked.

"You and I will just pretend we're on a desert island for the rest of the day. If they need us they can leave a message."

Holly smiled, although Dylan kept singing, and Tatiana looked alarmed, and asked, "*What?* What are you talking about, Mom?"

Her shoulder bumped into Holly's arm as she hurried past her toward the kitchen counter and the iPhone. She lunged at it as if it were in flight, as if she were trying to catch it rather than simply trying to snatch it off the counter before the call went to voice mail.

"Tatty," Holly said, "for God's sake. If it's Daddy we'll call him right back, and if it's not—"

Then, as if the phone *did* have wings and agency of its own, or as if it had been thrown, it flew off the kitchen counter and traveled, low and fast, across the kitchen and into the dining room, to the dining room table, where it smashed into one of Holly's mother's water glasses, which fell to the floor with a shattering finality that seemed predestined, or deliberate, or both.

"Tatiana!" Holly shouted.

What had happened? And it had happened so quickly! Apparently in her rush to grab the iPhone, Tatiana had somehow *thrown* it instead—swatted it, sent it flying across this room and into the next.

"For Christ's sake!"

Holly hurried out of the kitchen and over to the dining room table. The cell phone lay unharmed on the surface of the table, but her mother's iridescent water glass was no longer a water glass. It was a thousand shimmering, scattered bits. That water glass was nowhere now—and, also, everywhere. Who knew how far the glass slivers of it had flown? Holly would be sweeping and vacuuming those little billions up from the corners and from under the furniture and even off the windowsills for years. The water glass had *exploded* when it hit the floor. *Atomized*.

The iPhone, on the other hand, being utterly expendable (Holly had even bought the replacement insurance on it), was unharmed. In fact it was still lit up where it lay, displaying Holly's wallpaper—an image of Tatiana and Eric standing in front of a waterfall.

On the phone, in that photograph, the two of them were illuminated, in miniature, and the waterfall behind them looked like feathers instead of water—as if a few hundred pillows had just been broken open behind them while they stood smiling into Holly's cell phone. The precision of that photograph was incredible. Somehow Holly's iPhone camera had managed to capture not only the very second of those particular smiles on the faces of her husband and daughter, but the individual drops of that waterfall's frothing water in mid-fall. It revealed the scene for exactly what it was—something mild and violent at the same time, a moment rushing past them, while utterly frozen forever. And all of it on a device the size of a child's hand! Secured for eternity on a handheld electronic device! If this stuff weren't so ubiquitous, it would have seemed supernatural.

Holly stepped back, away from the scene of the water glass, shaking her head, and when she turned back around she saw that her daughter hadn't moved from where she'd been standing when the iPhone first sailed from her hand. But Tatiana held that hand to her mouth now, pressing it to her lips, as if the hand were injured or she were trying to stifle a scream.

"Jeez, Louise," Holly said—opting for levity, because what was the point of getting angry? She'd had twelve water glasses, until Tatty had broken three, and then she had nine, and, well, now she had eight. It was, at least, an even number again! Thuy's words came to Holly's mind: *You can't reason with a toddler, so why get angry with one?*

She'd said this in response to Holly's compliment—how incredibly patient Thuy was with Patty—and the words, the truth of them, had stung Holly, who immediately flashed on an image of herself standing over Baby Tatty, telling her to go directly to her room after being caught ripping the pages out of the *Webster's Dictionary* one by one. Holly remembered the way Tatiana had looked around her then, as if she had no idea where to go, which room was hers. She'd only been living in this house for six months, and still she woke up every morning calling out *Please?* in Russian: *Puzhalsta? Puzhalsta? Mama Anya?*

Why, indeed, get angry with a toddler, or a child of any age? When Thuy had laughingly tossed off this noble truth, Tatiana was already twelve years old, and Holly had wished herself, desperately, back in time. She wanted to take Thuy's advice—but all those early years were lost! All those little seconds she could have valued more, cherished better, in which she could have practiced more patience, professed more love, brought her daughter home from Wee Ones and taken her straight to the park—gone!

But Holly *had* tried, hadn't she? She'd sat on the floor countless times and played Candyland with her daughter, and Chutes and Ladders—the games that Holly herself had so wanted to play as a child, but which no one had the time to play with her. She *had* taken Tatty to the park. And the beach. And the zoo. And the *Nutcracker*! They'd gone horseback riding. They'd traveled. They'd eaten in expensive restaurants and little diners, and even if Holly hadn't attended a church with Tatiana (as Thuy and Pearl did with Patty), they'd toured a few of the world's largest cathedrals, attended Handel's *Messiah* at Hill Auditorium every December.

Still, by the time Thuy gave Holly this advice (which she'd never intended as advice, only the uttering of a fact), the past was already chiseled in stone, and unalterable, and every moment of Holly's and Tatty's lives together was recorded on that stone, and had been from the beginning, and would be until the end. Although Holly had, really, no religious or mystical views at all, she felt keenly, the longer she lived, the inevitability of every second of her life, especially since Tatiana had been in it.

❄

SO, THERE WAS certainly no sense crying over another broken water glass! No sense chastising Tatty about an accident! And it *was* an accident. Holly had seen the whole thing herself. Tatiana had not thrown the phone or smashed the glass on purpose.

Still, the mania of lurching to answer the cell phone—all that teenage-girl melodrama—was something Holly would have liked to challenge her daughter on. She would have liked to ask Tatty if it might not be possible to *take it down a notch.* But she wasn't going to say that. Not in the middle of this fragile day. She said, instead, trying to tease Tatiana, "That's quite an arm you've got there. Major league."

But Tatty didn't laugh, and did not take her fingers from her lips.

Holly swallowed a sigh. *More* melodrama. Still, she tried not to change her tone. She tried to keep it light—or "lite," as all her salad dressings might call it—and said, "You okay, Tatty?"

Tatty continued to utter nothing, and this time Holly did sigh. She managed, however, not to roll her eyes, and congratulated herself on that. "Okay, Tatty," Holly said, and touched her daughter's shoulder. "It's no big deal."

Still, no response. "Earth to Tatty." Holly snapped her fingers (playfully) near her daughter's ear.

Then Tatiana drew her fingers away from her mouth, and looked at them, studied them. Her dark eyebrows nearly met above the bridge of her nose, considering the fingertips.

Holly snapped more loudly this time, as if to summon Tatty from a trance. It worked. She looked up at her mother, and then she held out her hand for Holly to see.

Holly gasped when she saw the fingertips, and grabbed hold of Tatiana's wrist, looking more closely at the hand, and then spreading out the fingers so that she could see more closely.

They were burned! The middle three fingers. They were swollen, reddish, purplish. They were *blistered.* Holly found that she couldn't say anything, although she managed to pull her daughter by the wrist to the kitchen sink, turn on the cold water, and plunge her daughter's hand under the faucet. Tatty yelped, tried to snatch her hand away from it, but Holly held on, keeping the fingers firmly under the water's flow.

"Ouch, ouch, Mommy," Tatty cried out. "Please. Please, Mama!"

But, although she was crying out, Tatiana wasn't trying to get away any longer. There was no point. Holly was both panicked and ferocious now, and Tatiana could never have wrestled herself out of her grip.

Jesus Christ! What had happened? Could this be a second-degree burn? Or worse? The darkened, blistered skin was peeling away, ragged as lace now, exposing pale, new skin beneath the old. *Blanched!* Tatiana's fingertips had been blanched! As if she'd plunged her hand into a boiling pot, and kept it there.

"Oh my God, Tatty," Holly said. She held tight to her daughter's wrist but turned to look at her daughter's face. "Tatty, how did this happen?"

Tatty shook her head. Her eyes were enormous. She said, as if from far away, "I don't know, Mommy. I don't know. I never even touched it."

"Touched what, honey? What burned you?"

"Your iPhone." Tatiana stated it like a fact, but there was awe in it, too.

"No, sweetheart," Holly said, and looked over her shoulder at the stove behind Tatty. "You must have touched the stove. I thought I'd turned it off, but it must be burning hot somehow."

"No," Tatty said. "I didn't touch the stove."

"You touched something that was burning," Holly said. "But it'll be okay. We'll get some ointment on it. I'll look up burns on the Internet, and we'll see how serious this is. We'll make sure it doesn't get infected."

Tatiana looked away from Holly, back down to her hand, and then back at Holly. She did not look reassured. She looked as if she doubted Holly had any idea at all what she was talking about, or any power in a matter such as this.

Holly had a flash of anger that Eric wasn't here. He'd always been the only one of the two of them who'd ever been able to soothe or bolster Tatty. Tatty had *never* (infuriatingly!) taken Holly's word for anything. Holly's telling Tatiana that everything would be all right (whether it was a bruise or a bad grade or a tornado warning) had never elicited anything but this very expression of doubt she wore right now. Holly looked back down at the fingers, and she couldn't help but make a hissing sound between her teeth.

The burn looked terrible. It was quite possible, wasn't it, that they'd have to go to the ER later today? For only the second or third time in Tatiana's childhood did Holly wish that they had a family doctor, or a pediatrician she could call. But there'd never been any reason for one. Tatty was so healthy that they'd never even needed antibiotics or cough medicines—a lucky thing, because Holly was absolutely *not* going to subject her child to one more vaccine or unnecessary checkup in this life, after what she'd been through in Russia, and she knew that taking her daughter to a physician would open *that* Pandora's box. Despite what they said, this was *not* a free country, not when it came to making decisions about your own child's health care.

And poor Baby Tatty! She had suffered *so* much medical invasion already, with all the prodding and poking and sticking with needles she'd been put through during the adoption process. No. Holly would *never again* allow her daughter to be given vaccines for diseases that she would never be exposed to—rubella! polio! smallpox! And although their opinions differed when it came to dental care, she and Eric were in complete agreement on the medical establishment. Eric despised doctors, had only been to the one, once, in all the years that Holly had known him, and that was at her insistence because of the (benign, yet ever-growing) bump on the back of his hand. Eric firmly believed that it was the job of doctors to find diseases where none existed, and to exacerbate disease where they found it. So Holly and Eric simply, easily, lied about the vaccines and the checkups on the yearly school forms, and Holly signed her own name under "Attending Physician"—and in all those years no one had once called her on it because, as everyone knew, no one ever looked at those forms because those vaccines weren't necessary!

Of course, not to take your child to the doctor in this country was an unspeakable taboo, like corporal punishment, or like incest, so the only person Holly had ever confessed it to had been Thuy, who'd grown, herself, into a healthy adult without having seen a physician in childhood. The conditions under which Thuy had been raised certainly had not allowed for yearly checkups! And look at her! Her hair was blue-black glossy and down to her elbows when she didn't wear it in a bun. Her skin was flawless. She ran six miles a day. Her smile was the only smile Holly had ever seen that could have rivaled Tatty's for wholesome beauty. Thuy had promised not to judge Holly about it "as long as my Baby Tatty never gets sick. If that little angel gets sick, you're going to have to answer to Auntie Thuy if you don't get her to a doctor—or if it turns out she got sick because you *didn't*."

"That won't happen," Holly had said. "She *won't* get sick because I *won't* take her to the doctor. She'll be like you."

Thuy had considered this, twisting a pearl bracelet around on her wrist as she did, seeming to accept it, but then she said, "Well, honey, you must have *some* confidence in modern medicine." Holly knew that Thuy was talking about her prophylactic mastectomies, her oophorectomy.

"True," Holly had said, ready for this (she'd thought about it for years), "but that's all that can be done. The only thing modern medicine can do for you is rid you of body parts and tumors. After that, if you get a disease, you die. Believe me, Thuy. I know. I watched my mother and my sister and all the ways 'cures' kill you—slowly and horribly—of diseases you might not even have known you had if you hadn't gone to the doctors."

"See no evil, hear no evil, speak no evil?" Thuy had said, doing the monkey hand motions.

"Yes," Holly had said.

"And, Holly, not taking Tatty to the doctor isn't because you have, you know, regrets? I mean, all your talk of being a *robot* . . . ?" Thuy made an expression, half sadness, half mock horror. "You're not, you know, thinking you're going to spare Tatiana some similar fate?"

"I have a genetic mutation," Holly said. "Tatiana doesn't have one. She *has* no fate. My family fate is over. We're either all dead, or we're robots."

Thuy had punched Holly in the arm with playful force and then said, "Sorry that was so hard. But it didn't hurt, right?"

"I feel nothing," Holly had said, and they'd laughed.

❄

HOLLY LOOKED UP from Tatiana's fingers, having to blink in the blizzard-light blazing through the picture window. She said, as steadily as she was able, "Daddy will be home soon. If we need help or advice in the meantime, we'll call Thuy," as much to reassure herself as Tatiana.

"It doesn't hurt anymore anyway," Tatty said, pulling the hand out from under the cold water. Still, the expression on her face was pained, and the tone of her voice was that of someone who'd simply resigned herself to feeling pain.

"Come on," Holly said. "Let's very, very carefully towel the fingers off and look at them in the light, and then we'll find something to put on the burn."

She continued to hold Tatty's wrist, leading her daughter over to the picture window.

At least all this useless light would be good for something.

Seeing her daughter's fingertips in the better light, Holly tried to swallow down her alarm. She was, frankly, scared now. She considered the burning, and the blizzard. What if this was serious? What if she needed to get help for Tatty and couldn't back out of the driveway and Eric couldn't get home to help?

There were the neighbors, of course, but did Holly really know any of them well enough to be comfortable knocking on their doors in a snowstorm on Christmas Day to ask for help? Even in an emergency?

Well, it didn't matter what she was *comfortable* with, did it? She'd have to do it, for her daughter. After having vowed never again to speak to the neighbors on either side of them—both of whom had complained, bitterly, about the chickens, years ago—she would have to swallow her pride. She would have to do that, even if it was hard. The neighbors had not complained to Holly and Eric—that would have been one thing, a better thing—but to everyone else in the neighborhood instead. Holly had found herself one day walking down the street with Tatiana, finding out from every neighbor she passed that the two closest to them had called the police about Holly and Eric's chickens, that because of Holly and Eric's chickens they were demanding a repeal of the statute allowing residential homeowners to have backyard chickens.

Those were the next-door neighbors, but then there'd been Randa, in the house behind theirs, who'd openly blamed Holly for the traumatic death of Trixie, their cat. The worst part of Trixie's death, for Randa, seemed not to be the suffering of that sweet cat, but that her six-year-old had witnessed it:

"Why can't you take care of your pets?" she'd screamed at Holly, who had stood in her own backyard, helplessly, while Randa's voice shook with rage, as if Holly had done something hideous to an animal on purpose. She'd never spoken with Randa again. Or, really, to any of the neighbors. If she felt it would have done any good, she would have gone from house to house and explained to them that she, too, felt terrific shame about what had happened to the animals, and that it had happened while they were under her care, but anyone could see that these were mostly events out of her control, that they were things she would never, *never*, have allowed to happen if she could have prevented them. If she'd thought it would do any good, Holly would have agreed that, frankly, they were right.

She *couldn't* take care of her pets.

As a child, she'd never had anything even remotely resembling a pet. Not even a fish. Her mother had been sick. *So* sick. There had been sounds coming from her bedroom that no child should have to hear, and Holly had heard them all! Could there be no sympathy for a woman who'd had a childhood like that? It had been hard enough

for her sisters (children themselves, really!) to take care of
her, let alone a pet! No, they could never have had a pet!
So Holly really had no idea what she was doing with the
animals, just as the neighbors had accused her, and she
was willing to admit that. But she'd wanted the pets for
Tatty! So that her daughter could have what Holly hadn't.
And no one was sorrier than Holly that it hadn't worked
out. That it had been so disastrous.

But Holly would never have had the opportunity to explain herself to them, without appearing to them to be a
madwoman. So she avoided them instead of beseeching
them. It was a loss, though. Neighbors. She wished more
than ever that they were her close friends, that she felt comfortable calling them on Christmas Day, asking for help,
telling them that something might be terribly wrong.

Certainly, though, none of them were monsters. They'd
help, and gladly, if Holly and Tatiana needed help. They
held no grudge against Tatiana, of course. Holly knew
this for certain. Although Tatiana never talked to Holly
about it, Holly knew that Randa sometimes came out to
the waist-high fence when Tatiana was in the backyard,
and she and Tatty would have what seemed like long conversations with each other as Randa's little boy ran around
with a stick. The two of them seemed to be laughing. Occasionally Randa would touch Tatty's arm. Holly could
see that gesture from the window where she watched.

Randa would help. And Randa was a hospital

administrator—which didn't make her a medical profes-
sional, of course, but surely she would know what to do in
the case of a burn like this. If the snow was so deep that
they couldn't drive or walk around the block and had to
climb over the fence to get her, they could do that. It was
a low fence.

Holly looked back down at Tatiana's fingers and was relieved to see that they seemed to be changing color. They
were pinker now. Yes, a layer of skin had torn away, but
maybe the skin underneath it was undamaged. Maybe
this was just a superficial burn, like a sunburn. Maybe the
skin that was peeling away from the fingertips wasn't dark
because of the burn, but had simply been ashed black
from some sort of residue Tatiana had touched on the
stove. Admittedly, Holly didn't keep the top of the stove
as clean as she might. On many occasions, she herself had
come away from the appliance with dirt on a sleeve or a
smudge on her elbow or dirty fingertips.

To appraise the situation even more closely, Holly
squinted.

Now the peeled-away skin looked superfluous, and
the skin underneath did not look particularly tender or
overly exposed. It looked like the new skin had been waiting under the old skin for quite a while. There were even
fingerprints, it seemed to Holly, there beneath the old fingerprints, which had been there all along, in the shadows,
ready to take over.

But, of course, why not? Didn't their cells renew so quickly that, really, every year they were wearing an entirely new suit of flesh? Hadn't Holly read that somewhere? It was a miracle, really, the way, despite the shedding of the old skin, there were always those same fingerprints and birthmarks and scars floating to the surface, proof that you were the same person you'd been before your old cells had flaked away.

"It'll be okay," Holly said to her daughter. "It's going to be okay. We'll find some ointment and put Band-Aids on, and it might throb a bit, but we'll get you some aspirin. Okay?"

Tatty shook her head *no*, but Holly decided to ignore it. She led her to the bathroom, and Tatty followed—willingly, but sleepwalkingly, just the way she'd followed Eric and Holly out of the Pokrovka Orphanage #2, into the sunlight, and then into the dark car that would take them to the train station, to the airport, to all the stops between Siberia and Michigan—walking, walking, walking, as if it were all a dream, but also as if it were a fate there would be no point in resisting.

❄

SHE'D REFUSED TO be carried. Baby Tatty would not be picked up, even through the endless labyrinths of the Atlanta airport after flying, mostly awake, for nearly twenty hours.

And, of course, being only twenty-two months old, the steps she took in those little leather shoes (which Holly had bought for her in the States and laced onto her feet in the orphanage in Siberia) were tentative by nature—baby steps. Her ankles were wobbly. She'd never had hard-soled shoes on her feet until then. She'd never so much as stepped outside the orphanage—except, Holly and Eric had been told, once, when she and a few other ambulatory children had been allowed to run around in a fenced-in area out back. But that had been just the one spring day the year before, and, except for it, all the walking days of Tatiana's life had been spent inside the deep winter of Pokrovka Orphanage #2.

It took the three of them twenty-six hours to reach home from Siberia, and in all that time Baby Tatty spoke not a word, stared straight ahead of her, and was willing to go wherever the person who was holding her hand was going—but she would not be picked up.

Now it was like that again, pulling Tatiana by the wrist to the bathroom, telling her to sit down on the toilet lid while Holly started to search through the drawers, then through the linen closet, for—

For what?

Neosporin? Bactine? Would rubbing alcohol work? Witch hazel? Holly wasn't sure she'd ever in her life cleaned a wound. The only two scrapes that Tatty had ever had (once, scraping her knee open while running to greet Thuy and Pearl in the driveway, and another cutting her finger on a piece of broken pottery) had been tended to by Eric. But Neosporin sounded like something Eric had mentioned in reference to a wound—and, luckily, Holly found a tube of that.

She took the tube out of the linen closet and read the side of it. The description and the directions looked promising. She twisted the cap off and brought the tube over to Tatiana, who was still sitting, expressionless, on the toilet seat. Holly said, "Hold out your fingers, sweetie."

Tatiana did as Holly told her—just as she'd pulled down her panties to go potty in the tiny lavatory of the twin-propeller airplane that had flown them from Irkutsk to Buryatia. What could Baby Tatty have been thinking then? She'd walked on her own little feet so few times on earth, and now she was on a shaking thing in the sky over the earth. A stranger was telling her it was time to pull down her panties and to pee and that everything would be okay, but telling her this in a language she did not speak. Still, she had done it, peed in the potty, pulled her panties back up, returned with Holly to her seat, walking as steadily as she could on that wobbling craft, and she had not cried.

❄

HOLLY SQUEEZED THE clear gel onto her daughter's fingertips, and then she bandaged each one of them with a

Barbie Band-Aid. How long had they had those things in the linen closet? Or was it, rather, that Tatiana, despite how mature she seemed, had really just emerged from childhood such a short time ago that they were still surrounded by her childhood things?

"All better?" Holly asked, holding the hand with the bandaged fingers in her own.

Tatiana said nothing.

"Are you okay, Tatty?" Holly asked—and, yes, this time there was an edge to it. Her patience was thinning again. *Okay*, she thought—okay, so there'd been an accident, and Tatty had touched the stove, and her fingertips had been burned. But now it was time to *move on*, as they said. Right? "Tatty? Did you hear me?"

Finally Tatiana looked up and made eye contact with Holly, and this time it was Holly who found herself glancing away. Her daughter's eyes looked too shiny to her. Both too bright and too dark to stand. Tatty inhaled, seeming ready to say something she'd been holding in for a while, and Holly felt unaccountably worried about what it would be, could already feel herself beginning to form excuses, denials, but Tatty only said, "They called again."

"Oh," Holly said, sagging a little with relief.

The phone call. Her iPhone ringing on the kitchen counter before Tatiana had accidentally thrown it across the house, before she'd touched the stove and burned her fingers. She and Tatiana were back to the banalities of phone calls. "That's right," Holly said. "I already forgot. The phone rang, didn't it? I'd better see if that was Dad."

She began to turn toward the door, but Tatty said to her, "It wasn't Dad."

"Well," Holly said, "I need to check to make sure," and she left her daughter sitting on the toilet with her Barbie bandages, and made her way quickly back to the dining room, the phone, the little billions of slivers of glass. Seeing those shimmering on the floor in the light from the picture window, Holly hoped that she'd remembered to recharge the battery on the handheld vacuum. Often that wasn't something Holly remembered to do until the Cheerios had already been dumped on the floor, or something like this— like shattered glass—and the thing was dead in her hands.

She picked her iPhone up off the floor and looked at it, scrolled down through the recent calls.

Another Unavailable. It hadn't been Eric who'd called.

Still, she should call her husband, shouldn't she? She scrolled down her list of contacts until she found his name, and touched it with her index finger. She held the phone against her ear, where it felt warm, and imagined the vibration of it in Eric's breast pocket. He wasn't answering. Maybe he was already back in the car with his parents. Surely, if they were checking Gin into the hospital for the night, or anything serious like that, he would have called. The ringing went to what she thought at first was his voice mail:

Holly heard the double click that meant that no one was going to answer, that she was being passed on to a machine instead of her husband. But then, instead of a recording of Eric's stiff business voice saying "This is Eric Clare, and I'm away from my desk at the moment . . . ," there was—laughter.

A woman's laughter.

(A very young woman? Or perhaps a child?)

The laughter was not shrill, or hysterical, but a kind of simple, mirthful, amused laughter—sounding close, and intimate, and familiar in her ear. Still, the sound of it, the surprise of it, made Holly gasp and hang up before she even realized she'd done it, and then she quickly put the phone down on the table, where she just looked at it, not understanding, shaking her head. And, then, looking at the phone, she saw that the photograph she used as her iPhone wallpaper had changed.

By itself?

The froth and glow of the waterfall, and Eric and Tatiana smiling before it, was gone. Now there was just an image of Tatiana. Close-up. Her nose, and her eyes.

Holly picked up the phone and looked more closely at the photograph.

Apparently something had happened to the phone in its flight and in its fall. Had it broken? Had it rearranged her personal settings? Was that how she'd reached a stranger instead of Eric—connecting to that girlish laughter instead of his voice mail?

Apparently.

And her wallpaper photograph had been replaced with this—a fragment of another photograph. Nose, eyes, a photograph of Tatiana, but—

No.

Holly looked more closely. It wasn't a different photo. It was still the waterfall photograph, but zoomed in. The frame had narrowed so that the only part of the photograph that remained in view was this bit of Tatiana's face—her nose, her eyes. God. Technology. Its quirks and mysteries. Holly was baffled, but she was glad that the phone still worked at least. She picked it up and tried Eric again, and this time he picked up on the first ring.

"Sweetheart," Holly said to him, so grateful to hear his voice, to make this connection across the miles and through the blizzard. Being able to speak to him at that moment felt crazily almost as miraculous as having met him in this life at all. Having lived long enough to meet Eric, and to fall in love with him, and to bring Tatiana into their lives, and to become a family, as if there'd been no chance involved at all, as if it were fate—a fate full of near-misses and blessings and miraculous connections. "Are you okay, Eric? Is your mom okay?"

"I don't—Holly," he said. He sounded weary. He

sighed. He said, "She's confused, Holly. I mean, she's *really* confused. She thinks she's in Europe. She's speaking French to the doctors, and when they don't understand her she starts crying. She thinks they're Germans."

"Oh my God," Holly said. "Oh, Eric."

"And now Dad's having trouble breathing. All the stress, of course. So, he's in one room and Mom's in the other room, and Tony and Jeff and I just keep moving from one to the other."

"Your brothers are there?"

"Yeah."

"I thought the blizzard—"

"Well, you know, it was an emergency. They got here. Where there's a will, there's—"

"I should be there, too," Holly said. Her heart began to beat harder. He needed her. If his brothers could get to the hospital, she could have gotten there, too, and she hadn't even tried!

"You most certainly should *not* be here, Holly," Eric said. "The last thing I need right now is to have to worry about you and Tatty out on the roads in this. Please, please, don't do anything like try to drive here, Holly. Just stay where you are."

"Okay," Holly said—and although she did still feel guilty, remiss, she realized that she was also relieved. Relieved that this was Eric's problem, and his brothers'. Relieved that she could hang up the phone and simply wait for more news. Relieved that, truly, nothing at all was going to be required of her.

She talked to Eric for a little while longer about the awful doctors, the awful weather, the nature of Gramps's chest pains. They talked about Jeff and Tony, and about how hard it had been for them to get to St. Joseph's Mercy on the freeways. Eric asked about the Coxes and Thuy and Pearl, and Holly told him that they couldn't make it through the blizzard, either. He asked what she and Tatty were doing, and Holly chose to say nothing about the burned fingers. There was nothing he could do for Tatty's fingers now except worry. She said, "We're fine. We're just squabbling."

"Don't," Eric said.

"Don't what?" Holly asked.

"Don't squabble with Tatty. She's so excited about Christmas, Holly. She's got something really special for you. You haven't opened your presents yet?"

"No," Holly said.

"Well, this is a big one. Tatty's been working on it for—well, I shouldn't have even said this much. But we shouldn't have overslept, Holly. This is a big Christmas for Tatiana, I think. It's the first year she really took charge of getting gifts for us on her own. It's a kind of milestone."

"Oh dear," Holly said. How blind she'd been! How could Eric have known this, and so clearly, and not Holly? It explained everything! Poor Tatty! It wasn't the gifts she was *getting* that she'd been disappointed about, it was the ones she was giving! "Oh God, Eric. Okay. I'm so glad you told me. Consider the squabbling a thing of the past. I'm going to go make it up to her right now. I love you, Eric."

"I love you, too," he said. "Tell Tatty I love her, too."

"I will, of course. Of course I will. As soon as she wakes up."

"She's asleep?" he asked.

"Well, yes. She's been sleeping a lot today." Holly wasn't sure why she was lying. She'd left Tatiana in the bathroom, wide awake, of course, with her Barbie-bandaged fingers. "But I'll get her out of bed," she said. "We'll open a couple of presents without you if that's okay."

"I think that's great," Eric said.

They said their good-byes then, and when they were done Holly listened to the connection being severed, which was the sound of a very tiny ax felling a very thin-trunked tree.

❄

HOLLY TOOK THE phone away from her ear and looked at the photograph there again.

Tatty.

Those eyes.

It was as if the iPhone had decided that none of the rest of it mattered. Not the Jet-Black Rapunzel hair, not Eric, not the waterfall. Just Tatiana's eyes.

It was eerie, really. How many other parts of the picture could have been singled out? A button? A bit of white froth? Tatiana's perfect smile? Maybe, Holly thought, Steve Jobs had wired it this way, ingeniously arranged it so that even when your iPhone broke it did something to amuse and astonish you. "Tatty?" Holly called out. "Tatty, you should come and see this."

"See what?" Tatty said, and Holly turned around to find her daughter standing behind her, looking over her shoulder at the iPhone in Holly's hand.

"Oh," Holly said. "There you are. Look. The phone must have been damaged, and now the only part left of that image of you and Daddy at the waterfall is your eyes."

Tatty took the device from Holly's hand, looked closely, and then she shook her head and laughed.

At first, Holly was just relieved to hear the sound of Tatiana's laughter. The old Tatty, again! It sounded like the laughter that Tatty used to let loose at some funny cartoon on television, or at Trixie batting crazily at a peacock feather. It was the good old laughter of the preteen Tatty, laughing happily, unironically, at something funny, at something pleasing. *Thank God she's going to snap out of her funk*, Holly thought. It had been far too long since Holly had heard that laughter. She hadn't heard it in so long! In days! Weeks! Perhaps she hadn't heard that delighted little laugh since—

No.

Holly took a step back to look at her daughter, and realized that she recognized that laugh—not from Tatty's childhood, but from only moments ago. *That* had been the laughter on the other end of her iPhone when she'd misdialed Eric's number, hadn't it? That was the laughter she'd heard when she thought she was reaching Eric's voice mail. *That* laughter had been *this* laughter: Tatty's laughter!

Holly took the iPhone from her daughter's hand carefully and said, "Something's gone wrong with this phone, Tatty. This picture, for one thing, changing like that, and then when I called Daddy, I got a recording of your laughter instead of his voice mail."

Tatiana was still smiling. She shrugged and said, "Oh, well. Who cares? Still works, right?"

"Right," Holly said, looking at it, at her daughter's eyes on the screen.

Tatiana glanced back down at the phone, too, and then she looked from Holly's palm to the floor at her feet, at the place where the water glass had shattered, and said, "You'd either better put shoes on or sweep that up, Mom."

Holly looked down, too. Tatiana was right, of course. Holly was still in her stocking feet. If she stepped on broken glass, she would most certainly be cut by it, and she did not want to add *that* to the events of what had turned out to be a very dangerous day! She looked at Tatiana's feet then, to make sure that she, at least, was wearing shoes. She was. She was wearing unfamiliar little, black pointed shoes. Lace-up shoes with a low heel.

Vintage shoes? Junk shop shoes? Holly had never seen these shoes before, and if she had, she would have advised Tatiana to throw them out. They were very, very ugly shoes. Whatever material they were made of—some kind of material that might once have been shiny but was now very dull and scuffed—was cracked. Animal skin, she supposed, but not leather. And the laces almost appeared to be mildewed—stiff, ratty. Holly said, "Tatty, where did you get those shoes?"

Tatty looked down at her shoes, too. She laughed again, as if the shoes were a surprise to her as well, or as if they were a joke she might have been playing on her mother. She said, "I don't know. They're just shoes."

Holly continued to consider the shoes, which looked like something Dorothy might have worn in *The Wizard of Oz.* They weren't exactly Victorian, but a style fashioned after the styles of the Victorians—maybe in a place that had not been inhabited during the Victorian era, so that there was nothing left behind to compare them to. These were shoes that were utilitarian, but their maker had also attempted a quick stab at femininity— those pointy toes. It wasn't exactly that they looked old, Holly realized. These shoes looked as if they'd simply been worn on a few very long hikes through mountains, or across snowy fields. They looked as though, perhaps, many different girls or women had worn them over the course of a very long, bad year. They looked, Holly realized, like Soviet shoes: like the kind of shoes the nurses at the orphanage might have worn if they hadn't needed to wear flat canvas shoes as part of their uniform, or that the desperate-looking women Eric and Holly had seen around Oktyabrski would have been wearing, if Holly and Eric had bothered to go out into the streets and look at the shoes that the women in that town wore.

❄

THE ONLY TIME that Eric and Holly had spent more than a necessary hour (walking back and forth from the hostel to the orphanage) on those streets of Oktyabrski, had been on December 26. After having forgotten to bring gifts with them from the States, Holly had insisted that they go shopping. She thought she might be able to find something for Baby Tatty, something for the nurses, and for Marina Valsilevna, the orphanage director. She'd been told by the other prospective parents, back at the hostel, that gifts and money to the workers there might help to encourage them to take particularly good care of your child between the first visit and the second—during those long, required weeks between your first trip to the orphanage to meet the baby and the second one, to claim your baby. These parents suggested that the nurses might be bribed, in effect, to be attentive during those months that were going to have to be spent half a world away.

One of the would-be fathers, a Canadian man, had told Holly, "I don't want to scare you, but it's crossed my mind that there's not that much in it for them to take care of our kids once this first trip is over and the adoption's under way. I mean, right now they're dressing them up and all, trying to sell us on them. But once the show's on the road—I mean, maybe they'll figure, well, these kids are going off to live these rich North American lives, so we can neglect them in favor of the others."

"Not that they seem to be lavishing them with attention at the moment," Holly had said, and then had asked the Canadian man if he'd been, yet, into the wing with the older children—some of whom, in lieu of diapers, appeared to be spending the day on the floor, strapped to bedpans. And if that was happening in there, what in the world was going on behind the door they'd been forbidden to open?

"Well, it could be even worse, but those children aren't my problem, so I'm just going to do what I can to make sure our baby is taken care of in our absence," the Canadian had said, clearly annoyed at Holly's interest in the welfare of children who would not be theirs. "Before me and my wife leave we're going to give the nurses these." He opened up a shoulder satchel and showed Holly that it was full of iPods.

"Do they have computers here?" she asked. "To use these with?"

The Canadian appeared annoyed by the question, and it crossed Holly's mind that he hadn't thought about that until she mentioned it.

Still, it would be the thought that counted, wouldn't it?—along with the intimation that there would be more where that came from when they returned for the second time, if all was well while they were gone . . .

So Holly asked Eric to go into the town with her to see if there was anything worth buying for sale.

But they needed to enter only two or three stores to understand that there wasn't:

In that town there were nothing but bars, food stores, rows and rows of barracks-like apartment complexes, and a sprawling smoke-cloaked factory, in which something no one could describe to them was being manufactured. And the orphanage. There was certainly no place to buy flowers, or chocolates, or even cooking sherry. There were, instead, shelves and shelves and shelves of vodka, ranging in price from thirty rubles to forty thousand—and Holly and Eric agreed that a bottle of vodka was not at all what they wanted to give to the employees of the orphanage where Tatiana would be spending the next three months without them.

And, unnervingly, despite the factory and the rows of apartments, all the available vodka and all the children who had been born and dropped off at the orphanage, there seemed to be very few *people* in the town. The only vehicles parked on the streets were a bus that seemed to be made mostly of rust and two Zaporozhets, which looked like toy cars on roller skates (but cared for, it seemed from their gleaming cleanliness, lovingly). There appeared to be no men at all in town—although the few women, mostly young, were wearing short skirts and panty hose in the freezing cold, and jackets with fur collars and cinched waists, clearly intended for show, not warmth. These young women had pale faces, wore bright red lipstick, did not look at Eric and Holly when they passed them within inches on the sidewalk.

Perhaps if she'd bothered to glance down at their feet that day, Holly thought now, she would have seen that they wore boots like these on Tatiana's feet—boots that looked like they'd been made for institutional prostitutes, women who had a job to do, who needed to look as if they were sexual, but not as if they were glamorous, or spoiled, or used to bothering with fashionable, useless things. The kind of boots, perhaps, Tatiana's first mother might have worn.

❄

"THEY'RE AWFUL, TATTY," Holly said. "Those shoes."

"Why?" Tatty asked, looking down then, too, cocking her head a little, as if amused by what she was wearing on her feet.

"Well, first of all," Holly said, "they've certainly seen better days."

"Haven't we all?" Tatty said. Again she laughed, and Holly looked from the shoes to Tatty's face, and considered her daughter's expression:

Was she being sarcastic?

It was hard to tell because Tatiana's mood seemed so lightened from the one she'd been in only half an hour earlier. It was as if her daughter had come out of the bathroom with not only her blistered fingers bandaged, but also a new personality. It was like a metamorphosis—this shrugging, this laughter, this banter. Holly would have liked to have believed, as she had originally, that this was the old Tatty—but had Tatty ever been like this? Had she ever, really, been this lighthearted?

Certainly, Tatiana had, as a child, been eager to please, and been frightened of offending—but had it ever been easy to make her laugh? Certainly not since she'd grown out of childhood—not for her parents, anyway, although Holly had certainly heard Tatiana laugh and joke naturally enough with Tommy.

"Have you heard from Tommy?" Holly asked, remembering that Thuy had suggested that the bad mood might indicate that something had happened between Tatty and Tommy. If that's why Tatty had been so quarrelsome earlier, maybe her lighter spirit meant that she'd gotten a text, a few minutes earlier, and now they'd made up. Kids were in such constant contact with one another these days that the whole world could change in half an hour, and there would be no way for the adults in the household to keep track. In Holly's day it was a lot harder to quibble, and harder to reconcile. For one thing, the phone had to ring and to be answered in order for an argument to be started or ended. "Have you said Merry Christmas to him yet?"

"No," Tatty said. "My phone's dead. It was on when I went to sleep, and I never plugged it back into the charger."

"Poor Tommy!" Holly said, trying to make a joke of it. "Do you two ever go more than twenty minutes without a text? He must have been trying to reach you all day. Is anything wrong?"

Tatiana shook her head. She looked slightly pleased with herself, Holly thought, as if she'd played a trick on Tommy, and Holly went back to Thuy's hunch that there'd been an argument. An argument, and now Tatty was playing games with him. *Hard to Get* was the name of this particular game. Holly herself had played it quite a bit as a teenager.

"So you're not going to charge up your phone then, and text Tommy?"

"No," Tatiana said. "I don't think so." There was no indication in Tatty's tone of anything at all. Anger. Sadness. Bitter pleasure. She turned around then, and Holly couldn't see if she was smiling or scowling, and Holly remembered, once more, that they hadn't eaten, either of them, all day.

"We need to eat something, don't we, Tatty? We haven't eaten at all today. Soon it will be after dinnertime, and we never even—"

"I'm not hungry anymore," Tatty said. "Later."

She was heading back to her bedroom, or to the bathroom, with deliberate and obstinate steps. She was walking the way Holly recalled the Russian guards in the airport in Moscow walking from one end of a gate to another, neither hurrying nor taking their time, as if they knew exactly what you were up to and could haul you off for it whenever it pleased them. Holly felt her annoyance return.

"Hey, Tatty," Holly said to her daughter's back. "Go get the handheld vacuum, will you? In the basement? So I can clean up the glass."

"Okay," Tatty said, turning on her heel so quickly it was as if she'd anticipated the request. "Where in the basement?"

"I don't know," Holly said. "Plugged into the charger next to the Ping-Pong table I hope."

"Ping-Pong?"

"Yes," Holly said.

Tatiana snickered:

It was an actual *snicker.* As if she knew perfectly well that the vacuum was nowhere near the Ping-Pong table. "If you say so, Mom," she said. "What does it look like?"

This time Holly was the one who laughed unpleasantly, mostly through her nose. She said, "Well, first of all it looks like a handheld vacuum cleaner. In fact, it looks like *our* handheld vacuum cleaner!"

Tatiana nodded her head, as if this hadn't been a joke, and she turned then, heading back to her room instead of the basement. She was *willfully* ignoring Holly's request! Had this new, better mood all been a nasty joke? Was it all a ploy to provoke her?

"Tatty!" Holly shouted at her daughter's back.

"*What?*"

Tatty turned around as she growled the word, placing her hands on her hips. Her teeth actually appeared to be gritted, and her eyes were *huge*. They were the huge baby-eyes of Tatty (Tatty/Sally!), that first Christmas— and, looking at them, it occurred to Holly for the first time that maybe it *hadn't* been Tatty's face that had changed, but her personality. Maybe her eyes had appeared so large when Holly first held her because she was scared, or hopeful, or—?

Or what?

Who or what had that little girl been that she no longer was? Holly glanced instinctively from her daughter's glaring face in the hallway to the close-up of her daughter's eyes peering up at her from the iPhone in her palm, and she thought, suddenly, heart-stoppingly:

They were different eyes!

They were similar, of course, they were recognizable—but the eyes in Holly's palm were not the wild-animal eyes Tatty had fixed on her now. They were a different daughter's eyes. This daughter from two summers ago, standing in front of a waterfall, smiling beside her father, was not the girl standing and blinking at Holly now.

Holly looked away from the phone, and away from Tatiana. She could not think about this now, and she could not take Tatiana's bait. This was a day of bad surprises. There were such days in every life. Together they would get through this day, and in the morning, with Eric returned and the holiday over, everything would be fine again. In the calmest voice she could muster, she said, "Tatty, I asked you to go to the basement and get the vacuum cleaner."

"Fuck!" Tatiana said, and Holly flinched. "I *was* going to the basement to get the vacuum cleaner."

Tatiana hissed the *s* at the end of *was* and pronounced the *w* like a *v*:

I *vass* going to the basement!

"Okay, Tatty," Holly said, softly, although her hands had begun to sweat and shake. She was not, however, going to reprimand her daughter now. Now, she thought, was a time to model reasonable behavior, not to get angry, not to be punitive. Now was the time to take control of the situation, not to make it worse. "I'm sorry," she said. "If you fetch the vacuum, I'll clean up, and then

I'd really like to feed us both something, because we're getting hungry and irritable. Then we'll call Daddy and see what's going on, and if he isn't going to be back for a while, what do you say you and I go ahead and open a couple presents?"

Tatiana seemed to be trying to control her breathing as she stood in the hallway with her hands on her hips, regarding her mother. Maybe she was trying not to have a temper tantrum, or maybe she was afraid she might have a panic attack? Hadn't Holly been sixteen when she'd had her first panic attack? Weren't a panic attack and a temper tantrum one and the same? They just occurred at different ages.

"Sweetheart," Holly started, but Tatiana had turned (again, on the heel of that hideous shoe) to the linen closet by then, and she'd yanked the door open as if in a desperate hurry to find something in there, and, not finding it, she slammed it shut, and then she went to the basement door, yanked that one open, switched on the light, and straightened her shoulders, ready, it seemed, to descend the stairs as if she'd never seen *stairs* before. She took hold of the railing but seemed to hesitate before taking a step, and Holly said, "Tatty, honey, be careful on those stairs in those shoes. Okay?"

There was no answer at first, but when Tatiana was halfway down the stairs Holly heard her speak. But, surely, she couldn't have heard her correctly. What she thought she'd heard Tatiana say from halfway down the basement stairs was, "You didn't get me any presents."

"What?" Holly said, and went to the top of the stairs. Tatiana was at the bottom of them now, staring fiercely back up at her mother. Holly asked again, "What did you say?"

Tatty made her hands into fists and beat them against her thighs and screamed, literally screamed, "You didn't get me any *Christmas presents*!"

"What? Tatty! Have you lost your mind, Tatiana?! You picked out your own presents. You know you've got a treasure trove of presents under the tree! We must have spent two thousand dollars on Christmas presents for you this year!"

Holly had bought and wrapped so many gifts for Tatiana this Christmas that she didn't even remember what they were! Tatiana had gotten *everything* she'd asked for, from a list as long as her arm! Who was this spoiled stranger looking up at her from the bottom of the stairs, her face blue in the basement light? *No presents?* Clothes and shoes and electronics and books, and—

Holly looked away from her daughter to the living room, to the Christmas tree, to the thirty-plus boxes under it, wrapped in Russian paper. Holly had driven into Hamtramck, as she did every year, to buy the Ukrainian paper she always wrapped Tatiana's gifts in, always the same. (Holly had grown up with no traditions! Her mother had died! Her daughter would be raised with holiday traditions!) This was the first year she hadn't been able to find cream-colored paper decorated with Russian nesting dolls in neat rows. (The dolls were all dressed differently but all had black hair like Tatty's.) This year the store's owner told Holly that the Ukrainians, it seemed, from whom the shop owners got their shipments, were going in for the same sort of Christmas wrapping paper as the Americans these days—Santas, trees, trumpets, etc.—and that's all he had for sale, the kind of wrapping paper you could buy at any Wal-Mart. So Holly had come home and ordered wrapping paper directly from Moscow—ridiculously expensive, and exquisite. Shiny black paper with a variety of scenes from Russian lacquer boxes. Czars and knights and minarets and princesses. Holly had bought two hundred dollars' worth of that gift wrap, and now thirty or more boxes were wrapped in it under the Christmas tree, and Tatty was accusing her of not having gotten her any presents!

Holly was about to say something, maybe something she would regret, about selfish American kids and the wretched excess of American Christmases, and maybe something even more horrible, something about the Pokrovka Orphanage #2 and the children who were still there instead of here—but before the words could rise out of her, Tatty was gone, as if a trapdoor had opened and she'd been sucked into it. If Holly wanted to say something terrible, she was going to have to shout it. She sighed instead, but she was no longer feeling sorry for her daughter. Now she was furious, and her blood pressure—well, luckily there wasn't any heart disease in her family. She managed to make her way back to the living room, where the stringed lights on the Christmas tree looked, in the brilliance from the window, to be glowing with even more futility than they had been earlier, as if their whole claim to being *lights* was being mocked. "Sure," the blizzard raging outside the window might be saying. "Sure, in the pitch dark, a bunch of little electrical pencil-tips might look bright, but *this* is what brightness is."

Truly, those bulbs appeared, now, to contain no light at all, as if they'd been emptied of light. Sapped. Drained. And Holly stared at them for a full minute before she realized that, actually, they *were* no longer glowing at all. Holly went over to the tree and saw that the plug had been pulled from the socket. She bent over to plug it back in, and wondered if Tatiana had unplugged the lights, if this was yet another teenage passive-aggressive act. Was Tatty sending some message that Christmas was over, or ruined, or pointless, or—?

"Is this what you wanted?" Tatiana asked. Holly turned to find her standing in the living room with the handheld vacuum cleaner.

"Yes," Holly said. "Thank you."

"Not a problem," Tatiana said.

Holly expected her to turn on her heels then and head back to her room, but she didn't. Tatty stood close to Holly, smiling at her with what looked, hearteningly, like a bit of affection, or at least like sympathy, and then she asked, "How in the world did you break all this glass, Mommy?"

Holly sagged away and narrowed her eyes at her daughter, realizing that it had not been sympathy at all. It had been smug condescension. Holly tried to control the anger in her voice, but said, "You're hilarious, Tatiana. Really hilarious. Now, would you please just get out of here?"

Again, Tatiana shrugged. What was with this *shrugging*? Was this some new teeny-bopper affectation? Maybe some teenage actress had done this in a movie, and all the girls were imitating it now? Tatty turned around and walked slowly back to her room. *Sauntered* back to the room. Those ridiculous shoes with their hard little heels were going to scuff up the floors, Holly realized—and, my God, when had Tatiana changed back into that black dress? Hadn't she gone into the basement wearing Gin's red velvet? How could she have emerged in this black dress? And what the hell was the point of changing clothes four times for a party that wasn't going to happen?

Before Tatty could close the bedroom door (*slam* the

bedroom door) Holly called out, "When I get this cleaned up, we're going to eat. We're both cranky!"

The door slammed on the word *both*.

❄

FOR SEVERAL SECONDS Holly stood still, trying simply to swallow, trying to blink back the tears of frustration and rage that were threatening to fill her eyes. Then she turned to the task at hand, squinting her eyes at the splinters of glass on the floor. She tested the vacuum cleaner to see if the battery was charged, and, miraculously and thankfully, it was. She bent over:

It wasn't going to be easy to vacuum up all this glass. In fact, Holly was quite sure she never would. For years she would be finding little slivers of it in the cracks between the floorboards. She would find it in the most far-flung corners of the house, where she least expected to find it, long after this accident had been forgotten. A better housekeeper would have a whisk broom, and a dustpan, and would sweep the big pieces into that first. But Holly had no whisk broom. There was a broom—somewhere, surely. Garage? But she didn't know for sure because she never used it. It was quicker and easier, although perhaps less effective, to vacuum the wooden floors with the upright and, when things accumulated in the corners that couldn't be reached by the upright, to dash around with this handheld, assuming it was charged. There was something about the broom, motorless and primordial, that never seemed suited to any task Holly set out to do. And now, of course, she associated that broom with Concordia.

Black-haired Concordia, who looked so much more like a mother to Tatiana than Holly herself did. Is that why Tatty had loved her so much? The first time the housekeeper came for her weekly cleaning after they'd brought Baby Tatty home from Russia, Tatty had gasped as Concordia walked in the door with her plastic tote filled with sponges and sprays. Then Baby Tatty had rushed the housekeeper at the speed of light, and thrown her arms around her legs. When Concordia, laughing and speaking in baby-talk Spanish to Tatiana, had crouched down to take the child in her arms, Tatiana had clung to her neck, laughing with a kind of delight that Holly had not yet heard from her. And, after that, Saturdays were Concordia Day, and Tatty would sit near the front door like a loyal puppy waiting for her master, and then she and Concordia would play cleaning games all day.

"Seems like we're paying her to babysit, not to clean," Eric had said—not critically, for he loved Concordia, too—while watching the housekeeper chase after Tatiana with a broom, singing a nursery song in Spanish.

And then, the accident. The lawsuit. Their expensive lawyer had fended that off handily, but they'd never seen Concordia again. If she'd left that broom behind, Holly had no idea where it was, and simply thinking of it made her want to sit down among the tiny bits of glass and weep—for herself, for Concordia (whose ankle would never, apparently, properly heal because of the kind of fracture she'd sustained), and, of course, for Tatty.

Holly decided to pick up the big pieces first with her hands—and, naturally, immediately she cut her index finger. A drop of incredibly bright red blood snaked down the finger into the palm of her hand before she could stick the finger in her mouth. It didn't hurt, and when she looked at it, except for the mess in her palm (it was incredible how bright her blood looked to her in the glare from the picture window), there seemed to be nothing but the most superficial of wounds. A pinprick, really, would have been worse. Holly ignored it and continued to gather up the big shards. She carried a few of those, mixed with a little of her blood, to the garbage can under the sink and tossed them in.

The stem of the water glass had snapped into two nearly equal-sized sections, so Holly picked those up and put them on top of the dining room table. Then she bent over with the handheld and vacuumed up all the tiny bits and the glassy dust that could be seen with the naked eye. Still, those pieces and that dust didn't, in the end, seem to be nearly enough to have composed an entire water glass before it smashed, so she got back down on her hands and knees and felt around on the floor. A bit of blood from the cut on her finger smeared across the floorboards as she did so—and, indeed, some very finely ground bits of glass stuck to her palms, particularly the bloody one. Finally, Holly sat back on her heels, ran the vacuum over the general area, and then stood up and went to the sink to rinse her hands.

There was only so much she would be able to do.

Again, a better housekeeper would—what?

Well, maybe a better housekeeper would know some method for completing this task, some way to be certain there was no glass left on the floor. A damp microfiber cloth? Duct tape? This was the kind of thing that her sister Janet would have known. But Janet was long gone. Janet was as broken and dispersed as their mother's water glass by now.

No. For God's sake, do *not* think of Janet, today of all days . . .

It was easier than Holly had thought it would be for one to put people and events out of her mind. Until the few counseling sessions she'd had with Annette Sanders, Holly had thought that the mind had a will of its own, somehow, and ruminated of its own volition. But Annette Sanders had taught her otherwise. She had made Holly wear a rubber band around her wrist, and told her that, every time Janet's last days or Melissa's suicide came to mind, Holly was to snap the rubber band and think of something else.

Incredibly, it had worked. All those other therapists who'd tried to help Holly work through the despair and the unconscious sources of all her anguish, to drag them to the surface and observe them in harsh light: Ha! Total wastes of time! What Holly had needed to learn was how to *suppress* her feelings—something human beings had been doing successfully since the dawn of time, the evidence for which was that they'd managed to get out of bed, eat, procreate, despite death's unknowable horror potentially and inescapably waiting around every corner. Despite the fact that no one could really be sure that he or she would make it through the day, people did crossword puzzles and dug ditches and flossed their teeth. And, unlike the millions of Americans who needed prescriptions in order to do these things without panic or despair, Holly had been taught to do it with a rubber band!

Of course, she hadn't been writing poems, either, since Annette Sanders had cured her of—

Of what?

Of grief? Fear? The human condition?

Still, it was worth it, wasn't it? Rilke might not have thought so (*If my demons leave me, my angels will, too*—a quote one of her mentors in graduate school had hauled out every few weeks to warn the student poets—unconscionably?—against the psychotherapy and antidepressants some of them clearly needed), but, Holly felt sure, the cure had nothing to do with her writer's block anyway. Her writer's block had to do with how busy and cluttered her life had become with Tatty and Eric in it:

Married life! Family life! Motherhood! Work life! Her writer's block had to do with how many hours she spent behind the wheel of a car, getting to her office to write her ten million business-manager-memos a day instead of poems, and getting to the grocery store, getting back home, taking care of Tatty and Eric, going to bed to wake up to do it all again the next day. When would she have found time to write, whether she had writer's block or not?

Perhaps, in fact, writer's block was a blessing, since her life could certainly not have contained one more activity without shattering into a billion pieces. And Holly didn't care that (as Eric sometimes shouted at her if she whined too long about having no time to write) some poets had written, and perhaps still wrote, poems on the walls of their jail cells. That some poets were doctors, like William Carlos Williams, or insurance executives, like Wallace Stevens, and absurdly prolific. Sure, freshly written poems had been found in the pockets of the war dead of every war since time immemorial, and Miklós Radnóti wrote his last poems while in a forced labor battalion, despite having to endure beatings by the Nazi guards for it. When the mass grave in which he was buried had been dug up after the war ended, his wife found a book of poems written in pencil in a small Serbian exercise book in his back pocket. The pages had been soaked through with Radnóti's blood and body fluids, so she had dried them out in the sun.

Many of those poems had been love fragments written to Radnóti's wife, and in graduate school Holly had memorized translations of nearly all of them, although the only lines she could now recall were *Somewhere within me, dear, you abide forever—still, motionless, mute, like an angel stunned to silence by death or a beetle inhabiting the heart of a rotting tree. . . .*

It didn't help Holly's writer's block to think of these poets, or for Eric to remind her of the tales she'd told him of such poets. He didn't mean to be cruel, but he also didn't understand what *she* needed in order to be a poet. To be a real poet. To be the poet she'd wanted to be when she was in the MFA program. An American poet of the world, like Carolyn Forché, or a poet of the deepest interior, like Louise Glück, or a poet of love and loss, like Marie Howe, or a poet of humor and irony, like Tony Hoagland (whose poem "Hard Rain" had been the inspiration for her ringtone). Those were the poets she'd set out to be.

Now, with Tatty back in her room, Eric of course would say, "Go write a poem now! What's stopping you?"

He had no idea. He had no idea how much she wanted to do that. But she couldn't sit down and write a poem. A poem had to *come to her.* She couldn't *go to it.* And no poem had come to her for a decade and a half.

Fine. She was not a poet. She could admit that now. If she were, the poems *would* have come. She was not a poet like the ones she'd admired, or the ones who'd been in that MFA program with her. Even the fellow students who'd never published a word (which was most of them)—Holly knew that they were still out there writing. That they were scribbling in their studies some-where. That they managed to find poems while they were shopping at the mall, working at mindless jobs like Holly's. They were even managing to scribble on their lunch hours, or in the car while they waited for their kids' ballet classes to be let out. They could not even be discouraged by rejection. If they could not get their poems published in journals, they published them on websites they started themselves. Holly had seen those poems on those websites, and, she couldn't help it, had felt contempt for that self-advertising, that commitment by those poets to an art that had abandoned them. She hated, didn't she, that they continued to write, and to write, and to write?

Well, that was never going to be Holly's path, was it?

For Holly it had *always* been futile, hadn't it? She was fallow ground. She'd always allowed herself to believe that there *could* be something there—given the right amount of time, the right pen, the right desk—but she never got those things, because those were things she would have had to dig for with some tool she would have had to in-vent herself. Impossible. "Just sit down and write!" her husband would say, but Eric would never be able to understand this frustration, her frustration, the clear sense Holly had that there was a secret poem at the center of her brain, and that she'd been born with it, and that she would never, ever, in this life, be able to exhume it, so that to *sit down and write* was torture. It was to sit down with a collar around her neck growing tighter and tighter the longer she sat.

It was *the* collar:

When, at twenty-five, they'd told her at the Campion Cancer Center that (of course) she had the gene mutation they'd tested her for, Holly felt that collar being slipped over her head and put around her neck. The lovely red-haired oncologist had held her hand and said, "I really believe, Holly, that if you want to live to see fifty, maybe even thirty-five, or thirty, you need to have your breasts and ovaries removed."

They'd told her to take at least six months to think about it. Take six months to think about whether you wanted to die the way your mother and sister had. As if it would really take six months to choose between that fate or living to see fifty, or thirty?

Still, Holly *had* taken the six months—the longest six months of her life. They'd been a lifetime, those months. She'd been a woman at the top of a tower during that half a year, surveying the land in every direction for thousands of miles. That land was flat, and familiar. There were gardens full of cabbages. And the weather never changed. A lukewarm drizzle all night and all day. She could see her mother's and sisters' graves out there, from that tower, and she could also watch the children she wasn't going to give birth to playing on rusty, dangerous playground equipment. But she could see that she was out there, too—growing older, without disease, without passing her mutation on, and, except for this collar, for the rest of her life, nothing would be any different than it had been before:

That fifty-year-old woman she otherwise would never be—Holly would pass that woman on the road. That woman would be driving a ghastly little car, and Holly would drive past her until she could no longer even see in her rearview mirror.

She'd even quit *reading* poetry, except for happy nursery rhymes to Tatty.

❄

THEN, HOLLY REMEMBERED the inspiration she'd woken up with:

Something had followed them home from Russia.

As she'd known it would, that sentence had grown to mean nothing to her now. Now she needed to get on with things. Now she needed to put the roast in the refrigerator, so it wouldn't rot, so that it could be eaten tomorrow, when the storm had passed. Now she should again call Eric. And she also wanted to talk to Thuy—although she imagined her friend curled up on the couch, Patty between herself and Pearl, watching something on TV. *It's a Wonderful Life?* Or *Miracle on 34th Street?*

Pearl and Thuy were the kinds of mothers who seemed determined that every hour of their child's life be filled with memorable and seasonal pleasures and events. They took Patty to orchards and to cider mills and on hayrides in the fall. In the spring they walked with her through the woods to sketch the wildflowers they found (and did not pick!). There was the beach in the summer, of course, and Christmas began in late November with the *Nutcracker* (in Chicago) and the Ice Capades (in Detroit) and the stringing of cranberries and popcorn. Holly thought of them on the couch together now, snowed in and glorious, and she thought how much she wished she'd had their model for motherhood when Tatiana was still a child.

Because Tatiana was no longer a child, was she?

It was a terrible thought. Tatty's childhood was over! Holly walked over to the kitchen island and rested her hands on the cool and tomblike granite. It was a deep-sea blue, nearly black, but inside the smoothed stone there were tiny silver flecks. She wished she had more energy. She wished she felt strong enough to call out to Tatty again, to tell Tatty to come out of her room, to take off her terrible black shoes and that dress, to put on her white tank top and yoga pants, to wear her fuzzy slippers, and to bring a blanket. Holly would make hot chocolate, popcorn. If there weren't any good old movies on TV the two of them could sit and watch the blizzard outside the picture window. Holly would keep her arm around the thin blue shoulders of her daughter.

But she couldn't do it. She couldn't bear it. The thought of going to that door and knocking on it again, of stepping into Tatty's room—she couldn't even do that, could she? She couldn't even knock on the door. If the door were locked, if Tatiana had hooked closed that door on Holly with the lock that she herself had provided, what would Holly have to face then? And if it wasn't? That would be even worse. Holly could not bear that, either, to step into that room and find her daughter's cold back turned to her again.

Maybe later, but not now.

Instead, she went back to the picture window and looked out.

One must have a mind of winter.

Wallace Stevens.

Wallace Stevens was the insurance executive poet whose name Eric was trying to remember when he blamed Holly for her own writer's block, insisting to Holly that it wasn't motherhood and her job in corporate America that was giving her writer's block. ("Look at that poet, you know, that guy, the insurance guy . . ."). That her problem was, instead—

Well, Eric had a billion accusatory explanations for Holly's writer's block over the years, hadn't he?

Beyond the window, there was now a high wall made of snow. The flakes that composed it no longer had the individuality that snowflakes were always being ballyhooed as having. They'd come together in solidarity, instead. They were shrugging off any claim to personal distinction. They might, each one of them, be different from the others, but they were far too alike to be differentiated. They could never have been sorted, or given names. Together they formed a door, and closed themselves. *Wait*—

No.

That wasn't quite true.

There was no *door*, just the illusion of one.

What those flakes formed together was a *window*—a window behind this window, which Holly stepped closer to. She put her face to the glass, and cupped her hands around her face, and realized that if she narrowed her eyes against the light she could make out the fence between their yard and Randa's. She could even see the snowchild of the birdbath, and the cloth bags she'd tied around the roses in the fall against that fence.

Those cloth bags were gray-white, like the falling snow,

and were now covered with snow, so that Holly could only really see their outlines against the cedar boards of the fence back there. From here, obscured by blizzard, those sacks protecting her roses looked like heads, lined up, seven of them, against Randa's fence. Skulls full of roses, minds made of roses, hidden in there so that they could stay warm and dormant, so that her rosebushes had some chance of living through the Michigan winter:

One must have a mind of roses.

Now, it was hard to believe that, out there, covered in those bags and dormant (whatever *dormant* meant: somewhere between sleeping and dead?) were her Teasing Georgia, her Mardi Gras, her Cherry Parfait, her Falstaff, her Purple Passion, and her Black Magic—the one she called her Tatiana. Holly had placed the sacks over those herself, back in October.

Several years before, when she and her neighbor were still on speaking terms, Randa had asked Holly (politely, Holly had to give her that) what it was that Holly was spraying on the roses. Randa told Holly that she *loved* the roses, loved to see them blooming along the fence line that they shared, and loved being able to look over her fence and see them in all their glory and perfection. Still, she wondered, could whatever it was Holly sprayed them with poison her poodle? Or, say, Holly's chickens? Or the birds that came to their backyard feeders? Or anything else? *Her little boy, or Tatiana?* Randa's questions became more hysterical the longer she was allowed to ask them. Was it a pesticide? Was it a carcinogen? Were there any organic alternatives?

Holly had simply lied. In truth, she sprayed the roses with diazinon, malathion, and something else, something called Knock-Out. And, no, you couldn't grow roses like this without poison. There were no *organic* poisons—or, you might say, all poisons were *organic (of, related to, or deriving from living matter; of, relating to, or affecting a bodily organ)*. The earth itself was the ultimate poison, and the sun—they were all being slowly killed by radioactive fallout from the sun. She didn't bother to argue with Randa. Instead, she said, "Yes. It's all organic."

"Phew," Randa said. "Thanks for not being offended that I asked!"

But Holly *had* been offended:

She'd been offended by Randa's ignorance, and then been offended by her gullibility. She'd been offended that anyone could be so naïve as to think that roses like these might be able to fend off their own aphids and fungi and black spot without help from humans and the toxins they concocted in their factories. She was offended by Randa's innocent idea that Holly had any options (other than not grow the roses at all) but to spray them with something potentially deadly. Roses like this were worth some risks, weren't they? She felt a little guilty, yes, especially about Rufus the poodle, who spent most of his time sniffing around the fence between their yard and Randa's, where the roses happened to be growing. But, after all these years, Rufus was still alive, and Holly had felt much less guilty since Randa had confronted her (*attacked* her) about the cat.

❄

AH, TRIXIE:

Back there, near the roses, under the snow, along the fence line, there was a little grave mound in honor of Trixie, on top of which Tatiana had placed a small ceramic cupid they'd bought at Target.

Eric had been in California on business, so Holly'd had to dig the grave herself, and it had been winter then, too, and the ground had been so solid that Holly could hardly make a dent in it with Eric's shovel, so it had been a shallow grave. Really, a shamefully shallow grave.

Holly should have known that it wasn't deep enough, that something could come and dig the body up. But it had also been *so cold* that day that she'd assumed that Trixie's body, inside a cardboard box, would be frozen stiff by nightfall. No animal could have sniffed out such a frozen dead thing, surely, and by the time the body thawed?

Well, what did Holly know about dead bodies? It wasn't until the snow melted in March and Holly went out there to check on her roses, to peek under their hang-man's hoods, that she noticed that the grave *had* been dug up, and that the cardboard box was in damp shreds, and that the cat was gone. Luckily, she discovered this on a Saturday morning, and Tatty and Eric were still in bed, and Holly was able to hurry to the garage and to fake a grave mound and to replace the ceramic cupid, which had rolled on its chubby face beside the empty grave.

HOLLY STEPPED AWAY from the window.

She remembered, then, the roast, cooling now in the cold oven:

Twelve pounds at 12.99 a pound. She couldn't just leave it to spoil. She would wrap it, she decided, and put it in the refrigerator. If Tatty would agree to eat any of it with her later, Holly would just slice off enough for the two of them and finish cooking that on a tin plate in the oven or, if she was in a hurry, in the microwave.

But when she turned to face the kitchen she saw that Tatty was already there, and that the roast had been taken out of the oven. It was on the kitchen counter now, and Tatty was bent over it with a knife and fork, and she was chewing!

"For God's sake, Tatty!" Holly called out. "I kept ask-ing you if you wanted something to eat, and you just ig-nored me. Let me *cook* that before you *eat* it."

But Tatty didn't look up, and her mouth was, apparently, too full of raw meat to speak. She just chewed and chewed, ignoring Holly—and before she could possibly have swallowed the bloody lump of meat that was already in her mouth, Tatiana was carving off another piece, and stuffing that piece in her mouth. Witnessing this, Holly went from annoyed to alarmed:

"Tatty! My God! You're going to choke. Stop it! Please!"

She came up behind her daughter and yanked the carving knife out of her hand. She didn't really expect Tatty to grab for it, but she held it up and away from her daughter anyway. Holly knew how sharp this knife was. Only a few days earlier, foolishly, she'd left it point-side up in the dishwasher drainer and, reaching in to get a clean spoon for her cereal, she'd stabbed herself—quickly, but thoroughly—in the very center of her palm.

Tatiana's eyes were huge again. They'd never been larger, really. Had they? They were twice their usual size! Was this a symptom of something? Some sort of vitamin deficiency? Was this what the eyes of a person in a manic state looked like? Could Tatty be displaying symptoms of some mental illness she'd not yet presented? Mental illness had been something a few coworkers (not necessarily well-meaning, in Holly's opinion) had suggested to her when she'd first begun discussing her interest in adopting a child from overseas:

What about the child's mental hygiene? What about

her genes? Wouldn't a child in a state-run institution be likely to have alcoholic parents? Criminal parents? Schizophrenic parents? If the child were already nearly two years old, who could know what sort of abuse she'd suffered in an orphanage already and what that might mean for her psychological development?

Holly had been made furious by this line of questioning and reasoning, and, after the second or third such suggestion, she'd said, "Well, I guess if my own gene pool were perfect, like yours, I'd be more concerned. But since lethal gene mutations run the length of it, I have more compassion about that than some people might. I mean, unless you're suggesting that people with bad genes shouldn't have parents, or that people with bad genes shouldn't have children . . ."

Holly had managed, with this shaming tirade, to inspire a couple of abject apologies. And, after that, word must have gotten around the office because no one brought the subject up again.

Still, Holly would not have been human if she had not worried about this herself.

Something, of course, *had* gone terribly wrong in Tatiana's lineage. How else did a beautiful healthy blackhaired baby girl end up in an orphanage famous all over Russia—all over the *world*—for its stark interior, its lack of central heating, its meager food rations, its poor staffing (so poor that many of the children who spent their infancies in the Pokrovka institutions could be identified by the permanent bald spots at the back their heads, resulting from having been left on their backs in their cribs without being picked up or held for so long)?

No one in Siberia had ever been able (or willing?) to tell Holly and Eric one word about Tatiana's biological parents—except that Tatiana had been born "in the East," which might have been meant to imply that Tatty was of Romany or Mongolian descent, in other words "gypsy" or "Asian." Of course, this didn't matter to Eric and Holly. The only thing that concerned them at that point—after that first glimpse of Tatty/Sally's enormous dark eyes, after they'd fallen utterly in love with her—was whether or not there was anything they should know about her genetics in order to help her, not *reject* her.

But you couldn't blame the director or the staff of the Pokrovka Orphanage #2 for not trusting that. They'd seen hundreds of American couples pass through their doors, profess love for a child, find out that the child's birth mother was a drug addict, or a prostitute, or the victim of incest, or in some way genetically inferior to themselves, then leave the orphanage in search of another child to fall helplessly in love with. Surely it was concern for the children that kept the orphanage staff from divulging too much information.

Not until the very last hour of their last trip to Siberia— with the adoption finalized and Tatty standing stalwartly beside them (she would not be picked up), wearing a little white dress and coat that Holly had brought with her from the States (along with those little white leather shoes), with the first leg of their journey home (train to St. Petersburg) about to begin—would anyone even *listen* to questions about Tatiana's origins, let alone answer them:

"Do you believe her mother gave her up, or that she died?" Holly asked Anya, the nurse who clearly loved Tatiana the most, and who, coincidentally, spoke the best English.

Anya cast her blue eyes quickly up to the ceiling, and said, "To this world, the mother is dead."

This utterance revealed nothing, of course. *Dead to this world* did not necessarily mean *dead*. Clearly all of the children in the Pokrovka Orphanage #2 had been born into poverty, or into substance abuse that led to poverty, or they were the products of illicit relationships, or had been born to very young mothers, mothers who were themselves children.

These parents were dead to the world, whether or not they were dead.

There were also some orphans (a large roomful of them, in fact, which Holly had surreptitiously discovered for herself) who were so ill or disabled that even a functional family might have given them up. Those children were kept behind the door that visitors had been forbidden to open—a door that Holly had opened and stepped behind (how could she not?) when the scant members of the staff were occupied elsewhere.

❄

THERE HAD BEEN a sign on the door to that room, printed up professionally in Russian and then translated in sloppy but emphatic English in red pen below—THIS STAFF ONLY OPENS.

Holly would never have noticed or thought about it if not for that sign.

This was their first trip to Siberia, though, at Christmastime, when it still seemed important to know everything about the orphanage out of which they were adopting their daughter, to be suspicious of it—before Holly had come to the conclusion that blind acceptance at face value of whatever they were given or told would get them out of Siberia, and happily back to the States with their new daughter, more quickly, and with more peace of mind.

It had been December 26, their second day in Siberia, and there was no one at that moment around to stop Holly from opening the door. Eric was standing beside Baby Tatty's crib, holding her, as she slept in his arms and the two nurses on duty rushed around with armloads of sheets—all so gray or yellowed and rumpled it was impossible to tell if they were clean or dirty sheets— and black plastic trash bags into which they were either placing or removing those sheets. No one noticed Holly standing outside the door.

She put her hand on the doorknob and pushed it open, surprised to find that it wasn't locked, that no alarm sounded (she'd planned to say, if she were caught, that she'd gotten confused in her search for the bathroom), and Holly stepped over the threshold quickly, then closed the door carefully behind her so that no one would hear it.

Immediately she realized that it was a mistake, that she shouldn't be there, that she should have obeyed the command on the sign. This she was to have been spared, for her own good. Of *course.* She'd known this, hadn't she? If she hadn't understood it before, now she did, completely.

Not every secret should be revealed. Not every mystery should be solved.

Although the room, observed in a photograph, would have appeared not much different from the room full of cribs in which Tatty was kept—the same institutional light, the same curtains printed with faded blue stripes—to step into it was to understand that it was entirely different. Not just the smell of it (of vomit, of feces, of urine-soaked bedding) or the sound (complete silence), or the stillness, but the sense that some barrier between the living world and the rotting one just underneath it had been crossed at that threshold.

Holly closed her eyes, backed up, put her hand on the doorknob again, trying to unsee what she had seen in her quick glimpse, and certainly to see no more, but she couldn't open the door without opening her eyes again, and when she did she took in the room despite herself, its ten million terrible details blurring, blessedly—except for one:

A boy whose wrist was tied to a slat of his crib, his head twice the size of his torso, his eyes open and unblinking.

Then she was on the other side of that door, closing it behind her again, and resolving with the quick snap of a rubber band on her wrist not only never to open it again, but never to think about it again:

She heard Annette Sanders, as clearly as if she were standing beside her at the Pokrovka Orphanage #2, saying, "It isn't *repression* to acknowledge the horrors of this world and to let them go. It's *freedom*."

"IS THERE ANYTHING else?" Eric had asked Anya that spring day in Siberia, before they headed out the door of the Pokrovka Orphanage #2 to make their way home with their beautiful daughter. "We only need to know in order to know what she might need. In the future. You know. Was there any illness that you know of—in the family history?"

Both Eric and Holly had seen one of the nurses give Anya a sharp look when she replied, in her cryptic and strangely poetic English, "The sister, yes, born to die. Same sick as the mother."

Anya had put her fist to her heart then and given it a quick, light punch, as if to restart it, or to demonstrate for Eric and Holly the location and function of a heart.

Holly had decided then that something had been lost in translation. She wanted to ask no more questions. When Eric started to request some clarification, Holly had willfully muddied the waters by asking Anya a question she couldn't possibly answer or understand: "So, do you think there could have been a mitochondrial genetic disease?"

By then the other nurse's sharp look had caught Anya's blue eye—but it didn't matter. Holly hadn't asked it because she wanted an answer. Shortly after that, they said their good-byes, which were not nearly as dramatic as Holly had thought they would be.

Those nurses, who'd cared for Tatiana for the first twenty-two months of her life, bid her farewell with only a few terse nods and pats on the head—and then Eric and Holly left with Baby Tatty marching purposely, bravely, into the wan Siberian sunlight, as though to her doom, between them.

And as they walked out of the orphanage into the Siberian spring (such contrast to the winter landscape they'd left behind three months earlier), Holly again snapped a rubber band in her mind.

She would not let Anya be the wicked fairy godmother shoving her way into the back door of the christening. No one had the slightest idea what troubles had plagued

Baby Tatty's relations and ancestors, and never would. As with Holly's own forebears, it would have been a list of horrors, quite possibly, but Baby Tatty smelled of verbena now, and her cheeks were rosy red, and each little finger was perfect—and her hair was so long! What twenty-two-month-old child had hair so long? And, although her eyes were not as large as they had seemed at Christmastime, they were dark and wide and Holly was now going to devote her entire life to filling those eyes with beautiful sights!

Eric, however, still wanted to worry.

"Jesus," he said an hour later as they sat on a bench in the center of the nearly empty train station atrium. "What do you think Anya meant?"

The only other passengers waiting with them there were an old woman who seemed unable to sit down, pacing the station from one corner to the next as if she were looking unsuccessfully for an exit, and a young man in a blousy white shirt who stood and stared out the window at the tracks, devotedly chewing at his fingernails. "Did she mean that the mother died of some kind of heart defect?" Eric asked. "And that Tatiana had a *sister*? That the sister also died of—"

Here Eric mimicked Anya's fist tapping her chest, just above her heart.

Holly laughed, looking at the serious expression on her husband's face, and his pantomime. "Well," she said, "maybe they were stabbed to death, stabbed repeatedly in their hearts." Morbidly, Holly turned the heart-tapping gesture into a stabbing one. She wanted to show Eric how absurd it would be to guess at Anya's meaning. They would never know. Of course, it wasn't really funny, but the absurdity made Eric laugh—the idea that mild-mannered Anya might have been miming a fatal stabbing with that gentle thumping of her own heart with her fist.

Then, both of them being so close to the edge of hysteria already—exhaustion, joy, relief—they both laughed far longer than the joke warranted. They were so filled with an ecstatic terror they had never before experienced or even imagined! Their *daughter, their beautiful dark-haired daughter* in her little white hard-soled shoes was nodding in and out of a gentle, fitful sleep between them on the bench in the train station, and they could not contain their laughter.

Incredible, it seemed, that the nurses had simply let Eric and Holly walk out of the Pokrovka Orphanage #2 with a fairy princess! Just a calm farewell, and the door opened, and now they had this little girl all to themselves. Forever! (Of course, that it had cost them thousands of dollars, piles of paperwork, and nearly two years of their lives wasn't forgotten, but here it was! This day! Seeming sudden and miraculous and completely unearned!)

After they'd managed to stop laughing (trying to do so as quietly as they could so as not to awaken their restlessly dreaming daughter), Holly said, "Well, we'll never know what she meant. So maybe her mother had a heart defect. It doesn't mean Tatty does." She looked down at Tatty then, the little blue-pink seashells of her fingernails, her long dark hair. "*Clearly* Tatiana doesn't. And so maybe Tatty had a sister who died. Well, so did I. Two of them."

And after that, neither Tatiana's genealogy nor her mitochondrial DNA, nor her mother or sister was ever mentioned again. They never speculated whether Tatiana might have inherited her love of horses from some Mongol ancestor or whether her lovely singing voice had been passed down from a gypsy grandmother. They never again wondered aloud whether there'd been a sister, whether the sister had died or might still be out there somewhere, alive. Neither of them speculated as to whether there might be manic depression tucked away in those genes, as there was in Holly's, or heart disease, cancer, anything. Their daughter had come to them without a legacy. She was so beautiful and perfect she did not need one.

BUT, NOW, LOOKING into her daughter's face—her huge eyes, her mouth full of raw meat and a little pink rivulet of animal blood trickling down her chin—Holly felt terribly afraid.

She was, herself, the one holding the enormous knife over her head, but she was afraid. Afraid of her daughter.

No one is born without a legacy.

How had she let herself believe otherwise all these years?

Of all people, Holly should have understood that genes are destiny. That the past resides inside you. That unless you hack it off yourself, perhaps, or have it surgically removed, it follows you to your dying day.

It was why she'd wept inconsolably one night years ago when Eric had said, beside Holly in bed, after having passed by the open door of the bathroom where Tatiana stood at the mirror brushing her glossy black hair: "My, God, her mother must have been a beauty."

Holly had sat up fast, and found herself to be weeping before she even knew he'd wounded her.

"Oh sweetheart, oh sweetheart," Eric had said. "What a stupid, stupid, stupid thing for me to say."

He'd thought she was jealous! He thought that she'd heard in it the implication that she was not, herself, Tatiana's mother. But that wasn't it. He'd held her so tightly then that she thought she might break, but she let him, as she grieved there in his arms for the mother of Tatiana, for a woman she knew, in her heart, was dead.

Now Holly could see in her daughter's enormous dark eyes not only herself but the Christmas tree behind her, and the picture window filled with blizzard beyond that, and even her daughter's reflection in that window—and the girl in that reflection looked unfamiliar to her. She was not the same child they'd plucked, that first Christmas, out of her crib at the Pokrovka Orphanage #2.

"Tatiana."

Holly said her daughter's name quietly the first time, but when her daughter lunged at her, she screamed it:

"Tatiana!"

Tatty grabbed at the knife in Holly's hand, spitting the half-chewed meat out in her mother's face as she did, as Holly managed to swing away and to throw the knife over her daughter's shoulder. It clattered into the sink behind Tatiana, and Holly took hold of her delicate wrist and held it fast. And then everything seemed to stop:

They both stood still in the kitchen, breathing hard, neither of them saying a word. The only sound was their heavy breathing—except for what might have been, beyond that, the very light, sandy silence of snow falling on top of more snow. And, Holly thought, could she perhaps hear Tatiana's heart in her chest? Or was that the sound of her own heart?

The two of them stood like this for a long minute—so still it was as if a spell had been cast on them. Tatiana was not struggling to release her wrist from her mother's grip. Perhaps it was clear to her that her mother, the larger and stronger of the two of them, was not going to let go. She went very stiff, instead, and then she sagged, seeming to admit her defeat.

"What's the matter with you, Tatiana?" Holly finally

asked, in a voice that sounded so calm she hardly recognized it as her own. "Tatiana, what's wrong with you?"

Tatiana said nothing.

She closed her eyes, and Holly could see how beautifully and naturally blue her daughter's eyelids were. Until Tatiana, Holly had never seen anything like it. She used to stand over Baby Tatty's crib and gaze down at her daughter's closed eyes, and marvel.

She'd adopted a china doll! Or she'd somehow found, as if under a cabbage or in a nest near the chimney, a child so glorious in every detail that she *couldn't* be of this world. She *had* to be special. She might have supernatural powers, be immortal! Such a child would *have* to live forever!

Of course, she didn't. She wasn't perfection. No one was. But that was fine:

"Perfection is terrible," Sylvia Plath wrote in a poem. "It can't have children."

And this fact, that she wasn't perfect, revealed itself so gently as Tatiana grew older that, rather than being a disappointment to Holly, it made Tatiana even more magical. She wasn't, for instance, the first child in her kindergarten class to learn to read, but when she did Tatty was so wildly enthusiastic and so proud of herself that she read *everything*. She sat buckled into the child seat as Holly drove her to school and shouted out every word she saw that she could read:

Stop! For! May! See! Sale! One! Buy! Buy!

Holly tried to praise her after every word, but if she was distracted somehow and forgot, Tatty would reach up and touch Holly's shoulder with her little hand (the soft, pawlike hand of a five-year-old!) and say, "Mommy? Did you hear?"

Those hands!

They'd been sticky, sweetly sticky, no matter how clean they were. On weekend mornings Tatty would climb into Eric and Holly's bed and pat their faces until they were awake. Tatty would climb out of her own bed with her eyelids and lips ruby-blue, her hair a rat's nest. It would take Holly half an hour to brush the tangles out.

Tatiana's hair tangled. She tore pages out of books. She refused to eat dinner some nights, and then would wake up in the middle of the night hungry and crying. Her teachers said that she sometimes fell asleep on the playground at recess, slumped on the swing set, instead of playing with her friends. She'd never mastered fractions, and she had no interest until she was eleven years old in learning to tie her shoe. She lost her breath when she ran up the basement stairs. She sometimes caught colds that lasted for weeks. She *wasn't* perfect. She wasn't immortal. And, Holly thought, she was even more perfect because of it:

When Tatiana took ballet lessons, she wasn't the most talented dancer, but she was the one who looked happiest to be dancing. She would look around her at the other tiny ballerinas, smiling encouragement at them. And she'd pulled herself up out of the indoor public pool after her first swimming lesson and shouted what her teacher had said to her, for all the other mothers in the steaming and echoing chamber to hear: "Mom, I am like a *fish*!"

"Every day your daughter makes me happy," the secretary at JFK Elementary said to Holly. Miss Beck was an enormously obese woman whose hair was as long and black as Tatty's.

"There's no child here sweeter than she is. There never has been. There never will be."

Everyone had loved Tatty. Everyone had said how beautiful she was, how thoughtful, how special.

"Tatiana," Holly said. She loosened her grip, but she did not let go of her daughter's wrist. She said, "Tatty, honey. Please. You can tell me anything. I have always told you that. Please. Just tell me what's the matter. Please."

Tatty opened her eyes, stood her ground, let Holly stare into the eyes, but she did not seem to be staring back. Her eyes looked blank, as if they were turned inward—but they also appeared suspicious, as if Tatty were somehow looking beyond Holly's mind, seeing through the back of Holly's skull to something that was lurking behind her. Now that Tatiana had spat out the meat, her jaw was clenched, and her lips, now cerulean blue, remained sealed. When Holly smoothed a hand down her black hair, her daughter stiffened at the touch.

"My God," Holly said—and now that the whole awful

day seemed to be nearing some kind of culmination, her anxiety actually seemed to lift. There *was* something terrible happening, something terribly wrong with Tatty, some secret her daughter had been keeping. Now there could be no going back to slammed bedroom doors, and denial. Now it was here in the room with them, and it was dreadful, yes, but it was no longer *dread*. Dread was the slow approach of the injured cat dragging its hind legs across the yard. Dread was when, after listening to her mother wail behind a closed door, there was silence. There had been dread in that silence because there was still the opportunity to refuse the facts. It had, of course, been *dreadful* when her sister had come out of their mother's bedroom then and said, "Holly, honey. Come in here and kiss Mommy goodbye. She isn't suffering anymore"—but this was not nearly as terrible as dread. Mommy's eyes were closed in relief.

Now Holly was ready. She could face whatever it was. The dread had passed with the denial. She said, "Say it, Tatty. Tell me. I love you. I loved you from the first moment I saw you. I will always love my Baby Tatty."

Holly wasn't surprised that the words didn't change Tatiana's expression. She hadn't really expected that they would. Tatiana was beyond the reach of such sentiments at the moment. Holly let go of her daughter, and Tatiana stepped away. She looked from her mother's face to the blizzard beyond her. After that, she glanced at her hands, greasy and bloody from the meat, and then she wiped them down the front of her black dress, and then looked back at Holly, smirked, and said, without emotion, "That wasn't Baby Tatty."

"What do you mean?" Holly tried to control her voice. It was too loud, wasn't it? Her heart began to pound again, audibly. Anyone, she thought, in the house—maybe even outside the house—could have heard her heart pounding.

"You are so blind," Tatiana said.

"What are you talking about, Tatty?"

"You were so *in love* with me, with my big dark eyes, and when you came back you never even asked where I was."

"What?" Holly asked.

"You came back to get me and you never asked where I was."

"No," Holly said. "Tatty—"

"I'm not Tatty."

Holly gasped, put a hand to her mouth. She said, "No." She was ready to deny this with no idea what she was denying, and no idea why she was trying to grasp her daughter's wrist so tightly again. Tatiana broke away and ran back toward her room, and Holly ran after her, but she wasn't quick enough, and the bedroom door closed between them, and there was the sound of the hook in the eye, and Holly, hearing that, began to cry, backed up in the hallway, leaned against the wall.

"No," she said again, still denying, and she put her flooding face in her hands, tried to suppress the sound of her sobs, ashamed to have her daughter hear them, as if to cry was to admit something, to acknowledge the truth of it.

❄

AFTER THAT LONG winter back in the States, with their Baby Tatty waiting for them in Siberia, spring had come like a pastel explosion. It was so dazzling to look out the back door at the roses budding and the lilacs blooming that Holly almost couldn't do it, and finally the day came that they could return to the Pokrovka Orphanage #2:

Holly and Eric had walked through the orange doors, said a quick *prevyet* to the nurses, and gone straight to the crib.

Tatiana! Baby Tatty! Their daughter!

Her hair was longer, and her eyes were not as large in her face, but her cheeks were flushed, and she looked as healthy and beautiful as she had three months earlier, even if she was too thin—

But all the toddlers at the Pokrovka Orphanage #2 were too thin! None of them had the chubby cheeks of American toddlers. None of them had fat little arms and legs. There was only so much food at the orphanage, and only so many nurses to feed it to *so many* children. Holly and Eric had given the nurses an extraordinary sum of money before they'd left after their first visit at Christmas, at the advice of the Canadian couple. By Russian standards it had been thousands of dollars! They'd been sure to imply that, if Tatiana was well taken care of while they were back in the States without her, there would be even more money when they returned to fetch her. Anya, in particular—they'd paid her, when they'd left to return to the States, as much as the poor girl probably made in a year at the orphanage!

And although Eric and Holly were rich beyond the wildest dreams of these young Siberian women, Eric and Holly were not rich. It had been a sacrifice, that money. It had been paid so that the Tatiana they left behind at Christmas would be the Tatiana they returned for in the spring: happy, healthy. Well-fed.

They would leave their little Tatiana in her crib in that terrible gray orphanage over the course of a bitter winter, return to their comfortable home, and when they came back, she would be there, shining as they'd left her, the same baby they'd left, but with only those few subtle changes:

A little thinner. A little paler, bluer, with longer hair, with smaller eyes.

But they'd paid so much money, and they loved her so much. It was impossible to think that she'd suffered in their absence, to see the thin limbs as some sign of—

What?

THEY'D LOVED HER so much, from the first moment they saw her on Christmas Day in her crib. They would have taken her home that moment, if not for the Russian bureaucracy, the iron-fisted rule that they must leave her behind and return for her three months later. They'd been given no choices in that matter.

But how could you explain that to a baby when you placed her back in her crib in such a place, and left? How could you explain that, even later, even now that she was a teenager? How could you tell your daughter *We left you there without us, knowing how cold it was, how neglected you would be, that anything could happen to you—but we loved you, we loved you so much, we paid so much money for them to take care of you, so that when we came back you would be the same child we'd left behind us! Money was all we had to offer, and we offered it all!*

You could never explain such a thing to a child. But it shouldn't have mattered anyway! Tatiana could not possibly have any memory of that time, those months after they fell in love with her, and then left her, could she?

Holly forced herself to stop crying. She went to her daughter's door. She said, "Please. Tatty," to it.

But she felt panicked now, no longer in control at all, and as she lunged for the door she could smell her own adrenaline on herself, under her arms and at the back of her neck—the smell of damp children's sweaters in a small, institutional room.

Surely Tatty wouldn't do anything to harm herself, would she?

Holly pushed hard on the door, meeting with the hook and eye, and then she took a step back, realizing how little pressure it would take to break through the hook and eye:

It wasn't a security system. It was only a psychological divider. Holly had simply wanted Tatiana to feel that there was a place she could have privacy when she needed it—the way Holly had needed that when she'd wanted to write. When she'd needed to be alone. When, as stupid as it seemed to her now, she'd expected to uncover, in her private mind, behind a locked door, in a small room, a poem.

Oh, perhaps she'd expected Tatiana to write those poems! Perhaps she'd thought her daughter would write her own poems for her!

But Tatiana had no need of poems. And she hadn't wanted the door between them to be locked. *That* had been the problem all along, hadn't it? *Holly* was the one who wanted to be alone. She should never have had a child! She had been made barren for a reason—and she'd always known it, although she'd never allowed herself to think it! Once, she'd slapped Eric, hard, when, after she'd burst out crying on a Monday night when Tatiana was four years old and demanding macaroni and cheese instead of the chicken breast she'd been served (this, after work all day and ballet class all night), he'd said, "Maybe you never wanted to be a mother, Holly. What did you think it would be like?"

Yes, she'd slapped him. But he'd known!

Worse, *she'd* known: He'd been right!

No.

No. She *had* wanted it! *All* mothers became frustrated. All mothers had regrets. Holly loved her daughter. Her daughter was the one thing in this world that Holly had been born to love. Without Tatiana, there was nothing; there had never, ever been anything without Tatiana. If—

HOLLY PUSHED GENTLY on the door between them again, not breaking it in, but feeling how easily the lock she'd installed there would give way if she pushed harder.

She said to the door, loudly, her voice shaking, "Tatty, I'm so selfish. I'm a selfish person. But, God, I love you. I love everything about you. More than I ever knew I could ever love anything, I love you. Please, please, stay in this world with me."

There was no sense in trying to protect her pride now. Every minute of Tatiana's childhood had been leading to this moment, and the only thing that mattered in Holly's life now, the only thing that could ever matter was showing this beautiful creature how much she had been loved from the *very beginning*.

This child that Holly was so privileged to have—having cheated, having *cheated fate*, for this child she was so privileged to call her daughter!

To the door, again, even more loudly, Holly said, "I never wanted anything more than I wanted you."

Really?

Are you so sure?

Remember, you wanted to be a poet, Holly. Even this morning, after sleeping so late, you just wanted to be alone, you wished—

"No! I haven't been the mother I could have been, true, but please, Tatty, let me try again. Let me keep trying. Now I know. Now that I know, I—"

Holly pushed the door open a little more this time, but only enough to put her eye to the crack.

In there, she could see Tatiana lying in the bed, again with her back to the door. Pale arm, dark hair across the pillow. Now her back was bare, and the coverlet was off. Gin's red dress was on the bedroom floor, and the black dress was hanging over the back of her desk chair. Tatiana couldn't be asleep already, again, could she? Not with all the noise Holly was making in the hallway.

Still, her daughter didn't move at all when Holly said, "Please, Tatiana," and then screamed it: "Tatty! Please! Please open the door!"

Somehow she couldn't do it yet—break the lock, the *symbolic* lock—and barge into her daughter's room. She didn't know why. She had put it there herself so that Tatiana could escape her mother—hadn't she?—so how could Holly break that promise by breaking that lock?

And why would she? What would be the point? There was nothing in the room Tatiana could harm herself with, was there? No knives, certainly no guns, not even any scissors that Holly knew of. There were no medications, no Drano, no heavy rope, none of the things a teenage girl might use to cry for help, or to kill herself, or both.

So Holly backed away, feeling ashamed for having screamed. She sat down in the hallway. She put the knuckles of her right hand into her mouth. They were sore. From the knocking. Chafed. Not bloody, though. They tasted like dry bones, or stones, between her lips, and Holly recalled how, several months after her surgeries, after her breasts and her ovaries were gone, she'd felt so sure she would live forever, but also that she was completely empty—that she was nothing but a shell now. That she was not a woman with a future, but a mannequin, a statue, a *robot*. In one of her first outings after the bandages and the tubes had been removed, she'd gone for a walk along the beach, and had come upon two white stones, side by side, being washed around by a wave, and she'd bent over, picked up the stones, and put them in her mouth.

She had just kept walking, while holding the smooth stones between her palate and her tongue. They comforted her. They tasted rusty, like lake water, but also like blood. And she liked the way their cold lifelessness seemed to warm and soften as she sucked. After a while, Holly had tucked the stones side by side beneath her tongue.

They were her ovaries, she thought, crazily, but somehow

certainly. They were her ovaries returned to her! Her ovaries had washed up here from wherever it was the surgeon had tossed them when he'd plucked them out of her. And now they were back inside the soft fleshy tissue of her. She imagined that she felt them throbbing. She imagined she felt them breathing, almost, as if they had gills. She imagined that they were attaching themselves to her again. Eventually, Holly thought, she could swallow them and they would come to life inside her. They would sprout blood vessels, attach themselves back to her, disease-free.

She'd still been weak from the surgeries, Holly knew, that day. Surely that was the reason for such thinking. There'd been some complications, additional surgeries needed, and that had been the first real walk into the world Holly had been able to take alone for months. She'd not been right. After she spat the stones out, she gagged, and then vomited on the sand.

HOLLY TOOK HER knuckles out of her mouth and said, looking up from where she sat in the hallway to her daughter's bedroom door, "Are you asleep in there, Tatty?" She said it softly, not really having meant for Tatty to hear. If Tatty was sleeping in there, she should just be allowed to sleep. Tatty was tired. Tatty was hungry. Soon Eric would be home. He could talk to Tatty. He could talk to them both.

But Tatty did hear:

A few quiet seconds went by before, from her bedroom, there was an angry shriek—sounding part grief, part frustration—and a sound like a fist punching the headboard of the bed, and then Tatty screaming, "Go away! Leave me the fuck alone! That's what you do best!"

Holly stood quickly and, to steady herself, put one hand against the wall, palm laid flat between two framed photographs. She took a breath. She looked into one of the photographs. In it, Tatiana had her arms around Eric's neck. They were smiling. Behind them, a green riverbank. They were standing on the deck of a paddleboat floating down the Mississippi River. It had been a summer vacation, a family road trip they'd taken when Tatty was eleven. Holly had wanted to show her America! She'd wanted to show her Russian daughter America—as if, somehow, Tatty needed to see this country more than any other midwestern child needed to see this country!

But Tatiana wasn't like those other midwestern children, whose Americanness was utterly unremarkable. Unlike them, Tatiana might so easily still be in Siberia—or somewhere close to Siberia, not even Siberia! The nurses had said they couldn't be certain that her biological family was not from Kazakhstan, or even Outer Mongolia. They could have been northerners. Migrants. There were still nomadic tribes from that area who made their way south in the early summer—the time of year when Tatiana would have been born—for work, or with herds of animals. The woman, or girl, who gave birth to Tatiana could have come from the north, given birth in Siberia, and returned, leaving Tatiana behind.

But she could just as easily have taken Tatty back with her. Or stayed in Siberia to raise her baby. And, in that case, whatever concrete apartment block, or isolated wooden farmhouse, or yurt that mother was living in would be Tatiana's home now.

Eric always said, "We'll take her back someday. We'll travel all around the area. Maybe we can take the Trans-Siberian Railway, and—"

"Maybe," Holly would say, pretending. But she would *never* do such a thing! Tatiana should never see that place! Holly never forgot the nurses urging her to name the baby Sally, or Bonnie ("Bonnie and Clyde, right?") or *she will be back*. Holly had known all along, hadn't she, that they were right?

"Maybe," Holly would say. "But in the meantime, Tatiana needs to see the United States. It's more hers than ours."

Eric hadn't asked Holly what she meant by that, and Holly couldn't have explained it if he had.

Now Holly looked from the paddleboat snapshot on the wall to the photograph on the other side of her palm:

In this one Tatiana wore a reindeer-fur hat that Holly had bought for her off the Internet, imported from the Buryatia Republic. Tatty smiled thoughtfully in this photograph, looking like a very typical American girl, but with something ineffably exotic about her—some quality of her elegant face that was brought out by the fur hat and its implications of a vast, snowy continent far away, and long-lost blood relatives who may or may not have been wondering, at that very moment, what had happened to this little girl they had given away.

And they could never have guessed, those long-lost blood relatives, what had happened to that little girl.

How could they possibly have pictured a room like Tatiana's? The shelves of Harry Potter books and *Little House on the Prairie*. The iMac and iPod and iPad. The bin of stuffed animals, and the closet full of clean clothes, and the cabinet full of Tatty's Russian nesting doll collection, and all those lacquered boxes with Russian fairy-tale scenes painted on them?

No. Only the child herself, perhaps, would have been recognizable. The Jet-Black Rapunzel hair. The enormous dark eyes.

"That's our child!" they might have cried out, seeing her. "Sally! Our Sally!"

❄

"PLEASE, SWEETHEART," HOLLY said, taking her hand away from the place where it rested between those two photographs on the wall.

Now Tatty was quiet again in her room:

Hush, hush, little fish. Hush, hush, little fish. We are here on earth to make a wish. We close our eyes, and then we start, to make a wish with all our heart. . . .

Holly tiptoed away from the door, and then she made her way back to the kitchen.

There, the beef in its roasting pan was on the counter where Tatiana had left it. The carving knife still lay in the sink. Holly's hands were trembling, but she was able to bring down the aluminum foil and cover the meat with a silvery piece of it. Beneath that shiny foil, the roast looked like a model of a mountain range, or—much worse— like a severed head. The long head of an animal such as a horse, or a goat. That mound of meat was so large it would be hard to make a place in the refrigerator for it again, in its roasting pan this time instead of its wicked plastic bag. Perhaps, Holly thought, she should take it out to the garage, where it was certainly cold enough to keep the meat from spoiling. Though she didn't like the idea of the garage—the gas cans out there, the vehicle fumes and garbage pails.

Maybe she could just leave it covered in foil in the backyard?

She looked to the picture window, and beyond it to the snow. It looked sanitary. It looked like a place you could leave your Christmas feast and not have it poisoned. Although there were some dangers, of course. Even in a town as far from the wilderness as this one, there was some wildlife. Whatever had dug the cat out of its grave might come for the roast beef. But Holly wouldn't leave the roast beef out overnight, of course. She—

"Do it," Tatiana said. "Get that dead thing out of the house."

"Okay," Holly said. "Okay."

Holly did not bother to turn away from the window, to look around to see where Tatty's voice had come from. She must still be in her bed, surely. She could not be, as she seemed to be, so close to Holly's ear:

That voice—it could have come from anywhere. Her daughter's voice seemed to coming from the back of Holly's mind, from inside her. A mind full of roses. Or a mind of winter. Holly would do as her daughter's voice told her. She went to the coat closet and opened it.

Inside, their boots and shoes were lined up neatly. Keeping the coat closet tidy was Tatty's chore. It was the first chore she'd been given, as a very little girl, and she'd always done it carefully, taken it seriously. She'd given that closet, apparently, a special cleaning for the company that was to have come today. She'd put extra hangers in the closet for the extra coats, and she'd taken a pair of her father's work boots down to the basement to make room for the boots and shoes of the guests.

Hanging at the center of the closet was Tatty's red cloth coat. Beside it was Holly's white jacket, stuffed with the tiny white feathers of what must have been hun-

dreds of white birds. Sometimes those feathers managed
to escape from the jacket, and Holly would find them on
her sweaters and in her hair—small, magical surprises
from the sky. She slipped the jacket off the hanger and
put it on. She picked up her slip-on nylon boots and
set them on the floor where she could step into them
when she returned with the roast in her hands. So she
wouldn't have to walk across the house in them to fetch
the pan. Holly did not like shoes in the house. There
had always been tracks on her childhood floors from her
father's and brother's boots, and since no one had ever
scrubbed them off, those boot prints had accumulated
until it looked as if an army had been quartered in their
house for years.

Barefoot, Holly went back to the kitchen and picked up
the pan by the handles.

She returned to the hallway and slid her right foot
into her right boot, and then she lifted her left foot to
do the same with the other boot. But the platter of meat
was heavy. Much heavier, somehow, than Holly had
expected—although she'd been the one who'd lifted it
from the meat case at the supermarket and placed it in
her cart, hadn't she? And she was the one who'd brought
it from the car into the kitchen, and moved it from the
refrigerator to the roasting pan and the pan to the stove.

No one knew more about the weight of that meat than
Holly did, but, still, when it shifted in the pan at the

same time as Holly raised her foot above her boot, it was as if she'd stupidly believed that this enormous piece of solid flesh would be weightless, insubstantial, could defy the laws of gravity, and that somehow she would be able to balance it and herself in thin air at the same time.

Of course, she couldn't.

Holly lost her balance, and then she lost her grip on the roasting pan, and then it all fell away from her—the meat in the pan and the floor to which she collapsed—and the roast landed with the solid, awful sound of a baby being dropped. From a nurse's arms.

How many nights had she woken up, after that first trip to Siberia, from dreams that the baby she and Eric had claimed for their own, their Baby Tatty, far away in Siberia, left behind in that gray impoverished institutional place, had been dropped to the floor?

Sometimes Holly wasn't even dreaming.

She might be driving to work, daydreaming about the future, about the baby, about bringing the baby home, about the day she would finally have her daughter in her arms, and in her imagination was carrying the baby to her crib (the bumper and the comforter and mobile, all smiling ducks, hundreds of ducks smiling despite the fact that they had bills instead of mouths) and placing her baby into the crib, and teaching her the English word for *home*, and Holly would be seeing it all so vividly in her mind, bearing that sweet weight, that she would actually lurch behind the steering when she clearly saw a nurse, somewhere far away and in that other place, *dropping* the baby, the perfect Baby Tatty—

❄

"PERFECT," TATIANA SAID from somewhere beyond her mother.

Holly lay on her side now on the braided rug on the floor between the front door and the coat closet. She looked up. It seemed to her that Tatiana should be nothing but a silhouette above her, backlit as she was by blizzard from the picture window—but, instead, it was as if some spotlight from the floor where Holly lay was trained on Tatiana. Her daughter looked larger than life, standing there in more vivid detail than Holly had ever seen her before, looking down. Her eyes were sad. She was shaking her head. She was wearing Gin's velvet dress and Thuy's earrings again. "Mommy," she said. "What happened?"

"I dropped everything, Tatiana," Holly said. It was a relief to admit it.

Tatiana nodded.

Holly said, "I'm so sorry, honey. You must be so hungry."

"I told you, I'm not hungry anymore, Mommy," Tatiana said. She leaned over to offer Holly her hand, and Holly tried to take it, but it was just out of her reach.

Tatiana continued to hold it out, and Holly continued to try to take it, but she couldn't reach it, she couldn't catch it. The look on Tatiana's face grew agitated then, and impatient again, so Holly quit trying. She said, "I'm okay here, Tatty."

Tatiana nodded and turned away, making her way over to the Christmas tree. Holly could still see her from where she lay on the braided rug by the coat closet. Tatiana knelt down in front of the tree.

"Tatty?"

But Tatiana didn't answer her and didn't turn around.

Holly's back hurt more than perhaps it should have from such a short fall, but she managed to push herself up into a sitting position. Surely she hadn't injured herself very badly in such a minor spill. The floor was hard, but it wasn't as if she'd fallen from a great height. Even a baby falling from a nurse's arms to the floor from that height would not be seriously injured, would she?

It wouldn't even be something a child that age would remember, would it? Think of Thuy, who'd fled Vietnam with her mother and grandmother on an open boat. Thuy had been four years old, and she'd spent three days tucked between her mother and the body of her grandmother, who'd died in the boat in the middle of the ocean— but Thuy's earliest memory was of shaking the hand of Mickey Mouse at Disneyland.

After Eric and Holly returned to the States after that

first trip for those three long months before they could go back for their daughter, Holly tried never to think about what could potentially harm her baby still in Siberia— accidents, negligence, abuse, disease, spoiled food— during the long winter they were separated.

They'd done all they could do, hadn't they? They'd bribed the nurses to take care of the baby, and to call her Tatiana, not Sally. There'd been promises of more money to come if the baby was fine upon their return.

And she *was* fine!

Although she was larger (startlingly larger) and thinner and smaller at the same time, and although her eyes seemed to have shrunk and her hair had grown longer and shinier than it could possibly have grown in only those months, and although she was too pale (like all the children in the Pokrovka Orphanage #2!), she looked healthy. She had been potty-trained. Her cheeks were scarlet red, and although that flush had turned out to be rouge that had been applied by the nurses to the baby's cheeks, Tatiana did not look unhealthy even after Holly discovered the makeup on a white paper towel after washing, gently, her daughter's face for the first time in the airplane potty.

Of course, Tatiana did not look happy to see Eric and Holly when they arrived at the orphanage in the spring— but why would she? How could she possibly have remembered them from their visit at Christmas? A visit that was, anyway, so brief? She didn't *resist* them when they wrapped her in the blanket they'd brought with them, or when they changed her clothes into the little white cotton dress Gin had sewn for the occasion. When they left the orphanage together forever, Tatiana did not look back at the nurses—not even Anya, who had been, back at Christmastime, her favorite. Yes, that was a little disconcerting, that the nurse who'd cared for her for nearly two years seemed like a stranger to her. But Tatiana seemed unharmed. She seemed to have been well taken care of, for which they'd bribed the orphanage staff, although it did bother Holly that Baby Tatty did not look up when she spoke her name.

"Tatiana?"

Baby Tatty seemed not to recognize that name at all. So the nurses hadn't called her Tatiana, had they, as they'd been asked to do?

But of course that mattered so much less than everything else—that she hadn't been starved, or beaten, or dropped to the floor, or left so long in her crib that she had, as the orphanage's children famously had, a flattened skull, a bald spot.

And soon enough she began to answer to her name.

❄

ONLY ONCE, WHEN they had been home in Michigan for two weeks, did Holly ever say the other name.

"Sally."

Baby Tatty had been sitting on the living room floor, almost exactly in the place where Tatiana knelt now before the Christmas tree, and Holly, standing behind her, had said quietly, but loudly enough that she could have heard her, "Sally?"

Baby Tatty did not turn around.

"Sally?" A little louder this time, but still there had been no response.

Holly thought she should be grateful, that this child no longer answered to the name they must have called her in Siberia, that she had internalized her new name. But she didn't. Instead, Holly had felt a coldness spread across her chest.

It started behind her ribs—but the coldness also encompassed the area of her reconstructed breasts. She thought of the younger Tatiana, the one the nurses had called Sally, at Christmas, on that first Christmas Day, and how she'd looked into Holly's eyes as she cradled her, how she'd reached one small pink hand, with its perfect tiny fingernails out, and slipped it into Holly's reconstructed cleavage, into a gap between two buttons of her white blouse:

Her eyes.

Holly had never before and had never since seen such eyes.

Those had been Sally's eyes.

This child, who'd been brought home with them only weeks before, was not Sally.

❄

HOLLY TRIED TO straighten up. She pushed the white boots out of the way. They were splattered with blood from the roast, and there was a slick puddle of blood near the front door. She reached overhead, using the doorknob of the coat closet to pull herself up until she was standing. There was a shooting pain in her back, but Holly felt sure the pain would go away after a while. There could be nothing wrong with her spine, after all, if she was standing. She inhaled, gazing at her daughter's back:

All that dark, shining hair.

❄

EVENTUALLY, HOLLY HAD forgotten the coldness she'd felt that day when the child, who had not been called Tatiana—and who, then, surely had been called Sally—did not answer to her name.

No! Why would she? She answered to Tatiana now! How quickly a name, replaced by another, would be forgotten. No matter how long they'd called her Sally, now she knew herself to be Tatiana.

Forget *Sally*, Holly had thought, and she had gone so far as to name one of the hens *Sally*. It had seemed so innocuous, even charming. It was the name they might have given their daughter, but they hadn't. Now Holly gave it to her hen, and it secretly pleased her to hear that name on her daughter's lips. ("Sally laid an egg under the bushes!") Holly had never told Tatiana that Sally had once been her own name. Why would she?

She had never been Sally.

Holly shook her head, trying to shake that thought out of her mind:

Yes, she had looked like a different child, perhaps, when they went back.

Longer. Thinner, but larger. Older than they'd expected her to look, having grown and changed more over the course of those months than they'd known was possible. But there were familiar features! The eyes were smaller, yes, and the hair was longer, but they were essentially the same features. It was natural, surely, to come upon a child you hadn't seen for many weeks and to find her changed. To see her almost as an older sister to the child you'd left behind. Children changed so quickly, and in ways you could not anticipate. That Baby Tatty had changed so much, that she answered to no name that Eric or Holly or the nurses called her, that her hair—

Well, Tatiana hadn't been the only child with that kind of hair in the orphanage! It was surprising how luxurious a small child's hair could be! Behind that forbidden door, Holly had seen a girl with nearly such shining black hair. That girl, who seemed little more than an infant (although it was impossible to tell, as she was so malnourished), was sitting bare-bottomed, strapped to a plastic bedpan. Her face was pale and smooth as stone, and she stared up at Holly, and then—horribly!—she seemed to recognize Holly. That little girl had smiled at Holly with such a beatific expression it was as if she were trying to distract this onlooker from the horror of her situation—her broken and imperfectly healed limbs, her crooked spine.

Yes, Holly remembered now! That had *not* been their first visit when Holly had snuck into that room. It had been their *second*, when they'd come back for their baby!

And it had not been the boy with the hydrocephalic head that had sent her hurrying out of the room! It had been the smile of that familiar little girl with her enormous dark eyes, to whom something horrible had happened:

She'd been beaten. Or dropped. She would never walk. She was completely broken.

And Holly had hurried from the room, closed the door, heard the words of Annette Sanders in her ear so close and clear it was as if the therapist were standing beside her, and she had done it:

She had forgotten.

NOW HOLLY WATCHED as Tatiana pulled a present out from under the tree and seemed to read the tag on it. She said, quietly, to her daughter's beautiful back, "Sally?"

Tatiana didn't turn around, but she said, sounding disappointed, "I'm not Sally. You know that, Mommy."

Holly said nothing for a long time, letting the pain in her back turn into a numbness, until she finally managed to take a breath deep enough to speak, and then she asked her daughter's back, "Then where is Sally, honey? Where is Sally?"

Tatiana shrugged. But it wasn't the coquettish shrug from earlier in the day. It wasn't the shrug of teenage apathy, ennui. It was a shrug of sadness, of utter despair.

"Oh, Tatty," Holly said. "Was it Sally who tried to call, honey? Does Sally know my phone number?"

Tatiana shook her head. Maybe, now, she was laughing a little, or trying not to cry. Holly couldn't tell, seeing only her daughter's back. Tatiana said, "Sally doesn't need a phone number. The phone is connected to everything now, Mom. You know that." She reached up and waved a hand through the air, and then she turned around.

Now Tatiana was exactly the black silhouette Holly had expected earlier. She looked like a flat cardboard cut-out against the window, the blizzard shivering its brilliant static all around her. All of Tatiana's edges were sharp, but the rest of her was gone, and she said, again, more insistently, "You *know* that, Mom. Where are the wires, otherwise? It's all open now. It's everything."

Tatiana was right, wasn't she? Holly nodded. She *did* know, didn't she? Had she *always* known?

Still, she needed to know more:

"Where is Sally, then?" she asked.

"Oh, honey," Tatiana answered, sounding ancient, far away. "You left your little Sally in Russia, didn't you?"

Holly nodded again. Again, she'd known that. She'd always known that. No snap of a rubber band could have forced that from her mind, although she'd managed to keep that door locked for a very long time.

"Remember Sally? Behind that door? But I looked enough like Sally, didn't I? You brought me home instead."

Holly bent over then, holding her own face in her hands, and then she sank to her knees despite the pain that forked lightning up her spine. She was still denying it, that pain, wasn't she? She said into her hands, not yet crying, "Just tell me then, Tatiana. Just tell me. What happened to Sally?"

"Oh, Mama. What difference does that make? You were gone a long, long time. So much can happen. It was a very bad place. They broke that other baby. They dropped that baby, or they did something else, something terrible, to that baby. She would never be okay. So they put her away. You weren't supposed to go in there, remember? They gave you this baby instead, and you love her, don't you? They gave you Sally's sister, just a little older. You never knew the difference, did you? You loved me, didn't you?"

"Oh, yes. Oh, God yes, sweetheart. I'm so sorry for Sally, that they broke her, that she's still there. But we have you now! We love you. We don't know that other girl. You're our baby. We don't need any other baby. But Tatiana, why didn't they let us see you, the first time, at Christmastime? Why didn't they tell us that Sally had a sister?"

Tatiana sighed, sounding sad, weary, as if she were being asked to explain something for the hundredth time, or something so obvious it did not require explanation:

"Because Sally's sister was *sick*, Mom. Sally's sister had blue lips and blue skin and blue eyelids. Sally and Tatiana's mother died when we were babies. They told you that, even if you wouldn't listen. Sally was fine, until they hurt her, but they knew that the other sister was going to die, like their mother. And no one wants to take home a baby who will die, Mommy. Do they? They knew nobody wanted to bring me home to such a happy place just to die.

"But then they broke the other baby! They broke Sally! And you wanted *that* baby! I looked like her because she was my sister. And they knew you would be home a long time before you would believe that anything was wrong. You would pretend you didn't see it as long as you could. They rouged my cheeks, remember?"

Holly nodded. She remembered. She remembered everything.

"So what difference does it make, Mommy? If they hadn't broken Sally, they would have kept me behind that door. It was her or me. You loved your Tatty, right? Sally had bigger eyes and she wasn't sick, but I have more beautiful hair. And my skin is pale blue. For all these years you had your Tatty, and you loved her. Didn't you?"

Holly nodded and nodded, nodded and nodded, while tears spilled down her neck, under her dress, between her breasts:

Oh *God*, how much she had loved her daughter. *How much* she had loved her daughter.

"It's just that something followed us home from Russia, Mommy. Remember?"

"Yes." Holly sobbed it.

Tatiana shook her head. She said, "Oh poor Mommy. If only you could have found some time to sit down and write about it."

"Yes," Holly said.

"Poor Mommy. Poor Mommy."

"Yes," Holly said. She was no longer denying. She said, "What did they call you, honey? Before they let you out from behind the door, before they broke your sister?"

Tatiana shrugged. She shook her head a little as if trying to remember, but couldn't. "I don't know," she said. "Why would I remember? Jenny? Betty? No—*Bonnie*. But I'm Tatiana now." She laughed a little, and then stood up, holding a present she'd taken out from under the tree. She crossed the living room, bringing it with her. Still, she was just a flat blackness—the featureless, perfect cutout of a girl with graceful arms and flowing hair. Tatiana handed the present to Holly. It was something flat, wrapped in shiny green paper.

"I made it for you," she said.

"Oh, sweetheart," Holly said. "Thank you, Tatty." She took the gift from her daughter's hand. She said, "Daddy said it was something special this year. I'm so sorry I overslept, Tatty. I'm so sorry we didn't have time to open presents."

"Open it now," Tatty said, sweetly and gently. "Open it now, Mama. It's not too late."

Holly's throat filled with emotion—gratitude. The incredible kindness of those words: *It's not too late.* She peeled back the paper at the seam and let the green paper fall to the floor between herself and her daughter. It was a book. The covers were a soft and fawn-colored leather, and the binding was hand-stitched, and the pages were heavy, white, and blank. "Oh," Holly said, holding it in her hands.

"It's for your poems," Tatiana said. "The ones you never wrote. I made it myself."

"Oh," Holly said again, but by the time she had stood from her kneeling position to take her daughter in her arms, Tatiana was gone.

❄

SO QUICKLY, HAD she returned to her room?

Holly tried to follow, but it was hard to walk. She had to use her arms to try to swim through the air to get to the hallway, to get to Tatiana's room. She had to step over the piece of meat that lay unmoving on the floor where she'd dropped it, and by the time she got to the bedroom door, it was just about to close between them, and Tatiana was saying, "Now you have all the time you need."

"No!" Holly shouted, grabbing for the knob, trying to push the door open just as Tatiana slid the hook into the eye of the lock. "No! Please, honey!"

But suddenly there was no sound now on the other side of the door. Not even the sound of the bedsprings. Holly knocked, hard, and then she stepped back. She thought again about throwing her weight against it, and how easily the lock would snap away from the door and the frame, but even as she thought of it, she knew she would never do it. If she were the type of woman who could throw her weight against a door and break the lock, how many times would she have done that by now in this life?

It was like the rubber band! Holly's whole life, she'd protected herself, or she'd been protected. Her sisters used to cut advertisements for the Humane Society out of the magazines that Holly read so that she never saw the photographs of homeless cats and dogs. She thought of Annette Sanders, who'd died in a car crash, drunk, years after Holly's therapy had ended. She recalled how simple it had been to step out of that room in Siberia, to escape the hydrocephalic boy and the beautiful smiling girl on the floor, strapped to a bedpan.

One must have a mind of winter.

Holly lifted her hand to knock on the door again, and then, as if the sound had been programmed to stop her, "A Hard Rain's A-Gonna Fall" began to play on her iPhone from the living room, where it still lay on the dining room table.

❄

AS SHE HURRIED to the phone, Holly felt a piece of glass, a small one, but very sharp, stab her in her heel.

It hurt, but she didn't stop to pluck it out. She found her phone just before it stopped ringing (*And what did you see, my darling young one?*), picked it up, touched the answer button with her finger, and said, trying to keep her voice steady, "Hello?"

"Holly, honey."

"Thuy?"

"Yeah. How are you guys doing over there? Did Eric get back there with his parents?"

"No."

"No? Oh dear. Did they check Gin into the hospital then? Is she okay?"

"I don't know," Holly said. "It's been a while since I spoke to him. He was with her in a room. His dad was having chest pains, too."

"Oh my God," Thuy said. "*Stress.* Do they think she could have had a stroke?"

"I don't know," Holly said. "She's confused."

"Oh, Holly, I'm so sorry. This isn't the Christmas we thought it would be, is it? Have you been outside at all?"

"No."

"It's incredible. If it ever stops, we're going to have some serious shoveling to do. But we'll try to come over tomorrow, okay? Will you call when you get news from Eric about his mom? I mean, I know we only see her at Christmas, but we're all really fond of Gin. And Gramps, too, of course. I even wish we could have seen the Coxes today. And your sisters-in-law. Especially what's-her-name."

"Crystal."

"Ah, yes, Crystal. She's the one who says 'Gosh golly' when she drops something, instead of 'Oh, shit,' right?"

"Yes," Holly said. And then she said, "I also dropped something."

"Oh, shit. Or, I mean, 'Gosh golly!' What'd you drop, hon?"

Holly said nothing. She stepped over to the picture window again. She realized that it must be later than she thought. The sky behind the blizzard seemed to have turned pewter blue. Now, if she squinted, Holly could see that the hangman's hoods on her roses were casting long shadows over the accumulated snow.

Thuy said, "Are you still there, Holly? Are we breaking up?"

"I'm here," Holly said.

"Well, we ate tuna casserole and opened presents, and we watched *It's a Wonderful Life*. What'd you and Tatty do?"

Again, Holly said nothing. She saw a bird swoop from a branch of the dogwood tree in the backyard to the ground. It appeared, now, to be doing a little dance on the cat's empty grave.

"I'm going to take the hoods off the roses," she finally said. "They can't see."

"Huh?"

Holly got on her hands and knees, still holding the phone to her ear. She saw that, despite her vacuuming, there was broken glass all over the living room floor. This couldn't all be from the one water glass, could it? She stood back up, using her free hand to brush the sharp dust off her knees. It cut into her hands with its nearly invisible, razor-sharp flakes.

"You still there, Holly?"

"Yes," Holly said. She turned her palms down so that she couldn't see if they were bleeding.

"Well, before we get cut off, Patty wants to say hi to you, and I'd like to say Merry Christmas to my Tatty, okay?"

"Okay," Holly said.

"Okay, hold on then, Holly. Come here, Patsy Baby. Auntie Holly wants to say hi."

From the other side of town, but so close (so close it

seemed!) to Holly's ear, the little girl's voice was high and light and sweet, sounding like the rim of a glass ringing at the flick of a fingernail.

"Hi?"

"Patty, sweetie," Holly said. "Did Santa bring you any presents."

"What?"

"I asked if Santa brought you any presents."

"What?"

"Can you hear me, Patty?"

"What?".

After that there was no sound at all for a few seconds except for the little girl's breathing. She still sounded so close that Holly could even hear her swallow. Then Patty whispered something, and then perhaps she held the telephone to her chest because Holly could hear her healthy little-girl heart beating loudly in her ear. It was as if Holly herself had put her ear to Patty's tiny chest.

How small her heart must be!

You could probably fit it in the palm of your hand—and still the sound of it managed to fly through the air for twenty miles between their houses. *Please*, Holly thought, *please let it be that Santa brought her gifts, and that Thuy and Pearl can keep Patty believing in Santa for many years to come.* What a holy, simple pleasure.

"Holly?"

It was Thuy again.

"Is everything okay there? Patty said she can't understand you. She said you're not speaking English. Uh, you
are speaking English aren't you, hon?"

"I have to speak English," Holly said. "I only know a
few words of Russian. I tried to learn more. I'm no good
with languages."

Thuy laughed. She said, "Well, something's wrong with
the phone then. Let me talk to my Tatty before it goes
completely dead, okay? We'll try later, and we'll get over
there tomorrow if we can shovel ourselves out of here."

"Hang on," Holly said.

She held the iPhone to her own chest as she tiptoed
across the glass-strewn living room to her daughter's bedroom door. She touched the doorknob, carefully at first,
thinking it might somehow burn her hand the way the
iPhone had blistered Tatiana's fingertips. But the doorknob was cold. She turned it and pushed against the door,
thinking that she would hit the obstruction of the hook
and eye. But she didn't. The door was unlocked. *It's unlocked, Mom. I never lock the door!*

"Tatty?" Holly said to her daughter's naked back. Both
of Tatiana's arms were inside the sleeves of Gin's red velvet
dress, as if she'd tried to slip it over her head but it had
been too difficult, as if her arms were too stiff. As if she
were as unbendable as a Barbie doll. Her nightgown lay
on the floor, and her black ballet slippers were tucked under her nightstand.

"Tatty?"

Holly knelt down beside Tatiana's bed, but she was careful not to touch her daughter, who looked so naked, so vulnerable, so like a child, abandoned. Holly would never want to scare her, or to wake her, or to hurt her. There had been so many times since she and Eric had brought Tatiana home from the Pokrovka Orphanage #2 that Holly had thought to herself, *Thank God I didn't bring her into this world myself.* She'd thought, really, that it would have been a kind of sin to snatch a soul out of whatever other world there might be out there, to bring her into this one. Surely, she thought, wherever babies resided before they were born, it was more peaceful, less dangerous, than here. Surely the souls of the unborn and the dead were never again tucked into these bodies—so soft! so exposed! so defenseless!—and left to fend for themselves. What could possibly be worse than this? Than to place a soul as exquisite as Tatiana's into the body of a dying animal?

Because the moment she'd been born she'd begun to die, hadn't she?

But Holly hadn't done that, had she? It wasn't Holly's fault. She'd only snatched Tatiana out of a terrible orphanage, and brought her here, to the happiest country in the world. To a place full of technological amazement, medication, sanitation—no more garlic around anyone's neck when there was an outbreak of the flu!

Holly laughed out loud, remembering that.

Then she heard Thuy's voice calling out to her from the miraculous box she held in her hand (again, that voice, so clear, although her friend was so far away) and she thought of Thuy simply waking up one day from her infant slumber with her hand in the hand of Mickey Mouse. How wonderful. How blessed. How lucky Holly was to have such a friend. To her daughter's back, Holly said, "Thuy wants to say Merry Christmas to you, honey."

Of course, Tatty didn't roll over. She didn't even sigh in exasperation. She was so peaceful, despite the red velvet dress that looked uncomfortably tangled in her arms.

Tatiana had never opened the shades that morning, but Holly could see through the crack between the shade and the sill that it was growing darker out there.

Still, the whole night would be lit up by this blizzard, wouldn't it? Holly would turn up the heat. (The heat! Another marvel of their American life together! How well Holly remembered the cold, bare, hard floor of the Pokrovka Orphanage #2 that Christmas so long ago.)

But first she would pull the coverlet over her daughter's bare back, because she must keep that poor pale blue back covered.

❄

HOLLY PUT THE iPhone down on the floor and, with it, Thuy's tiny, crystal-clear voice.

Hearing that, Holly pictured her friend as a little girl

inside a whirling teacup at Disneyland, her long black hair whipping behind her:

"Becky! Are you having fun? Becky?"

Thuy's mother had changed her daughter's name to Becky when they took up residence in California, and it hadn't been until college that Thuy had changed it back, herself, to her Vietnamese name. It had been one of the reasons that Holly had wanted Tatiana to have a name that spoke of her origins.

Because you can't just forget where you've come from, can you?

Because it was important not to forget, not to pretend, wasn't it?

Wasn't that what Holly had been so sure of? Wasn't that why she kept a box of condoms in the linen closet for Tommy and Tatiana to use, despite Tatiana's tearful insistence that *We're not going to have sex, Mom. Why do you always have to push these things? Why can't you just let me be a kid?*

And Eric had been furious. He'd said, "Jesus, Holly. All the shit you seem able to keep your head buried in the sand about, and *this* is when you decide to have to be all open and groovy? She doesn't need this!"

But what had Eric meant? *What* did Holly keep her head buried in the sand about? What?

What do you think *you've kept so nicely buried out there, you bitch?*

Holly spun around fast.

She held her hand to her mouth to keep herself from screaming:

The girl in the black dress was back. She stood directly in front of Tatty's floor-length mirror. She wore the felt slippers of a child in the Pokrovka Orphanage #2.

How well Holly remembered those! They'd all worn such slippers. Those slippers had looked fragile on their feet, as if rags had been tied around their ankles simply to give the appearance of shoes. And this girl in the black dress, her legs looked as if they'd been broken and reset imperfectly. Her arms were limp. Her head did not look as if it rested properly on her neck. Holly had seen that, too! She'd seen children like that behind that door, tangled in their own misshapen limbs, not even bothering to cry. She'd seen them *smile.*

The girl shouted something at Holly in Russian—but, this time, Holly understood. It was as if she'd spoken Russian all her life! The girl, who was wearing Tatiana's broken body, screamed, "She has a bad heart!" This girl, even with her limp arm, managed to raise her fist to her chest and pound on it. "Even your fucking neighbor Randa told you! 'Your daughter's fingernails are blue! Her eyelids are blue! Why do her lips turn so blue? It's not even cold!' And *what did you do?* You stopped talking to her! You blamed it on how she reacted to the chickens, but you *knew* it was because of what she would say about Tatty if you ever spoke to her again: 'Tatty needs to see a doctor!' "

"There's nothing wrong with her," Holly said. "She was taken to a doctor in Russia. There was nothing wrong with Sally!"

"Fuck you," the girl said. "She *never was Sally*! You didn't even bring me a Christmas present! Where do you think *Sally went* when you left her there for months? Who do you think was taking care of Sally then? Who do you think is taking care of Sally now? No *American* wants a child with broken legs. A child who's been dropped, or beaten. Or a child who has a *bad heart*. That's why you pretended not to know until you *couldn't not know*!"

"That's not true!" Holly said desperately. "I never cared about any of that. I loved you. You were the sweetest, smallest thing I ever loved. I loved you *both*. I never cared! I would have taken either of you, or both of you! I would have taken you broken, I would have taken your sister with a bad heart. I would have, I *did*!"

No you didn't!

Although the scream was deafening, Holly didn't bother to put her hand over her ears. She knew where the voice was coming from, and she put her hands over her eyes, and she knew that, when she looked up, Sally would be gone.

❄

EVERYTHING, HOLLY KNEW, would be different when Eric got home, when morning came.

She swallowed, willing herself to cry no more. For the rest of the day, she would not make a sound. There was no sense upsetting Tatiana. She would never even have to know. Holly would never tell anyone. It wasn't something she would even share with Thuy. Just as she had never told anyone about the chickens, and the way, that summer, when they'd gotten the chickens from the farm outside of town, Holly had so stupidly believed they would be happy. That the chickens would stay inside the fence, peck at grubs, live in the lovely little Amish chicken coop she and Eric had mail-ordered for them.

She had never told anyone how, while Tatiana napped, Holly had been lying with a book in bed with the window open—because it was early summer, and beautiful, with a sky so blue it looked as though there were some kind of membrane over the world, pulled so tightly across space that it could have been punctured—and listening to the chickens under the bush outside the window, squawking.

She'd known, hadn't she, that the squawking was louder than usual? But Holly had allowed herself to believe that they were only squabbling over pillbugs, fighting to get at a worm. How Holly had loved the sound of the chickens! There was, truly, nothing lovelier than a few chickens in the yard. (*So much depends upon . . .*) Holly was sorry that the neighbors didn't approve ("Suburbanites don't understand farm animals; this will be a disaster!" one letter to the editor had admonished) but to have your own chickens, to scramble your chickens' golden eggs for breakfast—

It wasn't until much later that day that Holly discovered their squawking had been the noise of four hens pecking a fifth one to death. That the worst of it had taken place in Randa's yard. That they'd chased the victim—the one she'd stupidly, horribly named *Sally*—through a hole in the fence. By the time that hen made it to Randa's honey-suckle bush to hide, it was too late.

❄

CAREFUL NOT TO disturb her, Holly pulled the coverlet over her daughter's shoulder, patted it down gently, caressed her shining hair with the lightest of touches. Then she bent down and picked up her phone from the floor and held it to her own ear:

"Hello?" she asked, but the connection had been cut between herself and Thuy by then, and Holly was sorry about that. Tatiana would have loved to have talked to Thuy, to Pearl, to Patty. Tatiana loved Christmas. She loved to say Merry Christmas to her family, to her friends.

Holly turned around, leaned over Tatiana in her bed, slipped the iPhone into her daughter's hand, and folded the stiff fingers around it, just in case Thuy called back, and then she tiptoed out of her daughter's room, closing the door very quietly behind her.

REPORT #321-22-2-7654

DATE OF DEATH: December 25, 20--

TIME OF DEATH: Approximate 7:30-8:30 a.m.

DECEDENT: Tatiana Bonnie Clare

AGE: 15

PARENTS OF DECEDENT < 25: Holly E. Judge/Eric M.
Clare

LOCATION OF DEATH: Decedent's Domicile/11-- Great
Forest Road/----- ------
---------, Michigan 49---

CAUSE OF DEATH: Myocardial Infarction Due to Heritable
Congenital Defect/Hypoplastic Left Heart Syndrome

NOTES: Father returns to domicile approx 8:45 p.m.
after blizzard delay/family emergency. Finds mother
distraught/unresponsive in living room. Several minutes
later finds daughter deceased in bedroom. At first
suspects homicide. Signs of struggle: Broken glasses/
dishes/food and clothing strewn about premises.
Mother insists daughter is alive/will not leave room.
Speaks of intruder described as teenaged girl. "Sally."
"From Russia." Notebook/recent writing/references
to being "followed." (Acute stress-related psychosis?)
Violence/home invasion ruled out by police. Decedent's
clothes changed repeatedly by mother throughout day
postmortem. Decedent "force·fed," & moved repeatedly
from room to room throughout day postmortem.
Mother remains under observation.

ACKNOWLEDGMENTS

For assistance and support of all kinds, I am eternally grateful to Bill Abernethy, Jack Abernethy, Lucy Abernethy, Lisa Bankoff, Dominique Bourgois, Antonya Nelson, Katherine Nintzel, Carrie Wilson, and Olga Zilberbourg.

About the author

About the book

Read on

Insights,
Interviews
& More . . .

Meet Laura Kasischke

LAURA KASISCHKE teaches in the MFA program at the University of Michigan. A winner of the National Book Critics Circle Award for poetry, she has published seven collections of poetry and nine novels, two of which have been made into films, *The Life Before Her Eyes* and *White Bird in a Blizzard*. She lives in Chelsea, Michigan, with her husband and son. ⌒

A Reading List from Laura Kasischke

All writers are readers first. Laura Kasischke offers a list of books she loves, and some that influenced her in creating the unmistakable atmospheric spell present in Mind of Winter . . .

I COULDN'T BEGIN any list of haunting masterpieces without *The Turn of the Screw*. Henry James does, in this little novel, everything that can be done to cast a spell in language. This story should have been a lark, nannying two beautiful children in the English countryside, or it should have been a nightmare—rattling chains and ax-wielding madmen. Instead, it's neither. It's the psychological equivalent of a cold breath whispering something you're not sure you heard quite correctly—which you hope you perhaps did not hear quite correctly. No matter how closely you listen, you'll never know whether what you're afraid you heard is what you heard.

The Vet's Daughter by Barbara Comyns is one of the most potent and terrifying novels ever written, in my opinion. Part *Jane Eyre* and part *Carrie*, the novelist moves her heroine through a troubled childhood to strange new places. The combination of the realistic with the supernatural makes for terror that is all the more terrifying because it seems possible.

Graham Joyce has written half a dozen novels I'd put on this list, but *The Silent Land* is his most poetic and strangest and scariest. Every page contains a surprise followed by a gasp of recognition—until we are buried under a cold and thrilling avalanche of terrors.

No writer rivets and scares me more than Shirley Jackson. I still haven't gotten over my experience of reaching the end of "The Lottery" during silent reading time in my high school English class, and gasping aloud. Reading *We* ▶

A Reading List from Laura Kasischke *(continued)*

Have Always Lived in the Castle felt to me like being slowly lowered into a cold, dark lake. But in a good way. I'm not sure how Shirley Jackson slept at night, having an imagination capable of creating such people and places.

All of Guy de Maupassant is spell-casting, but his story "The Horla," and the mystery and specificity in his prose, is a perfect story. Like Poe, his genius is evoking madness that might not be madness. It's impossible for me to think of "The Horla" without wanting to turn on the lights, if it's dark, and lock the doors if they're not locked—and then I remember, from "The Horla," that this won't help . . .

Stewart O'Nan is another writer who seems to be able so effortlessly to combine events and atmosphere and language to cast that spell. *The Night Country* and *The Speed Queen* are masterpieces, but *A Prayer for the Dying* is his most beautiful, tragic, unrelenting tale. Its brevity makes its biblical proportions that much more uncanny.

The uncanny: Daphne du Maurier's book of stories, *Echoes from the Macabre*, is described on the cover as "Tales of Quiet Terror." Since having read it, I'm unable to travel without being accompanied by the sense of chill fever she conjures in her long story "Don't Look Now." Even the title—"Don't look now!" You can't not look, of course.

Strangers by Taichi Yamada is one of the most disturbing novels of delusion and/or ghosts I've ever read. Its subtlety is its strength. Imagine you find yourself alone in an empty apartment complex in a skyscraper in an enormous city. Well, that would be better than finding out that there is *one other occupied unit* in the building.

And just when you thought it was safe to move to a remote island in the Antarctic, Albert Sánchez Piñol wrote *Cold Skin*, and you realized that no matter where you lived, that spell could drop over you, because often it's far more frightening to imagine something than to see it, to be left wondering if you saw it than to know that you did—especially if amphibians are involved, and when the writing is as precise and accumulative in detail and dread as in this novel.

And I couldn't conclude a consideration of the haunting or spellbinding without Christina Rossetti's "Goblin Market." This is a poem, and its pretty music, underscoring its deeply frightening psychological complexity, has never left me from my first reading, either as a work of art or an experience. It's a nursery rhyme gone wrong, which, to me, is one of the scariest possible spells that could be cast. Luckily, it has a happy ending, unlike any of the other works on this list! ◞

Reading Group Guide

1. Over the course of Tatty's adoption story, Holly sees her as both cloaked in some sort of evil and at other times as a fairy princess. What do you think are some of the complicated emotions that go with adopting a child?

2. Kasischke does an excellent job of making the snow into a constant, ambient presence throughout the novel. What kind of metaphors can you ascribe to the mounting storm?

3. Though not the central focus of the book, one of the themes Kasischke explores is teenage sexuality. What sort of authorial observations does she make about Tatty's beauty and burgeoning sensuality? How do these observations tie into the other themes of the book?

4. What are some of the devices and motifs Kasischke uses to lend an air of eeriness to the entire narrative?

5. Why do you think the author chose to set the story during Christmas?

6. Relationships between mothers and their teenage daughters are famously contentious. In what way does *Mind of Winter* illuminate that dynamic? What point, if any, do you think Kasischke is trying to make about mother-daughter relationships?

7. How did learning the ending alter earlier aspects of the plot for you?

8. Do you think that Holly was always unstable or do you think it was her grief that broke her?

9. Finally, what are some other possible endings you considered while reading the book? Do you think the author intended for those scenarios to enter the reader's mind? If so, why? ∾

Excerpt from
In a Perfect World

IF YOU ARE reading this you are going to die!

Jiselle put the diary back on the couch where she found it and went outside with the watering can. It was already eighty-five degrees, but a morning breeze was blowing out of the west, sifting fragrantly through the ravine. She breathed it in, knelt down, and peered beneath the stones that separated the garden from the lawn.

She had been married, and a stepmother, for a month. In a bit of shade there, a tangled circle of violets was hidden—pale blue and purple. Small, tender, silky, blinking. If they had voices, she thought, they would be giggling.

She'd first noticed them a few days earlier, while raking dead vegetation out of the garden. That splash of color among the washed-out fallen leaves and other summer debris had caught her eye, and she knelt down and counted them (twenty-three, twenty-four, twenty-five) before covering them up again.

Somehow those violets had managed to stay perfectly alive through the scorching summer weather and all through the drought. The hottest, driest summer in a century. Maybe *ever*. They deserved special consideration, didn't they? If God wasn't going to give it to them, she would have to. Now, every day, Jiselle took the watering can outside, and was always surprised to find those violets alive and tucked away in their shady crack.

Still, she knew they couldn't last much longer—even hotter, drier weather had been predicted—so that morning, after watering them, she plucked just one. She covered the others up and brought the plucked one into the house, set it in a little souvenir shot glass from Las Vegas, with some cold water, placed it on the kitchen counter, and stepped back to admire it,

It was like a fairy tale: Jiselle almost couldn't believe it when Captain Mark Dorn chose her to be his wife. But as she settles into married life, Jiselle begins to realize that Mark is away, flying international routes, most of the time. And the Phoenix Flu, which Jiselle had thought of as a mere illness, when she had thought of it at all, has begun to spread in new and alarming ways . . .

deciding that she liked the little feminine gesture it made in the kitchen (Mark would be home in a day, and he would appreciate such a thing, as if she were settling in, getting comfortable, starting to decorate the place as if it were her own), until she turned her back on it, headed out of the kitchen to the bedroom to make the bed, and heard it *scream*. A high, piercing, horrible, girlish scream that made all the little hairs on Jiselle's arms rise and a cool film of sweat break out on the back of her neck. She whipped around, heart pounding, and hurried back into the kitchen, a hand covering her own mouth, to see.

Of course the violet hadn't screamed. It rested quietly where she had placed it, drooping over the side of the shot glass. If anything, it looked more defeated than it had a few seconds before—head bowed in acceptance over the shot glass, as if waiting patiently for the ax.

It would never have been capable of screaming. *That* had been Sara, howling at the news that Britney Spears was dead.

No one had said the word *epidemic* yet, or the word *pandemic*.

No one was calling it a *plague*.

The first outbreak had swept through a nursing home in Phoenix, Arizona, over a year ago, leaving the elderly miraculously untouched but killing seven nurses and aides. Some people fled Phoenix after that—taking their vacations early, boarding up their houses, staying in cabins in the mountains, visiting relatives—but they did not evacuate in droves. The Phoenix flu seemed contained, explainable. The new carpeting in the nursing home was blamed, and then the contaminated air ducts, in which a dead bat had been found. It was mummified. It was ashes. The biohazard men came in their orange jumpsuits and took what was left of it away in a plastic bag.

Then, a few celebrities nowhere near Phoenix died of what seemed to be the Phoenix flu—a soap opera star, Shane McDermott, Gena Lee Nolan, and the daughter of an actress who'd had a small role on *The Sopranos* years before— and although the non-celebrity deaths weren't made public, it was said that the nation's florists could not keep up with the demand for flowers. FTD changed its one-day delivery service to "Only two full days for most arrangements!" and it was reported that people were buying antibiotics and Tamiflu in bulk off the Internet, which resulted in shortages. But only the hysterical pulled their children out of school or left the country.

When a passenger fell ill after flying in a plane in which the body of a flu victim was being transported in cargo, a law was passed requiring airline passengers to be informed when human remains were aboard their planes. But, with the war on, this was such a common occurrence that it had no noticeable effect on travel habits. Flight attendants were encouraged to time their safety instructions to serve as a distraction while baggage-handlers loaded caskets, but on that side of the plane, the passengers, who had never been interested in safety instructions anyway, watched the procedures solemnly from their seats, sometimes pressing their faces to the windows for a closer look. ▶

Excerpt from *In a Perfect World* *(continued)*

No one had, to Jiselle's knowledge, ever demanded to be booked on another flight because of a corpse in cargo, and, in general, there was very little talk, public or private, about the Phoenix flu, although there was endless excited talk about what a strange year it had been.

Full of curious weather, meteor showers, and the discovery in rain forests and oceans of species thought to be extinct, it was the kind of year you might associate with an apocalypse if you were prone to making those kinds of associations, which more and more people seemed to be.

Sunspots. Earthquakes. Hurricanes. Tornadoes.

More than a year before, in what would come to seem to her to have been another life, lived by a different woman—Jiselle had been in a bar in a hotel in Atlanta, watching a Weather Channel meteorologist (bleached blonde, hot-pink suit) on the television. The meteorologist held a spinning Earth in the palm of her hand and predicted more crazy weather everywhere.

All across the globe!

It was March, which had come in that year, they were saying, like a lion being chased by a lamb. When Captain Dorn spoke to her, Jiselle turned from the television to him, holding a glass of wine in her hand—sipping from it, stem dangling between her fingers, the way the blond meteorologist held the world.

"Can I buy you another glass of wine?" the pilot asked. Jiselle was in her uniform—the pressed blue pencil skirt, silk hose, light-blue blouse—and the little brass wings were spread over her heart, as if her heart might have the gift of flight. She was wearing, too, a pair of beautiful shoes she'd bought weeks earlier in Madrid, at an old-fashioned shoe store in the heart of the city. A salesman with a thin black mustache and goatee had said, watching her walk across the wooden floorboards wearing them, *Perfecto!*

Sitting on the barstool, she had one long leg crossed over the other and was swinging the crossed leg slowly, trying to calm herself down after that terrible evening spent stuck on the runway in a driving rainstorm only to be turned back at the gate. It was nearly midnight. As Captain Dorn waited on the barstool beside her for an answer from her, one of the beautiful shoes, the one dangling from the swinging foot, slid right off her foot, and onto the floor.

In less than a second, he was on his knees below Jiselle, holding up the shoe as if considering it in the bar's dim light, and then he slid it with a swift whisper back onto her foot, while a group of businessmen at a table nearby laughed and clapped, and she blushed, and Captain Dorn stood, smoothing down his pants, and gave her a courtly little bow before he sat back down.

That night, Jiselle was thirty-two years old.

She'd been a bridesmaid six times.

It was always a surprise to her, being asked to be a bridesmaid. In truth, she'd had only a few close friends in her life, and none of them was one of these

8

six brides. But flight attendants made acquaintances quickly, and friendships became intense easily—a long layover, a blizzard, a terrible landing—and ended just as quickly and easily.

"You just look good in an ugly dress," one of her boyfriends had suggested when Jiselle wondered aloud about her popularity for the position.

And maybe she did.

She had a bridesmaid's shapely legs, wasp waist, blond hair that fell around her shoulders. The photographers at these weddings always seemed particularly interested in her, waving her over to stand by the cake, calling on her to kneel beside the bride and hold up the lacy train.

She'd worn green satin, and yellow chiffon, and something pink and stiff. She'd worn ribbons in her hair, or pinned to the top of her head, or down around her shoulders. One bride asked her bridesmaids to wear rhinestone tiaras, and although the last time Jiselle had been near a tiara was during a dance recital in second grade, *The Nutcracker*, she did—just as she obediently leaped to catch each bouquet as it sailed over her upturned face while the cameras flashed.

She'd been felt up by the drunken uncles of brides and been crushed on dance floors by their burly brothers. She'd been taken aside by a bride's mother and asked, "Jiselle, darling, when in the world will we be attending *your* wedding?" and had simply smiled, blinking.

"Always a bridesmaid," her mother had said on a couple of these occasions, "never a bride."

"Mom, I—"

"You don't have to explain to *me*," her mother said. "Do you think if I had a choice about whether or not to get married again, I would?"

"No," Jiselle said, clumsily, as if it had actually been a question. There *was* no question. After she'd kicked Jiselle's father out of the house, along with Bingo, the little dog he'd just brought home, Jiselle's mother had taken their wedding photos out into the backyard and lit them on fire one by one while Jiselle watched from the window over the kitchen sink. They shriveled up into black bats, and then into ashes, before her mother let them go.

Jiselle herself had fallen in love, too early, with two distracted boys—hockey and basketball, respectively. And then a few years escaped from her along with a married man. There'd been a British Royal Marine between scenes, and then a kleptomaniac. A drummer. A baggage-handler with a drinking problem. Then a few years passed during which she thought she'd given up men for good.

Already she'd buried the friend who would have been her maid of honor, and the father who would have walked her down the aisle. When people asked if she'd like to meet their cousin the doctor, their husband's shy best friend, Jiselle politely declined. She kept busy, pretending to herself and to everyone else that she wasn't waiting. ❧

Excerpt from
The Raising

Last year, Godwin Honors Hall was draped in black. The university was mourning the loss of one of its own: Nicole Werner, a blond, beautiful, straight-A sorority sister tragically killed in a car accident. Although a year has passed, as winter begins and the nights darken, obsession with Nicole and her death reignites. She was so pretty. So innocent. Too young to die.

Unless she didn't. Because rumor has it that she's back.

Prologue

THE SCENE of the accident was bloodless, and beautiful. That was the first word that came to Shelly's mind when she pulled over:

Beautiful.

The full moon had been caught in the damp bare branches of an ash tree. It shone down on the girl, whose blond hair was fanned around her face. She lay on her side. Her legs were pressed together, bent at the knees. She looked as if she'd leapt, perhaps from that tree or out of the sky, and landed with improbable grace. She was wearing a black dress, and it was pooled around her like a shadow. The boy had already climbed out of the smashed vehicle and crossed a ditch full of dark water to kneel by her side.

He seemed about to take her in his arms. He was speaking to her, pushing her hair out of her eyes, gazing into her face. To Shelly, he did not appear panicked. He seemed stunned, and rapturous with love. He was kneeling. He was just beginning to slide his arms beneath her body, to cradle or lift her, when Shelly came to her senses long enough to honk the horn of her car. Twice. Three times. He was too far away to hear her no matter how loudly she might shout, but he heard her honk her horn, and looked up. Startled. Confused. As if he'd thought that he and the girl were the last two creatures on earth. He was far from Shelly, on the other side of the rain-filled gash, but seemed to wait for her to tell him what to do, and Shelly was somehow able to tell him, as if they could speak to one another without bothering to speak. As if they could read one another's thoughts. (Later, she would consider this. Perhaps she hadn't spoken to him at all, she'd reason, or maybe she'd been shouting and hadn't realized it.) However it had happened,

Shelly managed to tell the boy, calmly, so he would understand, "If she's injured, you don't want to move her. We need to wait for the ambulance."

This was the one thing Shelly knew about accidents, about injuries.

She'd been married for a few years to a doctor, and that detail had stuck. "The ambulance?" the boy asked. (In Shelly's memory his voice was clear and close. But how could it have been?) "I called them," Shelly said. "From my cell phone. When I saw what happened."

He nodded. He understood.

"What happened?" he asked. "Who was that? In the car without headlights? Why—?"

"I don't know," Shelly said. "You ran off the road." "Help," he said then—a statement, not a cry—and the bare monosyllable of it was heart-wrenching. A cloud passed over the moon, and Shelly could no longer see him.

"Hey?" she called, but he didn't answer.

She turned off the engine. She opened her car door. She took off her shoes and waded carefully into the ditch.

"I'm on my way," she called. "Just stay where you are. Don't move the girl. *Don't move.*"

The water was surprisingly warm. The mud on the soles of her feet was soft. She slid only once, climbing up the opposite bank—and that must have been when she cut her hand on some piece of chrome torn from the wrecked car, overturned ten feet ahead of them in the road, or on a shard of broken glass from the windshield. But Shelly didn't feel it at the time. Only after the twin ambulances had flashed and wailed away from the scene would she notice the blood on her hands and realize that it was her own.

When she finally climbed out of the ditch and reached the boy and girl, the cloud had passed, and Shelly could see clearly again:

The boy was lying down beside the girl now, his arm wrapped around her waist, his head at rest in her blond hair, and the moonlight had made them into statues.

Marble. Perfect. Rain-washed.

Shelly stood over them for a few moments, looking down, feeling as if she'd stumbled onto something secret, some symbol in a dream, some mystery of the subconscious revealed, some sacred rite never intended for human eyes, but which she had been singularly and mysteriously invited to see.

Part One

There was a sad landmark on every block of that town: The bench they'd sat on, watching the other students walk by—with their backpacks, short skirts, iPods. The tree they'd stood under during a downpour, laughing, kissing, chewing cinnamon gum.

There was the bookstore where he'd bought the collection of poems by Pablo Neruda for her, and the awful college sports bar where they'd first held ▶

hands. There were the pretend-Greek columns that pretended to hold up the roof of the Llewellyn Roper Library, and Grimoire Gifts, reeking of patchouli and incense and imported cloth, where he'd bought the amber ring for her—set in silver, a globe of ancient sap with a little prehistoric fruit fly trapped in it for eternity. And the Starbucks where they went to study, and never opened a book.

Craig's father cleared his throat and slowed down at an intersection when a girl in tight jeans, flip-flops, and a low-cut tank top walked in front of the car without even glancing over. She was nodding her head in time to something she was hearing through the white wires plugged into her ears. Craig's father looked over and said, in a voice thick with emotion, "You okay, buddy?"

Craig nodded solemnly, straight ahead, and then looked over at his father. They both attempted to smile, but to someone seeing it through the Subaru's windshield it might have looked like two men grimacing at one another, each gripped suddenly and simultaneously by chest pains or intestinal discomfort. Sun slid through the car windows in the slanted, distant way of a bright day in early autumn; obviously, their side of the planet was tilting away from the sun. The girl passed, Craig's father stepped on the gas, and the car moved through the green shade of the huge, leafy oaks and elms that lined the road through campus, and which had been greeting new and returning students to the university for nearly a hundred and fifty Septembers.

"Take a left here, Dad," Craig said, pointing. His father turned onto Second Street. On the corner a girl with an old-fashioned bike was stomping at the kickstand near the curb. Her hair was so blond it glowed. It was the kind of hair that Craig had always distrusted—too seraphic, almost God-fearing—on girls. Until Nicole.

But this girl at the curb with the bike was nothing like Nicole. This girl had seen too many music videos, and was trying to look like one of the straggly, anemic blondes dancing behind the band. Her hair was greasy. Her nose was pierced. Her jeans sagged down over the sharp blades of her hipbones. She was the kind of girl Craig might have dated for a few weeks back home. Back then, before Nicole. "Take a right now, Dad," he said.

His father slowed down on narrow King Street. It was still cobblestone, somehow. Some strange nineteenth-century leftover. (Had they simply forgotten to pave it?) The tires of the Subaru rumbled over the stones, and the rearview mirror rattled.

Here, on King Street, the trees made a canopy overhead, and the houses sagged with their decades at the edges of the sidewalks. These decrepit mansions must have been, at one time, inhabited by the town's elite; Craig could picture women in bustled skirts, men with handlebar mustaches and bowties, rocking on the front porches, being brought glasses of lemonade by servants.

But it was a student slum now. The thudding bass of someone's stereo served as a heartbeat to the whole block. Couches sat on the porches and on the lawns. Bikes appeared tossed into piles, leaning into each other, locked up to wrought-iron fences. There were hitching posts for horses at the ends of the driveways, most of them painted the school's colors: crimson and gold. Two shirtless guys standing several lawns apart threw a football between them with what seemed like malicious force, while a girl in a bikini on a lawn chair watched it fly back and forth in front of her. Against the sky that football looked like the pit of some piece of bright blue fruit.

"It's this one."

Craig's father slowed down in front of the house, which had once been painted white but had weathered to gray. There were ten mailboxes beside the front door—the number of apartments—and there was Perry. Good old Perry.

How long had he been standing there, waiting?

Eagle Scout. Altar boy. *Best friend.*

The realization of that fact filled the back of Craig's throat with something that tasted like tears. He swallowed. He lifted his hand to wave. Perry was wearing a Pittsburgh Pirates cap, a clean T-shirt, and khaki shorts. New tennis shoes? Had his mother ironed that perfect crease in the shorts?

Perry saluted—sadly, ironically, the perfect gesture—and Craig's father's chuckle sounded vaguely like a sob. "There's your pal," he said, and pulled up to the curb, and Perry strode solemnly over to the car, yanked open the passenger door, and called in, "Hey, asshole, welcome back," and then bent down and looked past Craig to his father. "How are *you*, Mr. Clements?"

Dependable, presentable, sociable Perry. Just profane enough. Just polite enough.

"*Great*, Perry," Craig's father said in a voice full of gratitude and relief. "It's really good to see you." ❧